THE STONE WOLF

THE CHAIN BREAKER BOOK 4

D.K. HOLMBERG

Copyright © 2021 by D.K. Holmberg

Cover by Damonza.com

All rights reserved.

No part of this book may be reproduced in any form or by any electronic or mechanical means, including information storage and retrieval systems, without written permission from the author, except for the use of brief quotations in a book review.

Want a **free book** and to be notified when D.K. Holmberg's next novel is released, along with other news and freebies? **Sign up for his mailing list by going here**. Your email address will never be shared and you can unsubscribe at any time.

www.dkholmberg.com

CHAPTER ONE

The streets of Yoran were quiet, though there was energy in the air that left Gavin's skin tingling. He'd been feeling the trembling sensation of magic used throughout the city more often these days, ever since the enchanters had been able to operate more openly.

"Do you see anything?" he whispered into the enchantment.

He crouched along a building that was tucked up against one of its neighbors, feeling the stone pressing through the thin fabric of his dark shirt. The row consisted of mostly shops, some of them with signs hanging out front to advertise their wares. A few tall, narrow wooden buildings looked like they'd been added in between, filling the gaps where previous buildings had crumbled and collapsed. Occasional light from lanterns or candles glowing softly inside forced Gavin to be even more careful here. It was a partially residential area, which meant that he had to be cautious that he didn't raise the alarm.

Eventually, he would alert the constables that they had come through here, but he didn't want to do so until he knew exactly what they were dealing with. Head constable Davel Chan was temperamental about the idea of magic within the city, especially with the increased magic presence in the city. Gavin had tried to reach out to him earlier, but Davel sounded busy with another attack. That left Gavin even more on edge.

He watched the street, looking for signs of activity the way he had been trained to do, but saw nothing. Even the shadows were still.

"I don't see anything," Wrenlow said, his voice more high-pitched than usual.

This was one of the first times Gavin had asked Wrenlow to come with him out into the city—mostly to get him out of the Dragon, but partly so he could begin to implement some of the things they'd been working on. This was to be a fairly straightforward assignment, enough to give Wrenlow the opportunity to explore the city and get a feel for tactics he needed to use, though not so much that he would place himself in any danger.

"Remember what I told you," Gavin whispered. The scent of a nearby bells tree drifted to him, and he wrinkled his nose.

He appreciated that he didn't need to speak loudly with the enchantment. The thin metal earpiece that was curled around and tucked into the hollow of his ear was incredibly light, though surprisingly warm, regardless of how cool the night air was. A narrow chain ran down from the earpiece and ended with a small metal plate on his chest. With that, Gavin could adjust the volume, but he could also mute it so he didn't have to hear Wrenlow. There were times when such a thing was necessary, though he didn't want to admit that to his friend.

Tonight, Gavin doubted that he would mute anything. He needed to be there for Wrenlow to ensure he was safe.

"I remember," Wrenlow said. "You've been making sure I have no choice but to remember, so don't worry about me."

Gavin resisted the urge to chuckle. "Just get moving. Clear the street and I'll follow you."

He looked to the north. They had come to the outer edge of the city because there had been rumors of magic users that were not associated with the enchanters. Since the last time there'd been significant magic in the city it had been tied to Tristan, Gavin wanted to investigate each occurrence to make sure he hadn't returned.

Eventually he *would* return. As would the Fates.

That was Gavin's other fear. The only thing holding them back was the threat of the dark egg, but he didn't even know if he'd be willing to use that if the time came to do so. It was better to head them off and create the threat of his willingness to use it. Then he might keep the city safe.

There had been no trace of his old mentor, though. If he remained in the city, if he had anyone here on his behalf, he had not shown it. Gavin knew he should feel relieved, but with everything he'd gone through with Tristan, how could he?

His mind kept going back to the fight they'd had and how he'd nearly died. Tristan was still a skilled fighter, and given that he was part El'aras—the same as Gavin, really—Gavin doubted such fighting skill would ever wane.

Which meant that Gavin had to continue to improve.

Tristan had trained him and tested him, and his old mentor was *still* testing him. He wasn't training him any longer, though. Now this was on Gavin.

A different figure separated from the shadows near the end of the street and hurried away. Wrenlow crouched, trying to keep himself minimized, though in the darkness Gavin didn't think it even mattered. It was one more thing to keep working with him on. He really should have asked Gaspar to help train Wrenlow when it came to sneaking. Gavin was skilled enough, but Gaspar was a master thief. There were things even Gavin could learn from Gaspar.

"Stay along the buildings," Gavin whispered.

A soft grunt came in reply.

Gavin stepped away. He stayed in the shadows as his gaze skimmed along the street, constantly concerned he might encounter something or someone. But the streets were empty.

It wasn't late enough that people would have all turned in for the night in other parts of the city. In some places, the taverns would be busy, filled with the activity and revelry of men and women out for ale and wine. In this part of the city, though, all was quiet. There was nothing. Only them.

Gavin held out his El'aras dagger, which was a better weapon for this kind of sneaking than the sword. Still, he kept the sword sheathed at his side in case he needed its magical blade.

"I see something. Olivia's enchantment really helps," Wrenlow whispered. "I'm sure she can get you another—"

"Stay off to the side of the street," Gavin cautioned.

"I do understand the concept."

"There's a difference between understanding the concepts you were taught and implementing them. You're accustomed to being the one observing and not scouting."

And now that was Gavin's job. At least on this one.

"I know what I'm accustomed to doing." Wrenlow darted forward suddenly.

Gavin cursed under his breath. "Balls."

He lunged forward, hurrying along the street to catch up to Wrenlow before he did something too foolish. His friend had disappeared.

"Where did you go?"

There was no response.

Gavin swung his gaze from side to side. Nothing had suggested that Wrenlow would be in any danger, but there was the possibility he could have been surprised by someone. Gavin hadn't seen anything, but that didn't mean there wasn't anything out here.

The likelihood was high that there *was* something here, especially because of the reason Gavin had come here. There was magic. He was certain of it.

Standing in place, he could feel the tingling in the air, the cold washing of power over him that still flowed here. He just had to discover the source of it. Not enchanter magic, he was sure. Maybe sorcery, but would there be another sorcerer in the city already?

They'd dealt with far too many recently, and now Gavin had to believe that the Fates would leave them alone, especially with the threat that he might use the dark egg and release the semarrl.

"Wrenlow?" he tried again.

There was still no answer.

Balls.

For Wrenlow, this was supposed to be scouting. He wasn't supposed to get into any trouble. Gavin slipped along the street, looking at each of the buildings for anything that might be out of place. The buildings were taller here, mostly two stories and made of stone and wood. A few trees lined the street, as if someone had thought the razor-sharp leaves of the bells trees might deter activity here. Under normal circumstances, they might.

Gavin skimmed the roofline but didn't see anything. Many of these buildings had peaked roofs. They would be far too difficult for Wrenlow to have scaled without Gavin noticing.

Where had he gone?

"Wrenlow, if you're there, I need some sort of signal."

A faint breeze drifted along the street, carrying with it the smells of the forest just beyond the border of the city. The odor of the earth mingled with that of pine and the strange jestel trees that were scattered throughout the forest, though it wasn't the trees that carried the odor so much as it was their berries.

"I'm here," his friend said softly.

Gavin breathed out a sigh of relief, hating that he felt so unsettled and also that Wrenlow had put him through this.

"What were you doing?" Gavin asked, slipping back and following along a nearby building. This one was a low warehouse that stunk of dung and ash.

"I saw something and decided to investigate," Wrenlow said. "You said scout, so I'm scouting. Shouldn't I want to be more involved? That's what you're training me for."

Gavin could only shake his head. It was the same thing he would've done, so he couldn't get too angry with Wrenlow, especially as Gavin *had* been training him to be more independent. But he needed Wrenlow to recognize his limitations as well. Losing his friend and having him sneak off like that on a job where he was still trying to learn his skills left Gavin worried.

"Which building did you go into?" Gavin asked.

"It's not far from where I was. Looks like a warehouse. I saw the door swinging slightly ajar."

Gavin frowned. *He* was near a warehouse, though obviously not the same one Wrenlow had disappeared into. As he looked along the street, he found where Wrenlow had slipped off to.

"We were supposed to find information and then go in together."

"Come on, Gavin," Wrenlow said. His voice still

sounded hushed, as if he was concerned about what he uncovered. More than that, he sounded uncertain. Maybe unsettled. "I just poked my head inside the warehouse. Besides, we came here to find information together, didn't we?"

"Together," Gavin snapped. He could imagine Wrenlow grinning, and he shook the thought away.

He darted down the street, staying crouched and moving in the shadows of the night. At the end of the street, he could see only a bit of movement—barely enough for him to understand just what had caught Wrenlow's attention, but he realized why Wrenlow would've gone in. It was an unusual-looking building.

Gavin had explored quite a bit of Yoran in his time here. He couldn't be effective at his job otherwise, but he didn't remember this warehouse. It would have stood out to him. Warehouses were found all throughout the city, only most of them were made of wood. This looked to be made of a gray stone, almost completely smooth. There was something off about it, and it took a moment for him to realize what it was.

Magic.

These days, he was far more aware of magic around him than he had ever been before. Often, he could *feel* when it was used near him. The sensation was that of cold water washing over him. At least it invigorated him when he felt it.

Detecting magic *was* useful, though.

There were enchantments upon the building. Gavin would wager on that.

But why would there be?

In a place like Yoran—where magic had been exiled and where the constables had long had enchantments that enabled them to find magic—he would've expected that they would have sniffed out something like this. The constables wouldn't have tolerated any sort of magic like this in the city.

"Have you found the warehouse?" Wrenlow whispered.

"I think so, but it's strange."

"Because it's stone?" Wrenlow asked.

Gavin looked over to the door. There was just a hint of moonlight glittering through the clouds tonight, enough that he could make out Wrenlow standing in his dark jacket and pants, only a trace of the moonlight streaming down on him.

"Not stone," Gavin whispered. "It has more to do with the enchantments within the stone."

He headed toward Wrenlow. The time they'd been working together had given Wrenlow more of a muscular build, and the enchantments he carried granted him more fluid movement than he would have otherwise. Still, there was a jittery nervousness to him. This was a test, but nothing more, and Wrenlow was not supposed to have gotten involved in anything too dangerous yet.

Not like the magic Gavin detected out here.

He traced his hand along the wall, feeling for the enchantments.

Gavin hurried to the door and skimmed the rest of the building. There were no windows. The roofline was completely flat, low enough he thought he could jump and grab the lip of it and race across the top. Everything about the building itself screamed of a time before people had filled Yoran.

"It's an impressive structure," he said.

"You think all of it is magically enchanted?" Wrenlow asked.

Gavin tore his hand away from the building, and he turned to the doorway. "I think most of it is." That was unusual in Yoran. There were plenty of enchantments in the city, but he'd not seen many buildings that were themselves enchanted. If only he had enough control over his own magic to determine what those enchantments did. "Did you find anything when you looked inside?"

"Just the darkness. I figured I should wait for you."

"Now you decide to wait for me?"

"Maybe I should've waited for you before." Wrenlow grinned at him.

"We can go in together," Gavin said.

He slipped his hand into his pocket and reached for one of his own enchantments—a ring. The only other enchantment he used with any frequency was the one that allowed him to communicate with Wrenlow and Gaspar.

As soon as he slipped the ring on, his eyesight became enhanced and everything illuminated. Gavin appreciated this enchantment because he hated being trapped in the dark, even though Tristan had long trained him to operate and fight in it.

"So you didn't see anything?" Gavin asked, glancing over to Wrenlow.

Wrenlow had his own enchantment, which had come from the same source—the same enchanter. Though Gavin didn't like to rely on it, which was part of the reason he'd been willing to sneak through the city without the enchantment, there were times when he knew the enchantment offered him a benefit he couldn't have otherwise. By using this ring, he didn't have to be limited by darkness and could navigate through the warehouse far more effectively.

"It's empty, other than that door back there," Wrenlow said. "But for the most part, there's nothing."

Gavin took a step forward and could feel something shifting. It took a moment to realize what it was, but as soon as he did, he felt the power working around him.

He held his hand up. "More magic," he whispered.

He was thankful for the enchantment, thankful he didn't need to speak loudly, thankful that Wrenlow had the sense to stay close to him.

"Where?" Wrenlow asked.

Gavin shook his head. "I don't know. Everywhere."

It was different from when he'd gone looking for enchantments with Gaspar.

This was real power.

He immediately began to focus on the energy buried within him—his core reserves, a power he could reach for when needed. But it was a power Gavin hesitated to draw on often. While he could summon that energy and use it, weakness washed over him if he used it too much. He'd learned he needed to be careful.

Power filled Gavin. For a moment, the El'aras dagger

flared brighter, but he tamped down his connection to the power and the blade stopped glowing as much.

"What do you want to do?" Wrenlow asked.

With as much magic as Gavin felt around him, he didn't want Wrenlow to stay here. Or even in this city.

He also didn't think they could leave.

This was what he had promised Davel Chan. Gavin was going to stay and protect Yoran. Ensure that magic used against the city would not succeed. He was the reason that some of the powers had come here. He wasn't going to be the reason the city fell beneath the thumb of magic again.

"We need to keep moving," he whispered. "Be ready to fight."

"Do you really think it's going to be necessary?"

"I don't know."

"I'm just—"

Gavin glanced over to Wrenlow and held one hand up. "I know. You've been training. You can do this."

Wrenlow held his gaze with an unreadable expression in his eyes, but then he nodded.

Gavin needed to be careful. Maybe he should send Wrenlow back. Once he did, then he could investigate this warehouse. There was no doubt there was something here he needed to find, but what was it? And why did he detect it so significantly?

They reached the center of the warehouse, and Gavin paused for a long moment. He swept his gaze around him. He could feel the energy here, even if he couldn't see anything.

"I still don't like this," Gavin said.

"You don't like it because you don't know what it is?"

He frowned. "Because I fear I know *exactly* what it is."

He held on to the power within him; the deep-seated energy he could feel buried inside. As he focused on the power from his core reserves, Gavin began to realize something.

There was pressure against him.

"Somebody knows I'm using El'aras magic here," he whispered. He still didn't see anybody, though.

For the kind of power he felt, Gavin would've expected it to be considerable enough that he could detect it more easily, but somehow there was nothing else as he looked around.

The warehouse didn't have a high ceiling. The walls on either side stretched far apart. There weren't shelves or bins or anything else where someone could hide. It was simply empty.

"What should we—" Gavin glanced over, but Wrenlow was gone. "Wrenlow?"

How could Wrenlow have simply disappeared?

The magic.

Balls.

Gavin squeezed the hilt of the El'aras dagger and looked down at it. The blade glowed softly. He had been focused more on the strange pressure that he felt, focused more on what he could uncover, and hadn't paid any attention to *where* it was coming from.

And that was a mistake.

Gavin swung the El'aras dagger from side to side and felt something pressing on him. It had to be magic.

"Give me some sign, Wrenlow," he said.

He didn't like that this was now the second time on this stupid job where he'd started to be concerned about his friend. This was supposed to be an easy task.

"Wrenlow?" he called out.

A figure flickered at the edge of his vision, and Gavin spun. A man dressed in dark clothing swung a staff in a tight spiral.

Gavin glared at him. "You don't want to do that."

A whistling sound came, and Gavin dropped, spinning off to the side. He looked behind him at another man, a dark hood covering his face. He also carried a staff—which had whipped just above Gavin's head. These attackers were fighting in the dark, unless they were enchanted like Gavin was.

He sprang to his feet, twisted in a rapid kick, and missed. The nearest attacker was skilled enough to dart away from Gavin's attempt to strike him. Gavin positioned himself so that he could look around him better, but he still couldn't see Wrenlow.

One of the men swung his staff toward Gavin, who batted at it with the El'aras dagger. Gavin spun out of the way and came face-to-face with a third attacker.

Tricky.

"Gavin?" Wrenlow's voice came through the enchantment, panic within it.

"Where are you?" Gavin asked.

"Door," Wrenlow said. Then he grunted as if in pain.

"Wrenlow?"

Gavin ducked. One of the attackers spun his staff, coming close to Gavin's head, but he lowered it just in time and avoided the attack.

He had to get to the door. He had to get to Wrenlow.

It wasn't too often that he let his own anxiety guide his fighting style. Most of the time, he was in control. Within control was the key to his success; to knowing how he could react the way he needed and defeat the attacker.

Control equals precision.

Only, this time, Wrenlow needed him.

There were a few different fighting styles his mind raced through, but these men continued to jab their staves at him using the Bongan style.

They were Jind fighters from the far east. And skilled.

He would have to use a technique like Zar to defeat them, which had been taught to him early on. It was a high-risk, high-reward kind of fighting style, and there was always the possibility that somebody with enough skill could get past it. But when effective, it was incredibly brutal.

And in this case, the worst thing that would happen would be them striking him with one of their staves.

Gavin had been hit many times before. He didn't fear pain, but he also didn't want to welcome it if he didn't have to.

He jumped and spun, and given how low the ceiling was, he kicked in midair and came flying down toward one of the attackers while driving his fist out. The staff came at him, but Gavin's speed allowed him to slam his fist into the man's jaw. Gavin rolled, his legs catching the man around the neck, and he twisted hard until he heard a crack.

Gavin sprang back to his feet, and one of the men jabbed his staff at him. Gavin kicked, and the staff connected with his thigh.

It stung. Stars, but it hurt.

Gavin tamped down that pain, ignoring it. He had no choice but to do so.

He jumped again and drove his knee toward the man's face, but his opponent darted off to the side just in time. As the man nearly flew past him, Gavin grabbed the staff, twisted it quickly, and pulled it toward the man's head. The suddenness of the movement caught the attacker off guard, and Gavin jerked the staff with such force that it crushed the man's chin. When he landed, Gavin spun the staff quickly and connected with one of the other attackers, who blocked the thrust of the staff.

The enchantment started to flicker. The light it offered would fade soon. The attacker paused for a moment and twisted the staff, then tapped it on the ground.

Five others appeared out of the shadows.

Just then, another surge of magic struck, and everything plunged into darkness.

CHAPTER TWO

Gavin spun the staff. The ring's enchantment had faded, and Gavin could only hear his opponents now.

A whistling sound came toward him. It was quick, but Gavin was quicker.

He flicked the staff up and spun around.

These men were skilled, but from what Gavin could tell, they also only relied on their ability with the staff, not the way that Gavin could augment the Bongan style with other techniques.

And those other techniques were the key to victory.

Gavin spun again. In the darkness, the Zar fighting style wasn't going to be as effective. It was too risky.

He thought about how many attackers he knew were there. At least five.

No. Six.

There had been three, and Gavin had brought down

two, leaving the one remaining. But then there had been five more that had come right before his enchantment had left him in the dark.

Gavin had no idea if the enchantment had faded because it had been spent—something that was entirely likely, given what he knew about how the power waned over time—or whether the enchantment had been dampened by magic around him.

That was equally possible. He had been around sorcerers before who had the ability to restrict magic. If that was what had happened, Gavin had to find which person was responsible. If he did, then perhaps the enchantment would work again so that he could see.

A soft shuffle came near him, and Gavin whipped the staff around. He was rewarded with a sharp crack when the staff connected, and he spun it back around but met nothing.

He jumped toward where he had struck and drove his fist outward, fighting with a mixture of the Noru and Nor styles. The combination didn't always work well together, but in the darkness like this, Gavin thought this mix would be helpful. He had learned Nor from a master, and it was a style that Tristan didn't know nearly as well as Gavin did.

His fist connected with something soft, which he suspected was the man's stomach or perhaps his side. Gavin switched to the grappling style of Harjit. He twisted his legs and flipped his opponent down until he found his head, which Gavin lifted and slammed down as quickly as he could. The man went still. The darkness didn't fade, so this man wasn't responsible for holding the magic around Gavin and restricting his enchantment.

That left five.

Perhaps more, though in the darkness, Gavin wouldn't be able to know.

He jerked his hands around and brought his arms up, spinning the staff. He needed to create a bit of space around him to have a chance to figure out where the others were. Somebody could still sweep out from beneath him and trip him.

Gavin had to try a different technique. He knew the Bongan style fairly well and had worked with it long enough that he was comfortable—and more than competent—with it. These men were all masters, though, so he doubted he would be able to overwhelm them easily.

There were several different sword-fighting styles, though some of them involved more danger than he preferred. He flicked the staff, which connected, but there was nothing when he brought it back around.

Gavin had to figure out the spacing.

He continued to swing the staff and created a tight pattern around him, mostly so he could prevent anyone from getting close enough to him. He felt the wind shift.

Gavin ducked and brought the staff up, catching his attacker with a hard thud and a grunt. He switched his planted foot and kicked as hard as he could.

He heard the man collapse.

There was a part of him that actually enjoyed the fight. Were it not for his need to get to Wrenlow and find out what happened to his friend, Gavin might take the time to savor this fight. How could he not? It was so rare for him to get a good spar in, especially within Yoran. Few he'd faced posed him much of a challenge.

He felt a soft breath, little more than that, and he dropped. He twisted the staff in a quick flick of his wrist, augmenting the Bongan style with a hint of Sudo, and he connected. He followed through, making sure that the attacker was down, which left him with three.

Three men that he couldn't see in the darkness. Three men he had to find and eliminate to get to Wrenlow.

A soft grunt came through the enchantment.

"I'm trying to get there, Wrenlow," Gavin whispered. Something swept toward him and he crouched, spinning the staff, but he wasn't quick enough to strike. "I'm dealing with something here, though."

He sprang to his feet with the staff and felt it connect. Part of fighting with the Bongan style was turning the staff into an extension of his arm. Gavin had struggled with that aspect of the training. It had taken learning different techniques, including fighting with knives, for him to feel more comfortable using the staff.

Why were there so many attackers skilled at the Bongan style?

Tristan had known Gavin struggled with this.

Was this some sort of test from him? That bastard. He's still out there, isn't he?

Maybe he was even here. Gavin wouldn't put it past him to show up, to use his own connection to power, to somehow target Gavin with it.

There was pressure upon him.

Even though he couldn't see where it came from, Gavin had trained to fight in the darkness. It was a matter of sensing the shifting wind, the breath of air, the faintest sound, anything that might give him clues as to where his attackers would come from, but he had never felt the pressure around him he was feeling now.

Gavin had never trained to fight with his awareness of magic.

But why wouldn't he do that now?

He understood the basics of magic. He had felt that power, and he could use it. By holding on to the power within him, letting that energy flow through him, and allowing that connection to build, could he use something within?

He let the core energy fill him but didn't do anything with it. Gavin wasn't even sure that he would know how to in an effective way. That was one of the challenges he had, mostly because he had learned how to use that magic in only specific ways. Tristan had trained him to be the Chain Breaker, but not to use the El'aras magic that flowed within him in any other meaningful way. It was part of the reason Anna had welcomed him to the El'aras. Were Gavin truly sensible, he would've gone with her. Not only to learn about magic but for other reasons too.

He could feel pressure upon him nearby.

Gavin spun the staff out, whipping it toward what he detected. Something struck him in the back, and he staggered forward just a step, but it was enough that somebody caught him on the arm. He gritted his teeth, fighting back the pain. A blow like that could shatter an arm, but he didn't think his was broken.

Gavin spun the staff again and focused in front of him—what he needed to find and fight. He darted forward and swung the staff, lumbering a bit more than he would have wanted. If he wasn't careful, he'd stumble straight into somebody's weapon and end up with a staff smacking him across the face.

He continued spinning his staff. Surprisingly, he could feel the power from his core reserves flowing out from him, as if *it* were an extension of his arms.

Then his staff struck resistance.

Gavin twisted and jerked, and he felt somebody fall. He brought down the staff, now filled with the power from within him, and jammed it into the man's chest. The darkness around him dissipated.

He spun the staff around, and the two remaining attackers were just behind him. Gavin quickly whipped the staff around, catching one man in the head. The other seemed to recognize that Gavin could see again. The man tried to jump back, but Gavin darted forward, filled with the power he now possessed, and caught him in the shoulder. His weight carried through until he crushed the man's chest and slammed his fist up underneath the man's jaw.

Gavin jumped to his feet and twirled the staff as he looked around him.

There had been eight attackers. But now there was one more.

A dark figure stood and watched near the back of the warehouse.

He started toward the figure, and a warbled call came through the enchantment. "Gavin? I need you—"

Gavin gritted his teeth as Wrenlow's voice cut off. He stared at the figure and wanted nothing more than to go after them, knowing that it had to be Tristan.

But he wasn't willing to do so. Wrenlow needed his help.

Gavin spun toward the door. When he reached it, he looked back toward the figure and could feel cold washing over him, the sensation coming from them.

Magic.

Despite his temptation to go after them, he threw open the door. It was lit too brightly, and as soon as he stepped inside, the door swung closed.

Somebody jumped on him. Gavin grabbed at them, filled still with the power of his core reserves, and he tore them free and slammed them down.

A woman.

She bounded back up, her dark hair and delicate features reminding him of Imogen. She had porcelain skin, and she darted toward him, moving swiftly as if enchanted, but Gavin wondered whether she actually was.

He spun the staff he still held, though he hadn't accounted for the lower ceiling. The staff smacked into it, and he jumped back just as she lunged toward him. He rolled and crashed into a desk he hadn't seen. He tried to get up, but the desk was on top of him.

Gavin roared, filled with anger about the attack, about the fact that he had to leave Tristan behind, and about how Wrenlow was in danger because of him.

All of that rage consumed him, and he was left with no choice but to slam the power out from him. As he did, the desk crashed forward away from him.

Gavin bounded to his feet, quickly unsheathed the El'aras dagger, and flung it at the woman. She twisted off to the side and caught the blade.

Balls.

She tossed the blade away and darted toward him.

He dropped, and as she neared, he sprung up, filled by the power of his core reserves. Gavin grabbed her wrist, spun her around, and whipped her across the room. She slammed into the wall and crumpled.

"Wrenlow?" he said into the enchantment.

Where was he?

Gavin looked around. There were a couple of men lying motionless nearby. Had Wrenlow done that? Gavin had been working with him to improve his fighting ability, but he wouldn't have expected to see that from him quite yet.

It was difficult to see much else. Whereas the warehouse had been an empty space, this room was cluttered. There were boxes stacked all over, many of them blocking his view, and a layer of dust hung over everything. Another table created part of the maze he would have to fight through.

Why fight him here?

"This is stupid," Gavin muttered.

He jumped up onto the nearest box and surveyed the room. He had to crouch low, and he twisted the ring on his finger that provided light, but he didn't really need the enchantment. There was enough lantern light throughout the room, though it did cast pools of shadows that would likely lead to finding certain unwelcome surprises.

Gavin vaulted forward, landing on another box. The suddenness of the movement caught one of the other attackers off guard, and they looked up at him. Gavin flipped down, kicked the attacker in midair, and finished by driving his elbow down onto the back of their neck, dropping them completely.

He sprang back up and then began to sweep his gaze around him for any other signs of attackers. There was another fallen man, but nothing else.

Wrenlow couldn't have done that much damage.

He crawled along the boxes, making his way deeper into the room.

"Wrenlow, if you're there, I need you to say something so I know where to find you."

Wrenlow remained silent, and Gavin let out an exasperated sigh. He figured that once he was here, once he uncovered where they were keeping Wrenlow, he would find a way to get through the limitation they were using against Wrenlow and their communication enchantments.

Unless it was El'aras magic.

Tristan, of course, had El'aras magic, and he could use that against them.

Gavin gritted his teeth and jumped forward. All of this because he had been willing to let Wrenlow come out here on this job, because he hadn't pushed back when his friend had wanted some additional responsibility. Gavin had trained him and had been working with him well enough that Wrenlow might have enough skill, but there was still danger in coming out on any job. That was something Gavin had learned long ago. Any job could pose its own dangers. Any job had risks to it. Even the ones that seemed like they were going to be the most straightforward had the potential for danger, and those were the ones that he had learned to be the most careful about, knowing that if he wasn't, they might be surprised by something.

His jump carried him to the next box, and he had to stay low to ensure that he wasn't surprised by what was coming. He barely managed to keep his head from slamming into the ceiling.

Gavin swept his gaze around, searching, but he still didn't see any movement that suggested where his friend had gone. He had to believe that Wrenlow was here.

He'd said to go through the door, hadn't he?

Gavin followed the top of the boxes with his eyes, and then he saw him.

A dark-skinned man had Wrenlow penned into a corner.

Wrenlow was doing everything he could to fight him off, but he was slowing. The enchantments Wrenlow had were fading. They didn't last indefinitely, and they *would* fade when used quickly. Considering how Gavin's had been neutralized, it surprised him that Wrenlow still had access to his enchantments.

Gavin scrambled forward quickly, and as soon as he neared, another man darted toward him. He was tall and lean, with a scar on one cheek. His shaggy brown hair hung down to his eyes. His movement looked enchanted, especially with the way he seemed to glide toward Gavin.

"You made it through," the man said. He had a deep, harsh voice. "Didn't know if you would."

"Let him go," Gavin growled. "You only want me."

A shuffling sound and faint breeze suggested others were coming.

"Unfortunately, I'm not able to do that," the man said. "But I can give you something else." He grinned as he pulled a long, delicate silver blade out.

Wrenlow kicked past the first attacker.

Gavin pushed down the surge of pride. It wasn't a technical attack—relying instead on enchantments—but he'd defended himself.

When Wrenlow surged toward the man facing Gavin, the knife blurred.

Wrenlow's eyes went wide. With enchanted eyesight, Wrenlow would see the movement clearly. Without the necessary speed to stop the attack, there would be nothing Wrenlow could do.

Horror surged within Gavin.

People converged around Gavin, and he thundered, exploding the power of his core reserves out. The boxes were thrown back, the attackers were thrown away. He jumped, the suddenness of his movement carrying him forward, and he grabbed the thin man's wrist before he had a chance to reach Wrenlow. Gavin bent it back with a sharp crack until it shattered, then spun the man around to face him.

"Did Tristan send you?"

The man's eyes widened as he shook his head. "I don't know. I was just hired. They wanted to know what you've learned."

So that was what this was about?

The man tried to pull back. Gavin grabbed the man's head and jerked it in one sharp movement. There was a snap as he fell to the ground.

Weakness threatened to overwhelm him. He had called upon too much energy, too much power from his core reserves, but he had to hold on a little longer.

Wrenlow looked up. Gavin grabbed the man's slender knife from the ground and handed it to Wrenlow.

"You did good. Now we need to get out of here."

"What happened?"

Gavin glanced toward the door. The boxes that he had jumped across were all scattered, most of them against the walls, and there were half a dozen bodies lying among them. Gavin had no idea how many of them still lived, and at this point, he didn't even care.

As he tried to help Wrenlow up from the chair, he staggered. Wrenlow caught him and slipped his arm underneath.

"We need to get moving," Gavin said, sweeping his gaze around him. He didn't know how many of these attackers would get up, but he didn't want to be stuck here —and certainly didn't want to face any more fighters.

Wrenlow just nodded.

They neared the door, and Gavin saw the El'aras dagger on the floor. He stepped away from Wrenlow, nearly falling but managing to stay on his feet. He grabbed the dagger and held it up, but he didn't see any glowing from the length of flat gray. The lettering on the dagger glittered with the lantern light, and a warmth had started to fill the room from the rear of the warehouse.

Fire.

Gavin looked back. "We should really put that out."

It had already started to spread and now billowed with incredible heat. They weren't going to be able to put the flames out. Not without help.

"Do you have some way of doing that with your magic?" Wrenlow asked.

"Not this fire." Gavin was exhausted and felt a little drunk, which was a dangerous combination for a fighter.

"Come on," Wrenlow urged.

They stepped out the door, and Gavin hesitated, worried they would run into another attacker, but there was nothing other than the bodies. There was no sign of the figure he had seen lingering near the back of the warehouse, the figure Gavin was convinced had been Tristan.

Wrenlow held on to him, getting him through the warehouse, then back out onto the street. "What was that all about?" he asked, looking over to Gavin. "We had come out here because you detected magic."

"It *was* magic. Tristan used magic in a test. I don't know if I passed or failed, which is even worse," Gavin said, shaking his head.

Flames crackled from behind the door, granting enough light that Gavin could make out the fire that started to consume everything. He hoped the stone of the warehouse wouldn't let the fire spread far. He couldn't do anything—other than get help to put out the flames.

"When you get back to the Dragon," he told Wrenlow, "you need to let Davel Chan know what happened here."

"You want the constables to get involved?"

"For the fire," Gavin said. "They have to be. I promised him."

It was more than just the fire, though. He needed Davel and the constables to watch for any sign of another attack, to watch for magic and ensure that the city was defended against it. Davel Chan had to help him, because Gavin wasn't sure that he would survive another test like this.

Wrenlow pulled out a small ring-shaped enchantment from his pocket, tapping it. He whispered into the enchantment for a moment, then slipped it into his pocket again. "It's done. The constables will know."

Gavin sighed, staring at the gathering flames.

It was more than he could handle.

The fight had almost been more than he could handle.

And he still didn't know why they'd been here.

CHAPTER THREE

The Roasted Dragon was a comfortable tavern, and there was a level of vibrancy here tonight that Gavin appreciated. Given what he'd gone through and how he had nearly failed Tristan's test, having people—and the sense of life—around him gave him a feeling that he welcomed.

He lingered in the doorway for a moment, sweeping his gaze around the tavern. He looked for familiar faces—Gaspar, primarily, but he didn't see him. The old thief must have been on a job, or he was out with Desarra, hopefully rekindling their long-lost relationship.

Imogen was there, though. The dark-haired woman he had faced in the warehouse had reminded him of Imogen, with her porcelain skin and fast movements. Despite the similarities, the woman hadn't come at Gavin with a sword. Not like Imogen fought.

One of the tavern dancers whirled into Imogen's table

with a clunk. For a moment Imogen seemed to uncoil like a snake, but then she was smiling with the rest of the crowd. Gavin was suddenly reminded of her strength as she battled the Mistress of Vines. He suppressed a shiver.

Wrenlow nudged him from behind. "We have to go in. We can't stay outside if he's somewhere out there."

Gavin licked his lips. His mouth was dry, and though his strength had started to return, the power of his core reserves had not—at least not entirely. It would take rest and time.

Surprisingly, though, it wouldn't take nearly as much time as it once would have. Gavin could already feel that energy starting to trace back up inside, restoring him. There had been a time when he had believed that it was some part of his own strength, some part of his own energy, and he hadn't known that what he tapped into was truly magic. Even now, Gavin had no idea if he connected to magic all the time or whether some of it was simply residual strength that he had learned to access.

"He's not going to come after us again tonight," Gavin said, though he did take a step inside the tavern.

"Are you sure about that?" Wrenlow asked.

"He wants us to think he might, and he wants us to be afraid of him."

"*Are* you afraid of him?" Wrenlow kept one hand on Gavin and guided him inside.

Gavin didn't think he needed the support, though he did start to stagger a bit as he tried to separate from Wrenlow. He chuckled to himself, which earned a strange look from Wrenlow.

Gavin shook his head. "It's nothing."

"Which part is nothing?" Wrenlow asked. "What you did back there? How you're feeling? Or the way you're leering at me?"

"I didn't realize I was leering at you at all. I'm proud of you. You took what you learned and used it when you had to."

"You don't have to sound surprised."

"You never know until you're in that situation," Gavin said.

Wrenlow watched him a moment. "You have this strange look in your eyes. Sort of like you did when you killed that man." His voice lowered when he mentioned that, though not so much that Gavin couldn't hear the edge within it.

"If it's going to trouble you to see me fighting—"

Wrenlow guided him to a table, forcing Gavin to sit. Most of the tables within the Roasted Dragon had long benches, but Wrenlow walked him to one near the hearth that crackled with warmth in the back of the tavern and pushed him to take a seat.

"This has nothing to do with me seeing you fight," Wrenlow said, settling down across from Gavin. Wrenlow nodded to someone, and Gavin twisted to follow his gaze.

It was one of the servers that Gavin didn't know very well, somebody new that Jessica had hired. She was young, with auburn hair, full lips, and freckles.

"I think Olivia might get jealous," Gavin muttered, resting his elbows on the table.

"Olivia would be jealous of what?" Wrenlow asked, turning his attention back to Gavin.

"Of the way you're looking at that girl."

"Rebecca is a server, and I'm just getting her attention so I can get you something to drink. Look at you, Gavin. You look like you haven't had anything to drink in weeks."

"I think it's from using my core magic like that."

"Now you're calling it core magic?" Wrenlow leaned forward and twisted the enchantment in his ear, taking it out and resting it on the table.

Gavin did the same. It was easier to have a conversation at the table without hearing it reverberate. "It's magic, and it's part of my core energy, so I suppose that's what it is."

"Why do you hesitate to refer to it as what it really is?"

"What am I supposed to call it?" Gavin asked.

"You're supposed to refer to it as El'aras magic. *Your* magic."

Gavin grunted. "I've been trying *not* to think of it like that."

"Why wouldn't you? It's what it is, is it not?"

"I think so," Gavin said. "But just because that might be what it is"—that earned a sharp, raised eyebrow from Wrenlow—"doesn't mean that I can go around calling it that. Especially not in a place like this."

"The people in the city don't know anything about the El'aras," Wrenlow said, though he kept his voice low. Gavin appreciated that from him. "You know how hard it was for me to find out anything about the El'aras when they were first here? Stories and rumors more than anything else. They abandoned the city so long ago that no one even remembers them."

"I've had plenty of experience with the El'aras," Gavin said.

Wrenlow laughed softly. "Of course you have. That's what we're here about."

"That's not why."

Rebecca appeared at the table, and she flashed a grin at Wrenlow. She had a pretty smile that seemed to stretch far across her face, almost like a mask.

I really am *loopy.*

Fatigue from using magic. Fighting. From all of it.

He didn't even have to have a mug of ale.

"You're getting in late," she said.

"We were out at another tavern," Wrenlow said, smiling sheepishly. "Don't tell Jessica, though. She might get upset."

Rebecca leaned forward. Her dress wasn't all that low-cut, but it was enough that it drew Wrenlow's attention. Gavin chuckled.

"Your friend looks like he's had too much already. Are you sure you should let him have anything else?" she asked.

"Oh, I think he can have a mug of ale. Not much more than that," Wrenlow said. "I can't have him stumbling all over the city. Something like that is only going to draw the attention of the constables."

Rebecca laughed softly. "We wouldn't want that, would we? I think Jessica would be upset if we had the constables here. Do you know that they've stopped by three times this week?"

Wrenlow frowned. "Have they?"

"I don't think Jessica likes to talk about it, but I've seen them. They come through here, and they check the tavern, then the rooms up above. I don't think she's upset by it since she doesn't ever say anything." Rebecca stood straight, wiping her hands on her apron. "If it were me, I'd get angrier at the fact that we have the constables coming through here like that."

"You know Jessica," Wrenlow said. "She just wants to make sure her business thrives."

Rebecca nodded. "She's been good to me. I'm glad they guided me here. I wasn't sure where I would work."

"I'm glad to hear that. Maybe we could have a little food, in addition to the ale?"

"You've got it." Rebecca spun and headed away.

"Now you really *are* going to have some explaining to do to Olivia," Gavin said.

"And I said—"

Gavin chuckled. "I know what you said. And I'm just ribbing you. Can't I do that?"

"You can so long as you don't spread the wrong kind of rumors to Olivia."

"I know how to keep my mouth shut when it has to do with my friend and his dalliances." He started to laugh and realized that it sounded wild. Almost unhinged.

Wrenlow sighed. "What do you think is going on with the constables?"

"Probably what I asked them to do."

"You asked them to come through here and harass Jessica?" Wrenlow frowned. "I know the two of you have been a bit out of sorts, but I thought that you wanted to make sure that her tavern thrived."

Gavin grunted. "We haven't been out of sorts."

"You haven't come around here the way you used to," Wrenlow said.

"Because I've been searching for other things."

It was more than that, and Wrenlow knew it, just as Gavin knew he didn't have to explain it to his friend. But there was some truth to it. When he had first come to Yoran, the Roasted Dragon had been the place where he spent most of his time. It was somewhere he'd felt comfortable, somewhere he'd felt protected.

But then he'd ended up inviting attacks upon the tavern. Because of him, the Dragon was in danger. Now that he knew that Tristan was active in the city, he wasn't about to leave the Dragon as the target of Tristan's attention.

"You've been searching, but what have you been finding?" Wrenlow asked.

"I haven't found anything lately," Gavin muttered.

Rebecca returned to the table, carrying two large mugs of ale, which she set on the table in front of them. "The food should be out soon."

She smiled at Wrenlow, then turned away, heading back to the kitchen.

"Stop looking at her that way. You're old enough to be her father."

"I'm not that old," Gavin said. "Though I feel like it

because I have to deal with a pain in the ass like you as often as I do." He let out a long sigh, rubbing his eyes and trying to pull on his core reserves. It was difficult to do. A surge of energy came through him, and his mind cleared a little.

Wrenlow laughed and took a drink of the ale. "You might say you haven't been finding anything lately, but I know you have. I know you've detected magic in the city."

Gavin shrugged. "I've detected it, but I haven't been able to find much of anything."

"Much of anything like today?"

Gavin leaned back, and he took a sip of the ale. It was warm—a bit bitter, but tasty. Try as he might, he hadn't found many places in the city that had ale as good as Jessica's. Not that he had tried all that hard. He still did like the Dragon the best of all the places he'd visited in Yoran.

"Today was unusual," he said.

"Because you brought me along?"

Gavin shook his head. "I've offered you the opportunity to come along before."

"Right, but this was the first time you managed to actually get me out."

"I brought you on another job."

"Really? You mean the time you had me come with you to scout the edge of the forest?"

"Scouting is part of the job," Gavin said.

"The boring part," Wrenlow mumbled. He took another drink and glanced up as Rebecca returned and slid two trays of food to them.

She leaned up against the table as she looked at Wrenlow. "Where was the other place you visited tonight?"

"I don't want to get any other taverns in trouble," Wrenlow said, flicking his gaze across the room toward Jessica. "Most of the time it depends on where my friend likes to go." He glanced at Gavin. "He gets me into trouble."

She frowned a moment, looking at Gavin askance. "He does?"

"Too often," Wrenlow said. "And as much as I tried to keep him from some of the things he likes to do, he has a penchant for taking me to some dangerous places."

"Really? Some would say you should leave friends like that behind."

Wrenlow grinned at her. "I couldn't leave him behind. He needs me."

Rebecca regarded Gavin for another moment, as if trying to decide how to feel about him, before walking away.

"Great," Gavin muttered, taking another drink.

"What? I figured that with all the times you've harassed me, it only makes sense I get to do the same to you."

"I don't mind that," Gavin said, picking at the beets and meat on his plate. "It's more that I suspect the next time I come in here with you, she's going to spit in my food."

"Rebecca wouldn't do that. She knows I'm only kidding. Jessica helped her get set up. There have been a couple like her. All weak enchanters, you know."

Gavin hadn't known. Had his mind been clearer, he

might have seen signs of that himself. "You could have told me sooner."

Wrenlow shrugged. "Doesn't really matter. Zella asked for help; Jessica offered it. There are others throughout the city doing the same. It's a different place for them now. They don't fear using their magic, regardless of how strong—or weak," he said, glancing to the kitchen, "it might be." Wrenlow dove into his food. "Anyway, why are you so convinced this was Tristan?"

Gavin tore his gaze away from Rebecca. A minor enchanter.

How many had decided to reveal what they could do now—because of him?

He should feel pride, but it was difficult to do so with everything they'd encountered. The enchanters still had the general attitude about magic to deal with. Most within the city didn't want to know about magic. Most wanted to know they were safe.

Gavin sighed. He couldn't fix that. He could only give them a chance.

"Gavin?" Wrenlow asked.

"Sorry. You were asking about Tristan. I knew it was him because I saw him standing near the back of the warehouse, watching."

"He didn't get involved?"

Gavin picked at his food, taking a bite and chewing slowly. "He didn't get involved."

"Why would he watch?"

Gavin took a drink of the ale and shook his head. "This is Tristan. He does things certain ways."

"Even when he pits himself against you?"

"It's a test, like everything is with him. Even when we fight, there's still an element of that within it. I think, in his mind, he's looking for weaknesses."

"He trained you," Wrenlow said. "He'd know your weaknesses. Sort of like how you know mine."

"When it comes to fighting, yes," Gavin said in between bites, "but I'm not sure I would be able to list all of your other weaknesses."

"So this wasn't a test of your fighting style?"

Gavin wasn't sure. "He would've known that the fighting style was challenging for me."

"I didn't realize any fighting style challenged you."

"Most of them don't. There are a few that I never fully mastered." It wasn't an easy thing for Gavin to admit, even to a friend.

"So he sent a couple of people at you with a fighting style you aren't fully equipped to handle?"

"Is eight a couple?"

"There were eight there?"

Gavin nodded. "And he made sure I couldn't use the enchantment."

Wrenlow whistled, then took a drink of ale. "That's a shitty thing for him to have done."

"It might be shitty, but it's definitely the kind of thing he would do."

"But you passed?"

"Maybe," Gavin said, chewing slowly and staring at the mug of ale. He couldn't get past the idea that there was something more to this. Maybe it wasn't just a test. At least, maybe it wasn't the one he thought it was.

"Did you practice the style after leaving him?" Wrenlow asked.

"I practice all the styles," Gavin said.

"Even the ones you struggle with?"

Gavin set his hands on the table. "What are you getting at?"

"Well, if you're going to be tested by Tristan, do you think you should start to anticipate what more he might do with you?"

"I'm not sure there's anything more. He tried to find where I'm the weakest."

"So your fighting style is where you're the weakest."

"The Bongan style was never one that I fully mastered. Tristan would know that, which is why I'm going to have to keep working."

"I can help you," Wrenlow said.

Gavin forced a smile at him. "That would be great."

"I might need to borrow some enchantments to do it more effectively." Wrenlow chuckled. "I suspect that with enough enchantments, I should be able to pose even more of a threat to you."

Gavin held his friend's gaze. "You did well tonight. I'm glad the enchantments held out. That's why I've cautioned you not to depend on them."

"You know I'm not," Wrenlow said. "But I also need to practice with them, especially since there aren't going to be too many times when I'm not going to have my enchantments. Olivia makes sure I have all the ones I need."

Gavin took another sip of ale. "What happens if we face somebody like we did tonight? Somebody with the ability to suppress those enchantments?"

"I…"

"Exactly," Gavin said. "I want to keep you safe as possible."

"You'd just keep me on the fringes again."

"Are you on the fringes, or are you doing critical work for us?"

Wrenlow shrugged. "I suspect you'd tell me it's critical work."

"More than you know." Gavin finished eating and took a deep breath, leaning back. "Why don't you get some rest?"

"I'm supposed to meet Olivia tonight." Wrenlow slipped out of the booth, then stood at the edge of the table. "I appreciate that you came after me." Something about his demeanor had changed, and he flashed a smile at Gavin. "You didn't have to. I would've gotten out of there."

Gavin wasn't as sure. The attack had drawn both of them in.

"Of course I was going to go after you."

"I saw that look in your eyes, though," Wrenlow said. "One I don't know that I've ever seen before."

Gavin leaned back in the booth, and he closed his eyes for a moment. "I try not to go to that place very often," he said softly. "It's a place I was taught to go to. Tristan wanted to know if I still could, I suspect."

"So that was part of what he was after?"

"I don't know," Gavin said. "When it comes to him, I really don't know."

"Why doesn't he just come after you directly? If this is something he needs, why wait?"

"I suspect he's after something still. Maybe he wants the semarrl, or maybe it's something else." Gavin hadn't managed to figure out that part of Tristan's plan yet. Gavin opened his eyes, pulled the mug of ale in front of him, and took another long sip. "I don't know if he's just proving he can get to me." He shrugged. "Eventually, whatever Tristan wants is going to be made known, and I just have to be ready."

"You know you're not doing it alone. I'm going to work with you." Wrenlow left the table and walked to the door.

Gavin appreciated Wrenlow's offer, and yet there was another possibility—one he thought would help him even more.

He finished his ale and swiveled so that he could look around the tavern. It had been a while since he had spent any time at the Dragon, long enough that he couldn't deny that he now felt a little uncomfortable here. Maybe it really was what had happened between him and Jessica, though perhaps it was something else. Perhaps it was just that he had changed; that he had become someone else. Either way, he knew he needed to come to terms with it.

He could protect Jessica for only so long. He could ensure her safety for a while, and there was the possibility that Tristan wouldn't even come after her. That was what Gavin had to hope for.

On the far side of the tavern, Imogen sat across from a dark-haired man dressed in a black cloak, the hood pooled around his shoulders.

In all the times he'd been at the Dragon, he hadn't seen Imogen meet with anybody besides Gaspar. Despite being in Yoran for as long as he had, Gavin still didn't know much about her, and it was that ignorance that left him filled with curiosity about her—along with who she might be meeting with.

The man stood up and leaned forward, saying something quickly in a soft, flowing language that Gavin recognized but didn't speak.

Jalash.

Who would she be meeting with from Jalash?

The language was quick and fluid, as well as difficult to master. Gavin had learned only a few words in it, enough to get by when he traveled through the lands but not enough to understand what others were saying.

He frowned, but then Imogen stood up and slipped out of the tavern.

Gavin waited for a moment, but curiosity overcame him. He was still tired, and it was late, but he wanted to talk to her about the woman he'd faced in the warehouse who reminded him of her.

He left the booth, headed toward the door, and paused, looking out into the darkness. Her shadowy form moved swiftly along the street. He closed the door to the Dragon and followed her by staying in the shadows along the buildings. He turned the corner and thought he saw someone drifting down the street.

Gavin hurried toward it, and as soon as he got there, he realized it wasn't Imogen at all. He'd lost her.

Balls.

She was a thief, after all. At least, he thought she was. She worked with Gaspar enough that she would have to be trained in some way, enough so that she could sneak along with the old thief. Probably far more effectively than Gavin had ever managed to do—something Gaspar loved to point out to him.

There were lessons there for Gavin to learn, and if he was going to have to deal with Tristan the way it seemed he was, they were lessons he'd have to learn as quickly as possible.

The person he came across had the distinctive clothing of one of the constables, a dark gray bordering on a deep blue. The constables carried short swords sheathed at their sides and wore leather helms, signifying that they were there for the protection of the people. He didn't recognize this constable, but he trailed after him for a moment to see with certainty. He knew many of the enchanters who now worked with the constables, so he wanted to know.

Finally, Gavin turned away. Even trailing after this constable left him too tired to do much else. He didn't want to run the risk of encountering anyone with magic, forcing him to draw upon his core reserves—or his core magic, as he had told Wrenlow. He needed to recover through a good night of sleep.

He slipped off along the street, heading toward the place he'd been making his home and trying to ignore the feeling he detected in the city around him, which suggested there was other magic here. The feeling left him questioning whether Tristan was out there, following him.

And even if he was, there wasn't anything Gavin could do to stop him. That bothered him more than anything else.

CHAPTER FOUR

The lower level of the sorcerer's lair was dark. He had considered staying in the above-ground levels of Cyran's home, but there was a danger in him staying up there, especially now that Tristan was in the city. As far as Gavin knew, Tristan hadn't discovered the lairs. When there had been only evidence that Tristan was alive but not one of Gavin's opponents, it had been safer. Why shouldn't Gavin use a place that had been offered to him, that few others knew about? Now he was no longer sure it was safe, though there was a connection through it that he still needed to keep secured.

The darkness of the tunnels surrounded him, and he slipped the ring onto his finger for only a moment, long enough for him to find the door leading into the chamber. He pushed power out through his hand, borrowing only a bit from his core reserves to trip the magical lock on the door that allowed him to go inside.

Even that much weakened him.

He closed the door, pressed his hand against it, and let a little more of his core reserves flow from him so that he could seal it off.

He looked around the room. He'd been safe here. Separate from the others. It was possible that Gaspar knew where he spent his time. The old thief had every reason to know where he had gone, not only because Gavin had revealed this place to him but also because Gaspar tended to know things.

Then again, Gavin hadn't been spending that much time with Gaspar lately. Not because he didn't want to, at least not entirely, but because the type of job that Gavin had started to do—the urgency that he had as he looked through the city for evidence of Tristan—had taken him away from pulling jobs with Gaspar. The old thief also didn't need to get caught up in anything like this. Why should he get dragged into dealing with magic when it would force him to deal with power that he'd already told Gavin he wanted nothing to do with?

Gavin settled onto the small chair that stood across from a table. A few items were stacked on the table, most of them enchantments that Gavin had collected over his time in the city. He'd left them there, partly to ensure that he had additional connections were they to be necessary. He didn't like the possibility that he would need anything like that, and he certainly didn't want to rely on enchantments, but he'd learned that, if nothing else, being prepared was the only way to protect himself.

The dark egg also sat on the table, and Gavin could

practically feel its presence. He avoided touching it, not wanting to run the risk of inadvertently freeing the semarrl, though Gavin didn't even know if something like that was possible. As far as he knew, the dark egg needed to be intentionally activated.

He still wasn't entirely sure how to keep it protected. At least, not completely.

He would need to offer some real defensive measures for the egg, primarily to make sure that others didn't use it. More importantly, he had to ensure Tristan didn't come back for it. There was the possibility that he would make a play for the egg again, either to target Yoran or to go after the Fates.

Gavin unsheathed his El'aras sword and set it on the table. The absence of a glow reassured him that there was no magic in the room, but he also knew that wasn't a guarantee. He didn't know if it was possible to shield magic from the sword and the dagger, preventing them from detecting the use of power around him. Enchantments seemed to trigger it, though not nearly as potently as those who used magic intrinsically, like enchanters or sorcerers. The dagger hadn't glowed nearly as much as it should have earlier, though.

Despite his exhaustion, resting in the chair wasn't going to give him the sleep he needed. Neither would thinking about how Tristan was still in the city.

A small jar resting on the table caught his attention. Within it was the sh'rasn, but he had no interest in using that substance. It would allow him to tap into a greater source of power, but there were consequences to using it that he wasn't ready to endure yet. Were he to use the powder, Gavin would eventually be out for days.

It was better just to sleep; a natural way of restoring his connection to magic. There was no desperation here, though perhaps if he were to keep drawing upon power, he might find a need for the sh'rasn.

The draw of sleep called to him, and he started to question just how much of his power he'd really used. Gavin didn't have control over it, not nearly as much as he needed to better understand that magic. He could feel the energy in the core reserves and had drawn on that power enough times that he knew how to do so, but drawing on it and controlling it were two different skills.

It seemed to him that the dagger and the sword helped him focus the magic, but when he had pushed power out and exploded the boxes, along with his attackers, he hadn't used a focus like he had other times.

That had been the first time he'd done anything like that.

Hadn't it?

Gavin got up and paced, but soon had to stop as he felt a wave of weakness wash through him. He leaned on the table for support and then frowned to himself.

When he was the Chain Breaker, his abilities had involved magic. Gavin was certain of it now. At the time he'd first learned to do it, he'd thought it was tied to something within him, the core reserves of strength that empowered him.

Now he knew that Tristan had been trying to test him all along. Tristan had wanted him to use that power, had wanted him to find a way to access that magic, but there had to be some purpose behind it. Why would Tristan have taught him to reach for power that would only be able to be used against him?

It was times like these when he wished Anna was here with him. He reached into his pocket, holding the marker she'd given him. It was the same size as a coin, though it was warm to the touch.

He was tempted to use it. There had been several times since he'd defeated Tristan where he'd felt a desire to call to her so he could learn more about his magic, but it had also been a need to learn more about the El'aras. Were it not for his promise to protect the city, Gavin *would* have gone with her.

He had to be honest with himself, though. He wanted to learn more about Anna, not just the El'aras. And he suspected she felt the same way. She had stayed behind to watch over him after he'd been injured. That had to mean something.

But she was royalty. She was powerful among the El'aras, even though she had hidden in Yoran and stayed here until Gavin had been hired to bring her out of hiding. There had to be some reason that had kept her from returning to her people before, some answer Gavin did not know.

He took a deep breath and pushed away the thought of going to her.

A narrow bed that Gavin had dragged down here long ago was pushed against the wall. It wasn't nearly as comfortable as the beds in the Dragon, and the sheets weren't as clean as Jessica managed to keep them, but he settled into it. He missed Jessica's fragrant perfume, but he knew that staying here kept her and everyone else in the Dragon safe.

It also gave him an opportunity to have his own space. Alone.

This was one of the lessons Gavin had mastered above all—or at least he had until he'd started to work with Wrenlow, then Gaspar, and now even the constables.

He stared up at the ceiling. His mind raced, working through everything he had encountered, everything he had dealt with so far today. Despite trying to figure it out, Gavin still didn't feel as if he could come to terms with all of it.

There were no answers. How could there be when he had no idea what more he might have to face?

He had to slow his breathing, calm his mind, and settle into sleep. Gradually, he managed to do so, but it was not restful.

Dreams came to him. They were the same sort of troubled dreams he'd had ever since coming to Yoran—ones that filled him with memories of his youth, that left him knowing he'd been guided toward something, forced to serve in a way he hadn't chosen. Gavin stirred while he was sleeping and struggled through those dreams, trying to make sense of what filled his mind.

But he managed to curl up and relax, feeling warmth flow through him. It started deep in his belly, working from someplace buried within and making its way up, washing over him.

Gavin understood that to be magic. At least, that's what he understood now. The power connected him, guiding him to who and what he had once been. When he was younger, he had known about the power and connection he had, but he hadn't known why Tristan wanted him to be the Chain Breaker.

Tristan appeared in this dream.

Gavin had been almost fifteen. He had come into his skill and powers and had already acquired the nickname of the Chain Breaker. He'd been driven away from the other students he had trained with, making it difficult for him to feel as if he belonged anywhere. Tristan had forced him to take on increasingly challenging jobs—jobs that actually had meaning to Tristan and were no longer simple tests.

There had been dozens of them around this time. Gavin had been sent to take out targets, acquire items, and disappear. He was meant to be little more than the shadows, and in all those jobs, he had never struggled.

Until this one.

The dream settled around Gavin. He was aware that it was not real, as if there was some power within him that enabled him to know this was a dream but not to be able to act within it.

He would much rather have other dreams, even if they were of Jessica. Though, if Gavin were able to control his dreams, he would prefer to think of Anna—her golden hair, her soft and gentle smile, the connection he felt when he was with her.

He couldn't do anything about it, though. It felt as if he

were determined to have this dream, as if the magic were forcing him along the path of seeing this and knowing what was here.

Before him was a dark house set in the forest just beyond the borders of Nelar, the city where he and Tristan had traveled to for part of his training. Gavin had been forced to engage in several street fights, each of them with an increasing number of thugs that Tristan had managed to coordinate to come after him. None of them had been altogether challenging. Still, Gavin's fists were bruised and bloodied, and he thought he'd broken a bone in his leg. It hurt every time he took a step, but Tristan had not given him any opportunity to recover.

This job was too important to waste that kind of time.

When Tristan had assigned him the job, Gavin had asked why he had to take it, why he needed to attack when he was still so injured. Tristan had dismissed his concern, the way he often did.

"You think all jobs will go easily?" Tristan asked, standing in the shadows of a tree, his gaze lingering on the small home nestled within a clearing in the forest outskirts. Tristan had on a dark gray cloak with the hood covering his black hair, only his flinty gray eyes gleaming from underneath it and a hint of the lines on the corners of his eyes visible.

"I don't know if I can get through this quietly," Gavin said.

The home wasn't large, but it was isolated. His foot throbbed with a steady pain, but not enough that Gavin thought he had to pay too much attention to it. But it was there, and he was all too aware that it would limit him. Tristan had taught him to ignore pain, saying it was merely a mental barrier. Though it wasn't anything he truly struggled with, sometimes even mental barriers posed real challenges.

Still, he knew that Tristan wouldn't permit him to show any weakness. Which meant that Gavin would have to take the job and complete it successfully.

It was possible the job was a test, though typically when Tristan sent him after items, they were actual assignments. Knowing Tristan, though, all assignments were tests in some way, as if he wanted to gauge whether Gavin would be able to complete all of his tasks regardless of what was placed upon him.

Gavin looked around the clearing, and there was nothing that posed a challenge to him or said he couldn't complete the job. So, he hobbled across the clearing to the home and moved to one of the windows so that he could look inside for any sign of activity.

There was none.

He resisted the urge to look behind him and see whether Tristan was there, but he knew the man would be watching.

Gavin limped toward the door. He hadn't heard anything, and he tried to ignore the pain shooting through his ankle and the agony that screamed within him, but he couldn't. He winced and cried out.

It would be something Tristan would chastise him about later, but Gavin didn't care. For now, he just had to finish this job.

He pulled the door open, and something blasted at him. He dropped and rolled forward, driving out with a Sudo-style chop that connected with an older man. He brought his knee up as he spun and landed on his injured ankle, biting back the anguish that shrieked through him. The man tried to hold his hand out toward him again, but Gavin forced himself forward.

Something like a magical rope looped around him, and Gavin ignored it, trying to use his connection to the core reserves to blast past what was holding him and to destroy the energy that controlled him—and as it did, he struggled to fight past it. Gavin focused on the core reserves the way Tristan had taught him, and he exploded with an outward force. Whatever band of power this person held around him shattered. Gavin spun and drove his fist down on the old man, chopping through him.

Then the man stopped moving.

Gavin scrambled to his feet. Tristan had told him to fetch a small stone ring. He hurried and searched through the house. The inside was simple, sparsely decorated with a row of cabinets and a cookstove, along with a table and chairs. Gavin rushed through the cabinets, but he didn't find anything. The table was empty, and there was nothing along the flooring.

Finally, he staggered toward the back bedroom and leaned on the doorframe. There was a bed and a table but nothing else.

Where was the ring?

This had to be part of Tristan's test that Gavin had to complete.

But how?

He'd found nothing. Just the man who had attacked him.

The man.

Gavin hadn't checked him over.

He returned to the man, who was still lying motionless. His chest rose and fell, and Gavin wondered if Tristan wanted him to kill this person. He doubted it, though, because if Tristan wanted somebody dead, he typically told Gavin.

He crouched down and started sorting through the man's pockets, but there was still no luck. Gavin looked over his body, and then he found it. The man wore the ring on the third finger of his left hand. Gavin pulled it off and examined it. The pale white stone was warm to the touch, though not hot, and it was without any writing or symbols. Strange that Tristan would find that valuable.

Of course, some of the jobs Tristan had him do seemed strange, as if Tristan needed something but didn't want to reveal information in its entirety. Gavin tucked the ring into his pocket and nearly stumbled as he jumped to his feet. He staggered out of the house, closed the door, and then hurried across the clearing to find Tristan.

Gavin stumbled, his body aching, but he had succeeded. This wasn't the most complicated task Tristan had assigned, but it was odd enough that he thought there had to be some significance to what Tristan had wanted him to claim.

He hadn't gone far in the trees when something struck him from behind.

Gavin went sprawling forward. He tried to roll over but couldn't as a heavy weight pressed down on him, as if some massive boulder rested on his back. Then someone grabbed at him, tearing at him.

They left Gavin's knives. They left his coin. They took the ring.

The weight continued to bear down on him, long enough that Gavin could no longer breathe. He had trained to hold his breath, one more torment in a series of them, and he had learned to withstand this pain.

Now he fought, but not for long.

Gavin didn't have the strength to do so. At some point, he blacked out.

When he came around, it had started to grow dark. He gathered himself off the forest floor and stumbled through the trees, sweeping his gaze around for his assailant but saw no sign of them. He checked his pockets to make certain the ring was gone. He looked back toward the small house, but he knew he wouldn't find any information there.

He had failed.

Already he feared how Tristan would react. Gavin had never failed him so completely before. He had always managed to fulfill the assigned task or remove the target.

He staggered back toward the house and shook his head. He was in no shape to fight, and it was getting late. Time for him to return. Tristan would have to understand.

The walk back to the city took a long time. With the pain in his ankle, Gavin struggled to make it. The sun had fully set by the time he finally reached the city, and it was much after dark when he reached the tavern where they were staying. When he entered, Tristan sat at a table, drinking a mug of ale.

Gavin sat down across from him, and Tristan looked over to him. His eyes were unreadable and his dark hair neatly combed, as if he'd been relaxing the entire time Gavin had been working.

"Did you succeed?" Tristan asked.

Gavin wanted to snap at him, but fatigue and his own natural hesitation around Tristan gave him a moment to pause. Had Tristan been there, he wouldn't have lost the ring. "Why didn't you wait?"

Tristan glowered at him and looked like he wanted to strike Gavin. "You didn't need me to wait."

"You knew I was injured."

Tristan leaned forward, shaking his head. "Injury is not an excuse."

"I'm not making an excuse. You wanted me to pull the job while I was injured. That's what I did."

Tristan cocked his head to the side. "Then you got it."

"You didn't think I would?"

Tristan shrugged. "I wasn't sure."

"What is it?" Gavin asked.

"A trinket."

"The ring is just a trinket?"

Tristan shrugged again and took a sip of the ale. "A test, if that's what you need to know. But seeing as how you succeeded, I suppose we will continue."

"I got it… then lost it."

Tristan tensed. "What do you mean you lost it?"

Gavin swallowed. "I don't know what happened. I had it, Tristan. Then when I was making my way—"

A fist swung toward him, and Gavin ducked beneath it.

Tristan sat back as if nothing had happened. "How did you lose it?"

"Because I was injured. Beaten. And you weren't there."

"What makes you think someone will be there for you when you need them?" Tristan's voice was dangerous and low.

"They won't," Gavin said.

"No, they won't. You must learn to function on your own." Tristan clenched his jaw. "Had you succeeded, I would have let you rest."

Gavin tensed. Rest was what he needed now.

"Since you failed…" Tristan looked at him. "Go. Take this time to contemplate your failure. We will be leaving early in the morning."

Gavin got to his feet and fought back the pain exacerbated by the effort he had exerted to walk here. He staggered off and settled into the room to sleep. When he awoke, darkness still streamed in through the window, and he headed down to the tavern so that he'd be there before Tristan.

He paused in the doorway. Tristan was already sitting in a booth, talking to a dark-haired man. Gavin stepped back, but not before he heard a word that he couldn't quite understand, one that came from a language he hadn't learned.

Gavin waited until the man disappeared and then

stepped out into the tavern, joining Tristan. His mentor never said anything about it.

"It's time to go."

Gavin nodded and limped toward the door. His ankle didn't hurt nearly as much as it had before, and he tried to push the pain out, but even that was a struggle.

As they reached the horses, Gavin kept waiting for Tristan to say something more about his failure, but he never did.

CHAPTER FIVE

Darkness greeted Gavin as he came awake, and he stared up at the ceiling. That had been the last time he'd failed Tristan. Neither had spoken of it since, though the dynamic had changed between them after that. Gavin had never understood why, and he'd pushed himself in his training, not wanting to fail again.

He sat up, rubbing the sleep from his eyes. He slipped on the enchantment for just a moment, long enough for him to make out the contents of the room.

The night's rest had done him good. He had needed it, to get back to some semblance of recovery, and he felt as if he could finally reach for the power within him and use something of it to help him restore his strength. At least now if he were to face a test, he didn't think he'd struggle quite as much as he had before. But why did he have the dreams he did?

Maybe it was because he'd seen Tristan.

There were things about that time that had faded from him, but they had started to come back ever since he'd encountered Tristan in the city. Even before that, though, some things had started resurfacing when he had met up with Cyran.

Gavin got to his feet, and for a moment he expected a flare of pain in his ankle, as if the dream had been real. But there was no pain, other than the aches he felt from fighting through the attackers the night before.

It was time for him to work with Wrenlow. He headed out of the underground room and used his core reserves to seal the door. He looked around the street. From the way sunlight slanted along the buildings, it had to be midday, which meant that Gavin had slept longer than he had intended—hopefully, it had been only the one night, not more than that. He felt rested, which was always a challenge when he used as much magic as he had. It wouldn't be the first time he'd slept more than he thought.

Gavin headed toward the Dragon. A bright sun shone down overhead, streaming through a few wispy clouds and giving a warmth to the day that was not completely pushed away by the occasional cool gust of wind. A pleasing fragrance hung in the air from the flowers and trees on the edge of the city, as well as the vegetables, breads, and roasting meats from a nearby market. Gavin stayed clear of the market, mostly out of a desire to avoid drawing anyone's attention, but everything around him felt alive.

It was reassuring.

He had committed to offering Yoran a level of protection, and he was determined to do just that. These people didn't want to deal with magic, at least not the overt violence of the sorcerers they had once dealt with. They deserved something more, which was why he had stayed, to ensure that the city was protected from the Fates and any danger they might bring. Gavin had no idea if the Fates would even try anything more here, but he wouldn't put it past them to do so.

He reached one of the main streets of the city. The crowd of people started to increase, giving Gavin a chance to blend in and feel for any sense of movement that would signify somebody trying to follow him. He wouldn't put it past Tristan to track him down and send someone after him. Still, he didn't feel any sense of magic or detect anything out here whatsoever.

Maybe he was safe, at least for now.

By the time he reached the Dragon, he realized maybe he hadn't gotten nearly as much sleep as he had thought. He still felt tired, which suggested it had been only a single night of sleep.

Gavin paused in front of the main entrance. Though the wooden door was simple, an incredibly detailed dragon head was carved into it. He hesitated before pushing open the door, debating whether he wanted to go through the main part of the tavern or whether he wanted to sneak up and around.

Going through the tavern meant running into Jessica. Gavin had been careful about encountering her since he'd left the tavern, not wanting to have conflict with her, but also not wanting to raise the possibility with anybody who might be watching that he had any residual affection for her. It was for her own safety.

That's all it is.

He doubted that she would agree, but that was part of the reason he'd made a point of doing it. Jessica would tell him that she was safe, and though she might be, she didn't really understand the depths of the danger to her. Gavin also didn't want to put her in any more risk than necessary, especially considering how he had been responsible for so much of what had happened to her.

Which meant going in one of the side entrances.

Gavin ducked around the outside of the Dragon and made his way toward the kitchen door before pausing. Even that would potentially draw Jessica's attention, especially if she was the one cooking.

He could scale the wall, but he didn't really want to. It might be necessary so that he could get to Wrenlow, but then they'd have to sneak back out. That wouldn't be the worst thing in the world, and certainly not the most difficult.

Gavin scaled the wall and pulled himself up to the window of the room where he knew Wrenlow was staying, then tapped on it.

There was no answer.

He tapped again and peered through. Considering that it was midday, he wouldn't be terribly surprised if Wrenlow was already gone. There was another possibility, though, and as Gavin stared through the window at the still-made bed, he smiled to himself.

"That rascal," he whispered.

He started to scramble back down, when he slipped, landing with too much noise.

Gavin bounded to his feet, ready to hurry from the alley, only to come face-to-face with Jessica. She was a lovely woman about five years his senior, with deep brown hair pulled back in a ponytail. Grease stained her apron, and her arms were crossed over her chest.

"You're making all that noise sneaking back here?"

"I'm not sneaking," he said, though knew it wouldn't convince her.

"And you'd rather sneak up the side of my tavern than come through and visit with me?"

Gavin flashed a smile at her, though she didn't react to it the way she once had. "I was in your tavern last night, Jessica."

He looked past her, and immediately wished that he hadn't. When he turned his attention back to her, she watched him with a sour expression.

"You were there, but you didn't even bother to stop and talk to me."

He should have, and he understood why she'd be upset that he hadn't. "I'm sorry. I was out of it last night. Work. And other things."

She opened her mouth, looking like she wanted to say something, then shook her head. "What happened to us, Gavin?"

"I didn't realize that anything happened to us."

"We both agreed it was going to be casual. You're the one making this uncomfortable."

She was right, and Gavin knew she was, but it didn't

make it any easier for him. "I'm not trying to make it uncomfortable," he said. "It's just…"

"Just that you think you can protect me."

Gavin cocked his head, watching her before nodding slowly. "Is that wrong?"

"You know, you would be better able to protect me if you stayed at the Dragon rather than wherever you've skulked off to."

"I'm not skulking off anywhere."

"You haven't come around nearly as much. I remember the first night you came to the Dragon and needed a place to stay."

"You offered me your room," Gavin said.

"That doesn't need to be the case now," she said. "If you would prefer more traditional accommodations, I'm more than happy to provide them."

"I know you are," he said. He looked around the street before turning his attention back to her. "I'm… just worried. There." It was hard to admit. "There's a danger in the city, and I'm not sure it's the kind you would be able to handle."

"Is that right? I've managed to keep the Dragon under my supervision for the better part of twenty years. You don't think I can manage a little bit of trouble?"

"It's not that," he said.

"Then what is it?"

"It's just that… I know the kind of men we're dealing with."

"It's not just the *kind* of men we're dealing with," she said, tapping him on the chest. "You know the exact man."

"I do," he said. "And I know that we need to be careful with him. *You* need to."

"I have been. I've made sure we have enchantments all over the tavern. Is that what you wanted to hear? Did you want to know that I've done everything in my power to ensure the safety of the Dragon? Zella has been working with me to make sure we have everything we need."

"I didn't know that," Gavin said.

"Maybe if you came around more often, you might." She shook her head. "Or you might spend a little time with Gaspar. He's worried about you, you know."

Gavin smiled slightly. "I doubt he's all that worried about me. Gaspar and I have a working type of relationship, nothing more than that."

"Maybe that's how you view it, but I've noticed the way he's talked about you."

"With a lot of swearing?"

Jessica just shook her head again. "Come by and visit with him, would you? And maybe sit and have a mug of ale, and talk with me as if we're friends rather than whatever you've decided to make us."

Gavin took a deep breath before nodding. He really *should* be better with that. "I will."

"And don't go climbing the side of my tavern again to find Wrenlow. He never came back last night."

"I figured that. I saw that his bed was made."

Jessica smiled. "That boy. He keeps such a messy room, but I've been trying to pick up after him. Somebody has to care for him."

"I'm trying to help him learn to care for himself," Gavin said.

"I've heard," she said. "Teaching him to fight isn't going to turn him into you, you know."

"I don't think either of us wants him to be turned into me. Teaching him how to fight is helping him learn how to protect himself, nothing more than that."

"He's been spending quite a bit of time with Olivia."

"I know," Gavin said.

"Really? Seeing as how you haven't been coming around the Dragon, I wasn't sure if you were paying much attention to what he's been doing."

"I pay attention," he said. "Sometimes he lets me pay attention a bit too much, if you know what I mean." Gavin tapped the enchantment on his chest.

Jessica wrinkled her brow. "That's… unfortunate."

"You're telling me. I have to take it out so that I don't have to hear."

"Maybe they want you to listen." She winked at him. "Anyway, it *is* nice to see you, Gavin."

"The only way I can keep you—and the Dragon—safe is by staying away."

"It's isolating you," she said. "Is that your intent?"

He frowned. It hadn't been, but maybe that was Tristan's plan all along.

That bastard.

Gavin wouldn't put it past him to do that, to sever the connections he'd made in the city and break him away from not only Gaspar and his ability to help but also Wrenlow, Imogen, and now even Jessica.

And Gavin had let him do it.

"Damn," he whispered. "I'm sorry."

"There you are," she said, smiling and shaking her head. "It seems as if the great Gavin Lorren has decided to return."

"The great Gavin Lorren never left," he said. "But I think I'd started to let myself get manipulated."

"If you're worried about him, your best bet is to use the resources you've accumulated here. It's because of you that the city is safer and that the constables and the enchanters have decided to work together again. It's because of you that the Fates left."

"For now," he said. "The problem is that they'll return."

He had the dark egg. The semarrl. That was his deterrent.

They wouldn't come so long as they knew he had that.

But if he lost it…

Then the Fates *might* return. The city would suffer. Gavin didn't think even he was strong enough to handle the three Fates at one time.

"You don't know that."

"I don't, but I remember what they said when they left, the warning they gave me. They aren't done with Yoran."

"But you gave us time to ensure they can't keep targeting us," Jessica said.

Hopefully, it was time well spent. It was difficult to know, though. Were the constables training, or were they simply acquiring enchantments? But even if it was just about the enchantments, that was still a level of preparation.

"I'll come back tonight," Gavin said. "Is that good enough?"

"It is," she said.

He smiled at her and turned away, thankful she'd stopped glaring at him midway through the conversation.

He tapped on the enchantment, listening for a moment. "If you're there, Wrenlow, I would love to have a conversation with you."

There was no answer and nothing to suggest Wrenlow had his enchantment on. Maybe he was busy with Olivia.

Gavin meandered through the streets. He was in no hurry, but he needed to prepare.

There were specific types of preparations he needed, and some he could do now. He headed through the city, and he slowed as he neared the constables' building.

There was a distinct energy; a type of power that suggested magic use nearby. Gavin had grown accustomed to that magic here and the way they pulled on the power. The enchanters within this place drew on that magic, but he found that the power was used more openly than he had expected. There had to be others in the city who could detect the use of magic. It had to be more than just him who was aware of it, but it didn't seem as if anyone else cared.

He paused at the entrance to the constable barracks. The crowds that he'd seen elsewhere in the city weren't here. He lingered, holding his hand on the door, and then pushed it open.

The barracks had a different feel to them than when he'd

first come here. With the enchanters now working with the constables—and, in many cases, serving as constables themselves—the barracks had become a place where magic existed more openly than it did in any other spot within the city. Gavin found that amusing, though he noticed an occasional side-eyed glance from some of the constables and understood that old grievances would take time to resolve. Just because Davel Chan said a thing didn't make it so.

The inside of the building was awash with activity. Several constables looked up when he entered, but none of them reacted. He was a common enough sight these days. He recognized a man sitting at a desk near the door and headed over to him.

"Enrath," Gavin said to the man with long hair parted down the middle. "I'm looking for Davel. Is he in?"

Enrath nodded to the stairs at the back of the building. "Down. You know what he's doing."

Gavin grunted. "Still?"

"Most of the time. He has us making as many as we can," Enrath said, looking down at the stacks of wood piled on the desk.

Gavin shook his head. Enrath was an enchanter-turned-constable, a man he had come to know and interact with a few times. He suspected that Enrath was probably closer to forty than he was to twenty, despite how young he looked.

"He doesn't have you patrolling?" Gavin asked.

"Oh, he has us do that from time to time, but he's much more concerned about making sure we're all prepared."

Enrath shrugged. "I eventually get tired and can't make any more, so he lets us go out again."

Gavin chuckled. "Keep at it, I guess."

"Do I have much choice?"

Gavin laughed and made his way down the stairs. The farther he descended, the more he felt the walls pressing in on him. The stairs narrowed, and he could feel magic swirling around him, leaving the hairs on his arms standing on end.

He reached the lowest level. The magic here felt more potent than anywhere else in the constables' building; powerful enough that it filled him. He headed down to a set of closed double doors, and he pushed out a bit of power through him to trigger the enchantment required to open the doors.

Once he did, he saw three constables sparring with each other inside the room. They were nearly moving faster than he could track. They were all enchanted with speed and strength, and they appeared to have enchantments that made their skin nearly as hard as stone given the way knives bounced off them harmlessly.

"Impressive, isn't it?" Davel asked.

Gavin glanced down at the shorter man with a balding head. His muscles showed through his gray jacket and pants, but he had no weapons on him.

"How often do they spar?" Gavin asked.

"Quite a bit. Considering what we've been dealing with, it's been necessary." Gavin frowned, and Davel went on. "There have been more magical attacks within the city.

We keep waiting for the Fates to return. My interrogation of the Keeper has suggested that they will."

"Have you still been working with Zella?"

"She has been involved. She's less interested in questioning the Keeper than we are, though I think her reticence is understandable."

"What have you learned from the Keeper?"

"Very little. We have tried to push to find what the Triad intended beyond their simple attack—"

"Simple?" Gavin grunted. "I would argue that using the jade egg to create the dark egg to summon the semarrl to destroy the Fates is anything but a simple plan."

"Perhaps not simple. Straightforward, I should say. And it is not just about them, is it?"

Gavin clenched his jaw. It wasn't. It was about Tristan and whatever he planned, though Gavin had no idea what Tristan intended to do. He was still after something; Gavin was sure of it.

Maybe Tristan still wanted the dark egg. But without the Fates being able to attack, there might not be anything that Tristan needed the egg for.

Davel shrugged. "I don't know anything about this man, so I'm not sure." It seemed as if Davel read Gavin's mind. "Most of the time, we detect the magical intrusion as soon as it happens. As it's often nothing more than the intrusion, it feels like they're testing our ability to detect them, rather than planning any real attack."

"That's probably what it is," Gavin said.

"They haven't been able to do anything, though," Davel said. "They might have gotten past us a few times, but we stopped them as soon as they pressed too deep into the city."

"Did you detect a magical attack last night on the northern edge of the city?"

Davel looked over. "No."

Gavin frowned. "I thought your enchantments were designed to ensure that you picked up on all sorts of magic."

"You know that isn't how it works."

"Can you sense when I use any power? I used power last night," Gavin admitted.

"Let me guess. Because of this man you feel is targeting the city."

Gavin watched the fighting in front of them, which he found incredible. This was what he needed to be working on. This was where he needed to be practicing.

"He was there," Gavin said. "I don't know what he was after, but he targeted me."

"If he was targeting you, then he would've brought real force. We didn't pick up on anything."

"He brought eight men from Jind."

Davel frowned. "Jind? That's a long way away, and they prefer the style of… Anyway, we haven't seen any evidence of them."

Gavin chuckled. "That's how they like it. They're all skilled, but…"

"You took care of them? I don't need you leaving bodies throughout the city, Gavin."

"I doubt there were any bodies left. There was a fire in a warehouse on the north side."

"I received word," Davel said.

Gavin nodded. He remembered that much from leaving the warehouse. Wrenlow had seen to it that the constables would be informed so the fire wouldn't spread too far into the city. "What did you find?"

"It had burned out by the time we got there. It didn't spread, if that's what your concern was."

"A bit," Gavin said.

"If that's what you were worried about, then you could have reported the fire."

"I *had* somebody report it. I was busy recovering from the fight, which is why I'm here now."

Davel cocked his head, turning his full attention to Gavin. "You're here because of the fight?"

"I'm here because I realized something after the attack last night."

"About this man?" Davel asked, motioning to the constables behind him. They continued their sparring, though the intensity of the fighting increased.

"More about me."

Davel turned back to Gavin. "Are you leaving?"

Gavin smiled. "You don't have to sound so eager to get me out of Yoran."

"The longer you stay here, the more likely we face additional attacks. I realize you offer your own sort of protection, but there's been more activity in the city ever since the Fates targeted us. The enchanters are doing what they can to prevent any more attacks. They've been making enchantments that offer us a level of protection, far more than they had before, but there's still a danger in how many we've been fending off. Eventually, they may overwhelm our ability to protect the city."

It was the first time Gavin had heard Davel talk about that. "I can help."

Davel frowned. "I thought you *were* helping."

"I can do more to help," Gavin said quickly.

Davel grunted. "I thought you were."

Here Gavin had been worried about the Dragon, Jessica, and the people within the tavern, but maybe that wasn't all he needed to be concerned about. He needed to be more worried about the others in danger here. Not just those he cared about in Yoran, but also the city itself. Hadn't he promised to ensure its safety? Maybe there was no way for him to do that while he was here—not while Tristan continued to target it.

"I have been," Gavin said, "which is why I need something from you."

"And that is?"

Gavin looked over, smiling slightly. "It's something I'm sure you'll enjoy."

"Then I'm guessing I won't."

"I need you to fight me."

Davel pressed his lips together, studying Gavin. "Fight you?"

Gavin nodded. "Filled with your enchantments. I need you to use anything you think you have that can defeat me."

"I see."

"I've been growing complacent," Gavin said.

The fight the night before had made that abundantly

clear. He hadn't drawn upon the skills he knew he had, and there was only so much he could do practicing with Wrenlow or fighting against common street thugs. What he needed was somebody who would pose a real challenge.

He needed to be prepared for Tristan. Which was why he needed Davel.

Davel had proven he was skilled and knew various fighting styles, but Gavin also needed Davel's willingness to use enchantments so Gavin could test himself.

"I might be convinced to do that," Davel said. "When would you like to do it?"

Gavin looked over, and the other fighters had stopped to talk to each other. "Why not now?"

Davel chuckled. "Very well. I warn you, I won't go easy on you."

"No one ever has."

CHAPTER SIX

Gavin groaned as he stretched his muscles. He had sparred with Davel Chan for several hours, longer than he'd expected Davel's interest to hold. It had been useful for Gavin, but he had no idea whether Davel felt the same.

Still, Gavin had been pleasantly surprised by Davel's talent. He had used enchantments, but not nearly as many as Gavin thought he would have. It'd given Gavin the first real sparring session he'd had in quite some time. And now he was tired.

He hadn't used his core reserves during the fight, intentionally avoiding doing so. Even when Davel had struck him the first time and pain bloomed in his arm where he'd punched, Gavin had avoided doing it.

He wanted to be challenged the way Tristan would have challenged him, and he wanted to make sure he could withstand that kind of violence, to be ready the next time he faced Tristan. It was the entire reason he'd come to the constables' barracks.

Gavin remained convinced that all of this was some sort of test. Davel's explanations about what had been going on within the city, the other incursions that had attempted to press magic on Yoran, had done nothing more than reinforce that belief. And if that was the purpose behind it, Gavin had to question what more they might find.

What other tests did Tristan have in mind?

Any others that Tristan might attempt would likely be magical, but perhaps it was a mistake to think that way. As far as Gavin knew, any tests Tristan tried might not be magical but simply tied to the kind of power Gavin possessed.

He followed through the streets, sweeping his gaze along the buildings. He tapped on his enchantment. "Wrenlow, if you're there, I'd like to visit with you."

He waited a moment, but there was no answer. He passed a pair of men who glanced in his direction, and Gavin flashed a smile at them, making them turn quickly and head away from him.

The city felt different today. That might only be his imagination, but perhaps there was an urgency to it that had not been there before.

Could others have detected the magical intrusion?

He had little doubt that the people were attuned to it, at least in some ways. They had dealt with magic over the years, and many would likely do anything to ensure that they didn't have to face it again.

A small child scurried past him, chased by three others. They shouted before blending into the crowd in front of him.

Gavin paused. What would happen if he couldn't protect Yoran the way he intended? He had to push those thoughts away.

Wrenlow still wasn't available. Gavin had expected that when he'd finished sparring with Davel, he would hear from Wrenlow, mostly because he anticipated that Wrenlow would want to find him again.

Gaspar hadn't dropped onto the enchantment either. That wasn't altogether surprising, though. Gaspar rarely chimed in unless he was on a job with Gavin, which didn't happen these days.

A test.

Gavin couldn't get past that feeling.

He slipped along the street and found the forest stretching out in front of him. Gavin didn't go into the towering trees often these days, though not out of fear. It was more because he suspected that doing so would separate him from the city more than he wanted, as if going into the trees would create a division he needed to avoid.

Gavin made his way forward and slowed when he caught sight of Cyran's house. It had been a sorcerer's residence even before Cyran had taken it over. Gavin paused on the far side of the street from the house, sweeping his gaze along. In the distance, a pair of constables patrolled. He nodded to them, though neither seemed to notice him.

Gavin walked up to the door and paused. Each time he

came here, he tested for any sort of magic he might detect. He still didn't have a full grasp of his understanding of magic, only that the longer he worked with his core reserves, the more he became attuned to the magic he had, along with the magic that existed around him in the city. That had to matter.

He didn't feel anything this time, but it didn't stop him from hesitating.

Tristan had come here.

Not only that, but he increasingly felt that Tristan had been the one to send Cyran.

There was too much that seemed to overlap, and though Gavin wasn't entirely sure why Tristan had been interested in Yoran—at least, not before he managed to unearth the dark egg—he still felt as if he needed to know.

Cyran had come here for something. Maybe it was only for the sorcerers' lairs, but there could've been something more.

Gavin waited for a moment, then another, to see if anything would reveal itself, wondering if Tristan had brought another attacker here.

No other tests.

Some part of him was a little disappointed that there was nothing, though he knew he shouldn't be. He stepped inside.

"What are you after?" Gavin whispered. He stood in the middle of the room. Everything in Cyran's home had been picked over, and nothing remained. Gavin had taken any useful furniture down to the chamber below to set up a space for him to maneuver, but he hadn't been able to find anything else here. The cabinets were all empty, and nothing of Cyran's was left.

He unsheathed the El'aras dagger and began to push outward with his core reserves. He clutched the dagger tightly and swung it from side to side, illuminating the space. Even as he looked around the room, he didn't find anything more.

The enchantment in his ear crackled.

"Wrenlow?"

It fell silent again, as if the enchantment had failed.

Gavin focused on his power, and he tapped on the enchantment again. "Is that you, Wrenlow? Or is it Gaspar?"

No answer came.

He started to release the power within him, and the enchantment crackled again. This time, he was certain of what he heard, though he had no idea what it might mean. He'd never heard the earpiece crackle like that and didn't know if there was some part of it that was starting to fail. All enchantments' powers waned eventually. He didn't expect the El'aras enchantment to fail quite so soon, though.

Gavin tapped on it again and listened, but there was nothing. "If either of you is there, I'm at Cyran's home. I want to talk about our plan for these attacks."

Gavin released his hold on the magic within him, letting it fade. He turned and headed to the back room and the trapdoor that led underground to Cyran's lair, where Gavin had found the El'aras sword. He stopped in front of the trapdoor, holding his hand above it, and then pulled the door open.

Though he could use the enchantment that would grant him light even in the darkness, he hesitated. He needed to make sure he could use his own power. Gavin focused on the core reserves within him and pushed energy out through the dagger. Then he climbed down.

Something seemed different.

It was instinct honed over years. That was the only reason he felt that something was off. Even in that, Gavin didn't know if what he detected was real, but he thought it was.

He wasn't alone.

Gavin jumped the remaining steps down the ladder and paused at the bottom, sweeping his gaze around him. He didn't see anything.

He focused and pushed more power out through the dagger. The blade glowed, but something else happened that he hadn't expected. As the power flowed out from him, Gavin was aware of the energy that drifted along the ground.

It met resistance straight ahead.

Gavin darted forward.

Almost too late, Gavin realized there were three people with him.

Had he not already been connected to his own power the way he was, he might not have even detected it. Gavin jumped back, latching on to the core reserves. He tried to push outward as he would as the Chain Breaker, but nothing about the resistance shifted. Not the way he expected it to. Power exploded away from him, but he wasn't able to do it again when he tried. There was energy, but nothing beyond that.

Gavin considered switching to the sword, but in the small confines of the space, the dagger made more sense. He squeezed the handle, and then he jumped forward.

He slammed into an invisible barrier.

"Magic?" he whispered.

He hadn't felt anything.

These days, that was unusual.

The three people stepped to either side of him, getting close enough that he could see them with the light from the dagger. For a moment, Gavin feared that these weren't just any three attackers but the Fates. Then he remembered the Fates would not have been dressed like this—all in deep black leather. And from what he had seen before, the Fates weren't all women.

These attackers had matching red hair, tanned skin, and slender daggers. They stood before him, and yet they made no attempt to come at him. They just stayed there, waiting.

"Is this a trick?" Gavin asked.

Or maybe they weren't only waiting. They were holding on to power and weren't going to let him pass. All of this was meant as a way to prevent him from getting to the chamber.

His chamber.

This was where he had been the night before, though. Could they have had some way of tracking him?

They didn't seem to be doing anything other than

trying to hold him back.

That was it.

Why were they here?

That seemed beyond what he would've expected, but with all of the strangeness he'd experienced around the city these days, he supposed he shouldn't be altogether surprised. He pushed the dagger up against the barrier slowly but found too much resistance.

He sheathed the dagger and pulled out the sword. The entire purpose of the sword, at least from what Gavin had seen, had been to allow him to carve through magic that he couldn't before.

As he continued to press the sword against the barrier, the energy crackled, creating faint blue lines that worked along the surface of the barrier. The lines streamed away from it and stretched outward, toward the sword and along the blade.

Gavin forced the blade forward again. This time, he tried a different technique, pushing power out from him. That had worked before, and he knew how to let that energy flow out of him into the sword. The power left the blade crackling even more, pressing up against what these three attackers were doing to him.

One of them stepped forward.

"Why don't you just lower this," Gavin said, "and then the four of us can have a little chat."

"Head back out of here and you won't have any trouble." Her voice was soft, slightly accented, and it carried a hint of power.

He almost laughed at the comment. *He* was to head out

of here? Who was *she* to say that to *him*?

"Who put you up to this? Was it Tristan?"

"Stay away from here," the woman said. The others echoed behind her.

They moved in sync with her, their words matching hers. Which meant they were mirror copies. What reason would she need for that?

"All right. Maybe it wasn't Tristan," Gavin conceded.

That didn't fit, though. Why would they be here otherwise?

The dark egg.

That was the only thing of real value in the chamber.

And Tristan was the one after it.

They *had* to be with him.

Gavin brought the sword back and swung. The blade slammed into the barrier, and the suddenness of the blow forced the lead woman back a step.

Some part of her barrier shifted. Gavin took that as a positive sign.

"You might want to keep moving back," he said.

The woman frowned. She had a dark and lovely face, which Gavin had to ignore. He didn't often go against female attackers, though it seemed to him that Tristan enjoyed sending women after him.

Another challenge in how well he knew Gavin.

Tristan knew about Gavin's hesitation to attack women. It had been one that Tristan had fought against when Gavin had been training with him, trying to force Gavin to recognize this weakness that needed to be expunged.

Gavin brought the sword back again and swung it, this time powering through the blade and pushing as much as he could. Energy exploded and slammed into the barrier. All three women staggered backward.

Gavin hurriedly regrouped. He hacked at the barrier, lines of blue sparkling along it and along the blade. As he continued to batter at it, rage filled him. He slammed the sword forward again, and the women took another step back. He swung it one more time, and the barrier exploded.

The copies faded, leaving only one woman.

Maybe the barrier had only made it *look* like there were three of them.

Gavin darted forward. The woman held up her hands, twisting them in a strange spiral pattern, and another barrier formed around them. The copies didn't reform. He noticed something then. A pale, stone ring on one finger of her hand.

The ring from his dream.

When he had failed Tristan.

The first—and last—time that he had failed this completely.

"Where did you get that?" Gavin whispered.

The woman frowned again. She twisted her hands once more, and power exploded from her. It wasn't sorcery, at least not directly, but it was a sort of strange magic he had never seen or felt before. He tried to resist what she was doing, but the energy crackled against him, as if it were forming a stronger barrier.

"Why are you here?" he asked.

Her magic had surrounded him. She was going to trap him, and if he wasn't careful, she would use their magic to overwhelm him.

Gavin took a step toward the barrier.

"All we want is the *t'ranth*, and we'll leave you alive. We know it's nearby," the woman said.

We? And what was a t'ranth?

"Who are you?"

"It doesn't have to go this way," she said.

Gavin frowned at her. "Maybe we should take a break. I just want to rest. You can leave, come back later, and maybe we can talk."

He sheathed the sword and instead grabbed the dagger, then pressed power out through it. As he did, he realized something: the blade was not glowing.

Either she wasn't using magic, or she was concealing it somehow. Given what he'd felt, he suspected it was a concealment—unless her magic was different and not the kind the El'aras blade could even detect. If that was the case, then how was he supposed to survive this at all?

Gavin furrowed his brow and glanced down at the blade before looking back up at the women. "Not a sorcerer. And no talking. Great."

Then again, what if she was? He had seen the sorcerer, the strange ring that indicated that type of power—even though he didn't really understand what it meant, why she would have it, or whether he needed to be concerned about that ring.

"I need a few more minutes," another voice said.

Gavin spun toward it, though tried to keep his hands up. Who else was here?

All he saw was a trace of smoke. Nothing else in the shadows.

"I don't know if I have that long," the redheaded woman said.

"Give me what you can. I have to get through this door."

They were breaking into his room.

But for what?

A t'ranth.

That was what she wanted.

The dark egg was behind that door.

"I'm sorry, but I don't have a *t'ranth*. And you're not getting into my little lair. It's cozy. I like it. And you don't belong there."

He stabbed outward, trying to call on his core reserves at the same time.

She pressed toward him. There was more power coming, and Gavin focused on what he could feel. Their magic wrapped around him and attempted to squeeze him. This was something he could break free from.

He focused on the core reserves within him and ignored the energy of the El'aras dagger. For now. Power lingered within him. And then, much like he had in his training with Tristan, Gavin pulled the energy up through him and exploded it outward.

He expected something similar to what had happened the night before, when he had used a similar connection to blast outward. When he had done that, Gavin had thrown the attackers away from him and slammed them into walls, and the boxes had been strewn about.

This time, as he sent that power crashing away from him, he felt the resistance still there. It reminded Gavin of what he felt when trying to break through the chains. This was simply a type of chain, though it was a different kind than he'd ever dealt with before.

"Are you close?" the redhead asked.

"It's not working."

"Mine didn't either. We'll have to try something else."

Gavin wasn't sure how much time he had. Not much. Not enough.

They would get in and take what they were after.

They said *t'ranth*, and he worried that was the dark egg.

Maybe Tristan *had* put them up to it.

Gavin pressed outward with the energy he held on to, but even as he did, he couldn't feel any way to overwhelm this.

He looked at the woman.

What he needed was a way to focus it.

He pointed the dagger at her, and she simply frowned at it. Gavin began to push even more, and the power blasted outward through the dagger and struck her, throwing her back. The woman struck the wall of the cavern and collapsed. Gavin spun around, looking to see what had happened to the other, but she nowhere to be found. He turned back to the first woman.

She had vanished.

CHAPTER SEVEN

Gavin took a seat next to where the woman had disappeared, and he ran his hand along the ground. He hadn't imagined her, he knew, but there was no sign that any of them had been here, other than the residual energy that he still detected in the tunnel.

That residual energy lingered long enough that Gavin could still feel it pressing on him, some magic that seemed as if designed for him to detect.

The enchantment crackled again.

That's too often.

Something was going on with it. Whether it was fading or whether other magic was influencing it, Gavin didn't know—and at this point, he didn't care.

He got to his feet and spun the dagger around him, but he didn't sense anything more. The blade didn't glow, though given what he had experienced here, Gavin no longer expected it to. He slipped it back into its sheath and headed along the tunnel, pausing in front of the door leading into the hidden chamber.

Gavin started to question whether the women had any way of getting into this chamber. They had used a type of magic he didn't recognize, but it had not been potent enough to stop him. Which suggested that they didn't have any way of getting into the room, especially as he had sealed it with his own brand of El'aras magic.

Other than the sh'rasn powder that gave him a magical boost, there wasn't anything inside the chamber that he needed. Maybe this *was* all about the dark egg and Tristan coming for it again.

He would have to secure the room as well as he could.

At least they hadn't been able to get in. He didn't know if they would have figured a way had he not come. Which meant that he would have to come up with some way to protect it. Would that mean bringing the dark egg with him?

If Tristan were after it, he should keep it on him.

After slipping it into his pocket, hating the slippery surface and how it felt strangely warm, he slapped his hand against the door, pressing power out through him. At least he could protect the rest of the items he had in there. He swept his gaze along the tunnel one more time before hurrying back up the ladder and leaving Cyran's house. He didn't feel any sense of magic out on the street, but that didn't mean there wasn't anything taking place. In fact, Gavin remained convinced that there *was* something going on here, some sort of power that he had to be aware of—and perhaps even deal with.

The enchantment continued to crackle periodically. *What's wrong with it?* He wasn't about to take it out of his ear, though. By the time he reached the Dragon, it had crackled a few more times, though not enough that he'd been able to hear anything within it. *Could it have faded completely?*

He thumbed the marker Anna had left him. Would she be able to answer that question for him? He decided he wouldn't call her yet. Eventually, he might need her help, but Gavin didn't want to do that unless absolutely necessary.

He reached the Dragon and paused after pulling open the door. A minstrel sat in the corner, playing horrible music. He strummed a lute, and his warbly voice carried through the tavern, which elicited a smile from Gavin. Since Jessica knew that he was returning this evening, it seemed she'd decided to bring back the same torment she had often used on him.

He didn't see any sign of Wrenlow in the tavern. The only face he recognized was Gaspar, who sat alone at a table near the back. The same table Gavin and Wrenlow had sat at the night before.

After checking the dark egg in his pocket, Gavin weaved through the crowd, nodding to Rebecca when he passed her and getting an intense stare from her, then took a seat across from the old thief. Wrinkles deepened along his forehead, leaving Gavin wondering what worried him. Probably more than he would share, if Gavin knew anything about Gaspar. His gray hair was cut closer to his scalp than the last time Gavin had seen him.

But there was a sharpness to his eyes, and he flicked them briefly toward Gavin before turning his attention back to his mug of ale.

"Haven't seen you around here much lately," Gaspar said.

"Jessica told me I should come by."

"I kind of liked it."

"I kind of like having time away from you too," Gavin said.

Gaspar leaned back, taking a long drink of his ale before setting the mug down and resting his elbows on the table. "Where's your friend?"

"I don't know. I came here looking for him." He tapped on the enchantment. "I don't suppose you've been trying to get ahold of me today."

Gaspar tipped his head to either side, revealing his enchantment-free ears. "Not me."

Gavin frowned.

"By that look, I would almost say that you were disappointed."

"It keeps crackling on me," Gavin said. "I can't tell if it's finally fading or if there's some sort of interference."

"We've pulled more than a few jobs in the city without any interference," Gaspar said. "Even the Fates didn't interfere with it."

That was true, and they were some of the most powerful sorcerers that existed, so if anybody would've had a way of affecting the enchantment, it would've been the Fates. Even around Tristan, Gavin didn't remember any interference.

Maybe it *had* failed.

Gavin thought for a second. "The Fates didn't interfere with it, but the semarrl did."

"You think the smoke creatures escaped?"

Gavin shook his head, though maybe Tristan was trying to draw *more* of those creatures here. There *had* been smoke around the door to his lair.

That had come from the other woman.

Not semarrl.

And he had the egg on him. He'd know if something were coming.

"So, you worry it's finally fading," Gaspar said.

Gavin shrugged. "I guess I am."

"You still have that trinket she left you. Why don't you summon her?"

"I'm not calling one of the El'aras here just to have her make me a new enchantment."

"Seeing as how she lingered around you the last time, I can't imagine she'd be too disappointed if you do. You got a woman like that willing to come to your beck and call, you might as well take advantage of that, boy."

"We both know that it isn't a wise decision to call the El'aras for that kind of purpose," Gavin said.

"You've brought enough magic to the city, what would be a little bit more?"

"I haven't been trying to bring magic here. I've been trying to—"

"Protect Yoran, I know. In your own special way." He emphasized the word *special*. "And despite that, from what I hear, the constables continue to struggle with some strange influence. Anything you care to say about that?"

"Only that I don't know what's going on with it," Gavin said.

Gaspar grunted, and he glanced over, nodding to the server who appeared at the table. She was a bit older than Rebecca, though still younger than most of the servers who'd worked here ever since Gavin had started coming to the tavern. She had curly brown hair and wide-set eyes, and she frowned at Gavin before turning to Gaspar.

"Jessica wanted me to find out if you'd like anything," she said.

"You go ahead and tell Jessica to send out another mug of ale," Gaspar said. "Maybe two, if the boy decides he's going to drink."

"I wasn't supposed to get anything for him," she replied.

"Is that what Jessica said, or Rebecca?" Gavin asked.

The girl frowned again.

"Oh, don't be like that, Tinna." Gaspar chuckled. "The boy here can be rude—I've got more experience with that than anyone in the tavern, other than Jessica—but he means well."

"I suppose I *could* bring him a drink," she said.

"You do that."

Tinna scurried off, and Gavin shook his head. "She's going to spit in it."

"What makes you think a nice girl like that is going to spit in your ale?"

"Because Rebecca has eyes for Wrenlow and I was

giving him a hard time about it last night. I think. Everything last night was a little blurry. You know he can't keep his eyes off Olivia."

Gaspar's face turned even more sour before his expression faded. "I suppose I should be kinder to that one. I know he means well, and I know he can't help it that he's as simple as he is at times."

"You're calling Wrenlow simple?"

"You've seen the kind of trouble he likes to get himself into. That foolish kid keeps chasing you all over the city." Gaspar said nothing for a long moment while twisting the mug. "Have you found anything?" he finally asked.

"You mean when it comes to Tristan?"

"What else would I mean, boy? Have you found anything?"

"Only that he continues to attempt to infiltrate the city." Gavin told Gaspar what he had heard from Davel, along with the events of the attack the night before. Finally, he ended with what had happened in the tunnel underneath Cyran's home. He avoided telling him that he had the dark egg on him.

"You sure that's all him?" Gaspar asked.

"I don't know who else it would be," Gavin said. "It might not be him, but it fits the kind of thing he'd do."

"I suppose it might. That is, if what you've told me about him is true."

"Why would it not be?"

"This is a man who decided to train you for some mysterious purpose," Gaspar said. "You come up with an answer as to why yet?"

Gavin shook his head. "Because he thought I could be used."

"Fine," Gaspar said. "He thought you could be used, but the real question is *why* did he think that?"

Gavin leaned back as Tinna brought the ale over to their table, setting it in front of them. She sloshed it a bit more aggressively in front of Gavin before placing it gently in front of Gaspar. When she was gone, Gavin sighed and used his sleeve to wipe the spilled ale off the table.

"You're going to stink like it," Gaspar muttered.

"There are worse things than that," Gavin said.

Gaspar shrugged.

"It seems like a lost opportunity for you there, Gaspar."

"What do you want me to say? That you always stink?"

"It would be typical for you, so I suppose that's what I want you to say."

Gaspar grunted. "Maybe don't go around upsetting the waitresses and you wouldn't have to wipe up the table."

"And I told you I didn't do anything."

"Maybe it's just the way you look. Can't say I blame them all that much for it either."

"They think I did something to Jessica," Gavin said.

"Didn't you?"

Gavin ignored the question and looked around the tavern. It was busier than it had been in quite some time, though he wasn't sure if he would even know how busy it had been recently. The sound of the musician's voice carried over the crowd, and a couple had even gotten up to dance in front of him. Most of the people were seated around their tables. Some of them were playing games, others leaned close and talked, and there was one circular table with half a dozen chairs around it where the conversation was far more boisterous, an occasional shout ringing out.

Gavin turned his attention back to Gaspar. "I've been trying to protect her."

"That's what you told her, at least."

"Yes, that's what I told her," Gavin said.

"And how does she feel about it?"

"About the way I expected."

"You did spend quite a bit of time with her before you decided to move on, so can you blame her?" Gaspar asked.

"We both knew it was short-term."

"I wonder if she knew it as well as you did."

Jessica emerged from the kitchen and swept through the tavern. She stopped at one table, then the next, before finally making her way over toward them.

"She knew," Gavin said before she reached their table. "Gods, I think she even wanted to warn me early on."

Jessica pulled a chair over and sat at the end of the booth, leaning forward and resting her elbows. "Boys, it's awfully nice to see the two of you seated here like this again."

"We're not planning anything, if that's what you're asking," Gavin said to her.

"And why would I think there was anything going on here?" She glanced at Gaspar. "Did you get it?"

Gaspar nodded quickly. "Got it, secured it, and made sure it won't get away from me again."

Gavin looked from Jessica to Gaspar, curiosity weighing on him. "What are the two of you talking about?"

"Nothing you need to worry about," Jessica said. "Just something I asked Gaspar to do for me."

"A job?" Gavin chuckled. "I suppose since I left, you had to find somebody else to do your jobs."

"I wasn't trying to *get* you to do any jobs," Jessica said. "I just wanted you to be happy." She studied him as he took a drink of the ale, then set the mug down.

"I'm surprised I haven't seen Wrenlow," Gavin said.

"He's off with Olivia." She waved her hand. "Don't you go disturbing him."

"I didn't plan on it. I just figured I'd see him before now. Besides, it's not like him to go as silent as this."

She furrowed her brows. "That young man and his lady don't need to be disturbed. I would think you'd understand, Gavin."

He frowned. The enchantment crackled again, and he looked over to Gaspar. "There it was."

Gaspar shook his head. "The damn enchantment again?"

"What's wrong with it?" Jessica asked.

"The boy here thinks his El'aras enchantment is fading."

"I would expect that kind of enchantment to last longer," she said.

"Me too," Gavin replied.

"I'm sure Olivia can help find those who can make you other enchantments."

He just nodded. It wasn't so much that he was worried about finding somebody else, it was more about what had happened to *this* enchantment.

"I still worry this has something to do with Tristan," Gavin said. "He sent some strange women after me." That elicited an arched brow from Jessica. "Nothing quite like that," he added quickly.

"I would've figured that you wouldn't mind having a few women come at you," she said.

"Would you stop?"

She chuckled. "Magic, I presume?"

Gavin nodded. "Unfortunately. And what's worse, I'm growing concerned that the constables aren't aware of all the magic in the city."

"They have enchantments to protect them," Gaspar said.

"That they *believe* will protect them. But we don't know whether those enchantments will work the way they think they will."

"You don't think the enchanters can give them all the protections they need?"

Gavin cupped the ale and took a sip. "When I was at the constables' building recently, I didn't have that sense."

"Why did you go there?" Jessica asked.

Gavin glanced to her. "Not to intervene in whatever arrangement you have with them." She didn't show any glimmer of emotion at his comment. "I needed to speak with Davel. And I wanted to spar."

"With the chief constable?" Gaspar asked.

"What can I say? After the attack that Wrenlow and I

dealt with, I started feeling like I haven't faced the kind of challenge I need to keep my skills sharp. There's only so much that running through forms and patterns can do for me."

"How did you fare?" Gaspar asked. "I imagine you had him use some of his enchantments."

"As many as he felt he needed."

"And how many did he need?"

Gavin shrugged. "Speed. Strength. Impervious skin. I think he got that last one from the Captain."

At least, that was the first place Gavin had seen anything like it.

"That's it?" Gaspar asked.

"I don't know how many enchantments he had on him," Gavin said. "It's not like he shares that sort of thing with me. I told him to use whatever he felt he needed to fight me."

"You realize that allowing him to size you up that way takes away any advantage you might have if you have to deal with them," Gaspar said.

"I considered that. But I don't know that there was anything I could do about it."

"Why not?"

"I needed the practice, and besides, I faced him without any of my own enchantments." Gavin focused on the ale, his gaze lingering on it with far more intensity than he really should have.

"What else do you intend to do?" Gaspar asked him.

"I'm not exactly sure. I know there's something more going on here, but I don't know what."

And he couldn't shake the feeling that Tristan was behind all of this, regardless of anything else he had seen. It seemed too likely, and far too much like Tristan, for it to be something different.

He took a deep breath and leaned back. As he looked around, he noticed a dark-haired man sitting near the door that he hadn't seen before. The man was watching them.

"Who's that?" Gavin tilted his head in the man's direction. He had a sharp nose and narrow eyes, and there was something almost animalistic about him.

"That's why I came by, actually," Jessica said. "He came in here looking for you."

Gavin sat upright. "Was he asking for me by name, or was he just looking for me by reputation?"

Jessica frowned. "Does it make a difference?"

"A little." Especially with everything else that had been going on.

"Relax," Gaspar said. "It wouldn't be the first time somebody came here looking for you."

"That's true, but don't you find it odd that I haven't been here all that much lately, and suddenly somebody shows up looking for me?"

"Anything that deals with you is always a bit odd."

Gavin chuckled and got to his feet.

"What are you doing?" Gaspar asked.

"If someone's looking for me, I should go and have a conversation with them, shouldn't I?"

He headed across the tavern toward the beady-eyed man.

The man glanced up as Gavin approached, and a wide grin crossed his face, leaving him looking even more rat-like. "You him? Gavin Lorren?"

"Do I know you?"

"Can't say that we've met. I think I'd remember a face like yours."

Gavin grunted. "I feel the same way."

"Yeah? Well, I was sent here to tell you something."

"And what exactly is that?"

"A message," the man said. "Had to do it in person, you see, as that's how I'm going to get paid."

"By who?"

"The man who paid me is who. Now, don't go snooping around my business like that. I'm just telling you that I'm here to give you a message."

Gavin tensed, holding on to the El'aras dagger with one hand, ready for the possibility of an attack. It would be just the kind of thing Tristan would pull. And if that was the case, he would have once again brought violence to the Dragon.

"What's the message?" he asked.

"I came to see if you would take a job."

Gavin raised an eyebrow. "What sort of job?"

"Hey, I can't say that I know all the details. I was supposed to give you this." He reached to his side, and Gavin raised the dagger. The man quickly raised his hands, shaking his head. "Come on, man. I'm not jumping on you, so you don't need to go jumping on me."

"I'm not jumping," Gavin said.

"You aren't being kind, that's for damn sure. I have

something for you. Let me get it and give it to you, then you can decide if we need to have words." He grinned.

Gavin glared at him.

The man shrugged. "Be my guest. Anyway, I'm supposed to give you this." As he pulled the paper from his pocket, Gavin recognized the sigil on it.

How could he not? He had lived beneath that sigil, that marker with a small swirl surrounded by a triangle, for the better part of his childhood.

Tristan.

If there was any question that Tristan was the one lurking in the warehouse, Gavin now had his answer. He was even more thankful that he had the dark egg on him now. If Tristan came, maybe Gavin would unleash them on him.

"What's the job?" he asked.

"I wasn't privy to it," the man said. "Just supposed to bring you that. And so I did, and…" His gaze drifted to the dagger in Gavin's hand. "Maybe I just need to get going. I don't want you to get too excited about that, you know."

"I'm not going to attack you. Where did you get the letter?"

"It came through several intermediaries, you know. Sort of the way things go with me. I'm too new to get the jobs directly."

Gavin doubted that to be the case. That was never how Tristan did things.

He started to step away, and the man got to his feet. Gavin spun and twisted his arm behind his back, and he shoved the man toward the far side of the tavern.

"What's this about?" the man sputtered. "I told you I don't know anything."

"We'll see. But you aren't going anywhere until I find out about the job, and then we can decide how much you know—or don't. Either way, you're sticking around for a bit."

Gavin walked his captive to the table where he'd sat with Gaspar, and the old thief looked up at him.

"A job," Gavin explained. "From Tristan."

Gaspar nodded, and he quickly flourished a pair of knives and got to his feet. "Sit," he said to the beady-eyed man.

The man shrugged, and Gavin shoved him forward into the booth. He unfolded the letter, and his gaze skimmed across it.

"Well, shit," Gavin muttered under his breath.

"What is it?" Gaspar asked. "What's the job?"

"He has Wrenlow."

CHAPTER EIGHT

Gavin stared at the page in front of him, trying to figure out just what Tristan wanted out of him, but other than a location—a familiar one, at that—Gavin couldn't tell anything. The paper itself was thin, which meant it wasn't from Yoran, where the paper mills tended to make a much thicker stock. It reminded him more of something Tristan would've brought from the south.

He pushed those thoughts away. That wasn't the issue now.

Wrenlow was gone.

After everything they'd done together, *this* was how he'd disappeared. There had always been the possibility that something would happen during one of their jobs, but Gavin had hoped to protect Wrenlow from most of it. By only having Wrenlow scout, he should have been able to protect him.

Now…

He was another casualty of Tristan's planning.

"Are you sure about that?" Gaspar asked, looking over to the man and shaking Gavin from his thoughts.

"He has him," Gavin said.

"Hey," the beady-eyed man said, "I was just sent to give you a message, nothing more than that. You can't blame me for any of this."

Gavin reached for the El'aras dagger and then paused. "I need to know what you did before you came here."

"I didn't do anything," the man said. He looked over to Gaspar, and he flashed a sardonic smile. "Maybe you can get that point across to him. All I did was take a job. Is that so wrong?"

"All you did was help abduct his friend," Gaspar growled. He twisted one of the knives in his hand, flicked it around, and jammed it into the tabletop. "If you want to live through this, I suggest you tell him everything he wants to know. I've seen him pick apart a man. He starts with your fingers, carving them off. Then he works his way up, taking your hand off at the wrist, then at the elbow. And then he starts with your lower portion, going from your toes, all the way up—"

"Enough," the man said. "I told you, it was just a job. Nothing more."

Gavin continued staring at the paper. Just a job. That was all Wrenlow was to him.

And *Wrenlow* had been the test.

That had been the reason Tristan had targeted the warehouse in the first place. All of it to gauge Gavin's weaknesses, trying to determine whether he cared. It hadn't been about trying to test Gavin's fighting style after all. At least, it hadn't been entirely about that. That might've been a portion of it, but would Tristan really have cared?

No. This was for something else.

"Go," Gavin said to the man.

Gaspar frowned at him. "Are you sure about it?"

Gavin nodded. "Go."

The man slipped out of the booth and turned, looking at both of them. "I might be able to help you trace this back."

"Trace it back?" Gavin asked.

"To the man who hired me. That's what this is about, isn't it? You want to know more about the man who pulled me into this job."

Gavin snorted. "I know everything about the man who hired you. Probably more than anyone else alive."

"Is that right? He went about things pretty roundabout with me. Didn't want anyone to know, you see. It's like he wanted to keep it all secret. Hush-hush, if you were."

"Go," Gavin said again.

The man walked away toward the entrance to the tavern, and Gaspar leaned over to Gavin. "You're just going to let him go like that?"

"No. I don't suppose you have somebody nearby who might be able to follow?"

Gaspar frowned. "I might."

"I was hoping so. Just keep tabs on where he goes, and then we can see who he's been in contact with."

"Even if you know what Tristan wants out of you?"

"*Especially* if I know what he wants out of me."

Gaspar slid out of the booth, moving more quickly than Gavin had seen him move before, which suggested that he wore an enchantment. He slipped through the kitchen and then disappeared.

Gavin sank down into the seat and stared at the paper. Wrenlow had been captured. And now Gavin had to go back to a place he had not been in a long time.

Why Nelar, though?

For whatever reason, it seemed that Tristan had decided to bring up the past, to play a game. But the problem was that Gavin had no idea what game Tristan intended to play, nor did he know the reason behind it. Whatever it was, it involved Gavin doing something for him.

And it would be something he didn't want to do. He was sure of it.

Gaspar returned from the kitchen and sat in the booth, nodding to Gavin. Worried lines creased his brow. "Done."

"Imogen?"

"Yes."

"Good," Gavin said. "I don't think Tristan would have accounted for her."

"You said this man is an incredibly gifted planner?"

"He is."

"Then what makes you think that he isn't aware of the people you've been interacting with?"

"He's probably gifted at that too," Gavin said.

"So he would know about Imogen."

Gavin smiled. "Seeing as how *I* don't know anything

about Imogen, I'm not so sure that Tristan knowing something about her will make much of a difference at this point."

"She's probably the finest damn sword fighter I've met. And she's discreet."

Gavin had a hard time telling which of the two mattered more to Gaspar. Probably the discreet portion, though. Given what he knew about Gaspar and what he valued, the sword skill would've come into play a few times, but discretion was even more important.

"How would he have gotten Wrenlow?" Gaspar asked.

"He probably followed us back to the Dragon," Gavin said. "And then when Wrenlow disappeared again last night to meet with Olivia, Tristan might have snagged him then."

"And you've heard no word from Wrenlow in the meantime?"

It seemed so long ago now, but not so long that Gavin felt he couldn't retrace the steps. He got out of the booth and looked around the tavern. Everywhere around him were the sounds of merriment—the minstrel still strumming his lute and bringing his annoying warble above everything, and the shouting of the crowd that mixed with the boisterous calls of others around them. Some cried out for the serving staff to join them. None of it fit Gavin's mood.

And maybe that was more of a reason why he hadn't returned to the Dragon. There was too much happiness here, far more than he felt the mood to take part in.

"I need to see where Wrenlow has been," Gavin said.

"His room?"

Gavin nodded. He walked to the door leading up to the sleeping rooms and tapped on the enchantment. "Wrenlow, if you're listening, I need to reach you."

He had no idea whether Wrenlow would even be able to respond. Even if he still had his enchantment—and if Tristan was involved, he probably would've stripped the enchantments first—there was still the issue of getting through whatever magical restrictions had been placed around him.

"No answer?" Gaspar asked, climbing up the stairs behind Gavin.

"There hasn't been any."

"What about that crackle?"

He wasn't even in the mood to make a joke on Gaspar's behalf.

"Probably not, but I don't know what else to do," Gavin admitted.

"Focus on the task in front of you. And then move on. That's all you can do. All anyone can do."

Gavin glanced back at the old thief. "Why are you helping?"

"Who said I was helping? I'm just going up the stairs."

"This is you helping," Gavin said as they reached the landing on the second level, where Wrenlow's room was. "You care about him."

Gaspar grunted. "Care about the kid? You should know better than that by now."

"I thought I did," Gavin said, shaking his head. "But maybe I had you right from the start."

He reached Wrenlow's room along the hallway. There were half a dozen stout doors, each of them a brown, stained oak, and Wrenlow had one at the end of the hall. Gavin tested the handle, finding it locked. He started to push on it, but Gaspar grabbed him and pulled him back.

"You don't need to force it open, boy. Not everything has to be brute strength with you."

"Go ahead, then," Gavin said. "I suppose we *could* ask Jessica for the spare key."

"Don't have to do that either." Gaspar slipped out his lockpick set and made quick work of opening the door. When he was done, he rolled up the lockpick set back into the leathers and returned it into his pocket. Gaspar waved his hand. "There. Was that so hard? You didn't need to try to force it open."

"Thankfully, I have you here."

"Thankfully," Gaspar muttered.

The inside of the room was relatively neat, which showed Jessica's involvement. The bed was made, and the basin nearby emptied. A table at one end of the room had a stack of books, the only sign of any disturbance. A lamp rested next to the books, and Gavin sniffed for a moment.

"Are you going to light the lantern?" Gaspar asked.

"Something smells off," Gavin said.

Gavin looked around. Maybe it was just that Wrenlow's presence was missing from the room, but Gavin was left with a strange feeling.

He sorted through the large wardrobe, the clothes neatly folded—another of Jessica's traits. There wasn't anything near the bed or the side table. Gaspar looked through the books, flipping from page to page. Which left only the desk and Wrenlow's belongings.

"I always see him working on these books, but I never know what he's doing," Gaspar said, turning from one page to the next.

"He keeps notes," Gavin said. "He likes to keep track of the jobs we've done, and of any resources he has."

"Maybe this has nothing to do with Tristan."

Gavin held out the paper. "This has *everything* to do with Tristan."

"Why would he go after Wrenlow?"

"Because of me," Gavin said. Gaspar looked over at him, and Gavin shrugged. "Tristan would have wanted to determine whether I'd go after him. It's part of the reason he caused the trouble in the first place. He would have used everything he could to test my willingness to press after somebody like him."

"Why would he think you wouldn't?"

"The problem is that, before all this, he didn't know if I was willing to go after Wrenlow." Gavin sighed. "That was part of what he was after in the warehouse if he couldn't defeat me. I didn't realize it before now." He nodded to the stack of books. "Anything there you think might be useful?"

"If the kid were here, I'd tell him that none of this was useful." Gaspar closed one of the books, placed it on top of the others, and grabbed the entire stack. "But the truth is, he has some interesting observations." He glanced over to Gavin. "Don't tell him I said that."

"What are you doing with his journals?"

"I'm going to use them to see if we can come up with anything that he might have been involved with."

"And I told you this doesn't have to do with anything he was tied up in."

"That you know of, but how many of his assets were you aware of?"

Gavin shrugged. "I don't know. I let Wrenlow run his own side of the operation. There wasn't any point in digging into what he was up to, especially as he didn't need me intervening."

"Didn't need you? You were the reason he got involved in most of these jobs, so that suggests he needed you quite a bit."

Was that true?

Gaspar started flipping pages before stopping. "This one was recent. It talks about a fight." He looked up at Gavin. "He was surprised at how well he did. *Gavin said he was proud of me. I've never felt better about myself than when he said that.*"

Gavin swallowed. Wrenlow had written that about what he'd said?

"I *was* proud of him," he muttered. It was hard to get the words out, though he knew they were important. "He's been training. Getting better. He's not a fighter, but he *fought.*"

"I know," Gaspar said.

His throat was dry, and he licked his lips. "He would have fought."

"He would've."

Gavin knew what to do. There was only one thing he

could do. Push it down. All of it. Emotion wouldn't serve him now. Tristan had made sure that he knew to put that aside and be ready for what he had to do.

"I need to speak to Olivia." Gavin nodded to the journals. "Where are you going to store those?"

"Jessica can keep them safe, or we could even have Olivia watch over them if you would prefer," Gaspar said.

Gavin wasn't entirely sure what he wanted. At this point, the only thing he needed was to figure out what Tristan was going to do and how much time he had to find Wrenlow.

"You still haven't said anything," Gaspar pointed out.

He took a breath, getting himself ready. He *would* be ready. "What's there to say?" Gavin asked.

"About what he's asked you to do. You haven't really told me anything."

"It's a job, like that man suggested," Gavin said, holding out the paper.

"And?"

Gavin arched a brow at him. "You know what he trained me to do."

"So it's that kind of a job."

Gavin nodded.

"And where is it?"

Frustration surged in him. "That's part of the issue. He wants me to go to Nelar."

It would take him from the city.

If Wrenlow were here, there would be no way of looking for him.

Gaspar frowned. "That wouldn't be too far from here."

Nelar was north of Yoran, probably a week or more by foot. Less if they took horses. Still, it was far enough that it would pull Gavin away from the city.

"I can have Jessica lock up the room again. And I'll make sure that nobody else gets inside," Gaspar said. "We're going to get the kid back."

He looked to Gaspar. "Thank you."

Gaspar nodded. "I care about him too. He's a good kid. Got a solid head on his shoulders despite who he's learning from. We'll get him back, boy."

Gavin struggled with the lump in his throat.

Tristan had beat that out of him. Why did he fail now?

Because it's Wrenlow.

They headed down the stairs and back out into the tavern, where Jessica greeted them. She looked from one to the other and turned her attention to Gavin. "What's wrong?"

He shook his head. "We have to find Wrenlow."

When he told her what happened, she gasped, covering her mouth.

She cared about him too. There were probably others in the tavern who felt the same way. Gaspar was right. He *was* a good kid. And Gavin didn't know how long they had before something happened to him, only that he was going to have to act quickly to find his friend.

She twisted the fabric of her dress for a moment, then straightened. "What do you need me to do?"

Gavin had been worried about who would look after Wrenlow as Gavin left him and snuck off on his own, but he shouldn't have been concerned. Wrenlow had people around him, like Jessica, who cared about his safety. Olivia was also certain to worry once she found out what had happened. Even Gaspar did; a man who'd teased Wrenlow about his abilities from the start.

"You plan to go after him." Jessica cocked her head to the side. "And from the look on your face, he's not in the city."

"You can tell that from my face?"

"I've seen that look before, Gavin. You might like to think that I don't know you, but I did spend quite a bit of time around you. You're planning, and in this case, it's something different than what you've done before."

"He's out of the city," Gavin agreed. "He's not far from here, though."

"That's good, isn't it?"

"You would think so." Gavin glanced over to Gaspar. "Can you track down Imogen? See what she uncovered from that rat-faced man. We need to know who he might have interacted with and see what he knows of Tristan."

"If he was just an intermediary, he wouldn't know anything," Gaspar replied.

"That's just it. I don't think he was just an intermediary. That's not generally how Tristan does things."

"You think the man actually knows Tristan?"

"It would fit," Gavin said.

"Then why did you let him go?"

"Because I knew somebody else would follow him. And I needed to make him believe I was too distraught to go after him."

"You *were* distraught," Gaspar said.

Gavin shrugged. "That's right, but he didn't need to know that."

Gaspar shook his head. "You know, there are times when I don't even know what to make of you, boy."

"Go and figure out what Imogen found. I'm going to talk to Olivia."

"Okay, but then I'm going with you for that," Gaspar said. "I don't know how she's going to take you suddenly springing in on her in the middle of the night."

"Middle of the night? It's barely midnight," Gavin said.

"Not everybody has your job." Gaspar shook his head again.

"Olivia would understand. I can do this."

They stepped out of the Dragon, and as soon as the door was closed, the music and the noise from inside became muted. Gavin felt a strange mix of emotions. He was glad to get away from the revelry of the tavern, but he also felt some regret at losing that vibrancy from within. Another part of him felt the same thrill he often did when it came to getting ready for a job. In this case, the job was personal, something that he wanted to ensure he did as well and as accurately as he could. But the thrill was the same.

Gaspar looked over to Gavin and seemed as if he wanted to say something, but he didn't. He turned away, slipping off into the darkness of the city before fading completely from view.

Gavin placed the enchantment back in his ear, making sure that he had it on him so that if Wrenlow or Gaspar were to speak to him he would be ready for it. He had gone only a little ways when the enchantment crackled again, the same way it had several times already.

"Wrenlow?" Gavin whispered into the enchantment.

There was no response.

He fingered the dark egg in his pocket, feeling the smooth surface.

That might be the real reason Tristan wanted him out of the city.

He would have to make sure the egg was safe before he left.

"Tristan?"

It might have only been Gavin's imagination, but there was a shift in the energy over the enchantment. Had he been listening? There was that danger, which meant he'd have to use the enchantment carefully when reaching Gaspar—if at all.

He ran his finger along the surface of the marker Anna had given him, once again debating whether he should use that to summon her. Finding Wrenlow meant using every advantage he had. Gavin tried to activate it—but nothing happened.

Not that Gavin expected it to work. Why would Anna come running because he wanted her to help him with the enchantment? This was something he had to do on his own.

Gavin stayed in the shadows as he navigated through the streets, and he started to slow as he neared Desarra's home. He didn't visit her often, but he knew the way.

Desarra lived in a nicer section of the city. Most of the homes along this street were much larger than they were in other parts of Yoran. They were all built of stone and several stories high. Like all the homes in this area, Desarra's house was surrounded by a low wall to keep out unwelcome visitors.

There were no lights glowing in the windows. Gavin stared at the iron gate for a moment before shaking off his hesitation, then pushed it open. The air smelled of the flowers growing in her garden. In the darkness of night, the flowers looked like inky black death, though he knew they were red and purple and even deep green—strange colors for flowers, but ones that Gaspar had once suggested that Desarra preferred. Gavin wondered if the unique colors had anything to do with her enchantments.

He took the cobblestone path that led up to the door and knocked. There was no answer, which didn't completely surprise him, especially as he was visiting late at night. He knew he should turn away, but this was about Wrenlow. Gavin needed answers.

He tested the handle.

It was unlocked.

Under other circumstances, Gavin might have been relieved at the possibility of getting into a building without having to force his way, as Gaspar liked to tease—but this wasn't any normal circumstance.

Desarra was not the kind of person to leave the door unlocked.

His heart pounded as he reached for his El'aras dagger and unsheathed it. The blade didn't glow, so there was no sign of magic, unless it was shielded from him. He twisted the door handle, pushed it open slightly, and listened.

There were no sounds inside.

Gavin stepped through the doorway and then backed up to the wall. Everything was dark. He reached for the enchantment that would grant him enhanced eyesight and slipped it on his finger.

As if a dozen lanterns had suddenly been lit, the darkness faded, and everything in the room became clear. Including the body lying on the floor in the center of the room.

Gavin darted over to Desarra, her dark hair splayed out around her. He touched his finger to her neck and let out a relieved sigh when he felt a pulse.

He slipped his arms underneath her and carried her to the plush sofa that was angled toward the hearth. She moaned softly but didn't awaken.

She needed help. She needed healing.

Worse, he now worried that Olivia might have gotten involved in this as well.

Gavin tapped on the enchantment, hoping that Gaspar would have it on instead of leaving it inactive. "Gaspar, if you're listening, Desarra needs your help. And a healer."

There was a moment of nothing, and then a slight crackle.

"I'm coming."

CHAPTER NINE

Gavin searched the home for any signs of Olivia, but he didn't expect to find anything. He figured that, given what he had seen and how Desarra had been incapacitated, there would be nothing else here.

Gavin found only a few enchantments in various states of creation, the carvings along the enchantments incredibly skilled. They were certainly nothing that would make him believe that Olivia was still here.

After surveying the home, he returned to the living room just as the front door opened and Gaspar hurried in.

"Are you here, boy?" Gaspar hissed.

"I'm here." Gavin realized that he'd still been wearing the enchanted ring that gave him enhanced eyesight. He made his way to a table, lit a lantern, then slipped the ring off his finger.

Gaspar blinked a moment before darting over to the sofa where Gavin had set Desarra down. He stroked the side of her head, tracing his fingers through her hair. "What happened?" he asked without looking up.

"I got here and found her lying on the floor."

"She doesn't look injured."

Gavin had taken a chance to run his hands along her, looking for any sign of injury. That wasn't his skill set. He knew how to assess for minor injuries and could bandage certain wounds, but anything more than that required a healing touch that he didn't have—especially because the types of things he'd done for Tristan involved harming, not healing.

"She has a pulse. She's breathing."

Gaspar turned to the door, and Gavin glanced over to see Imogen standing there. She had on a black cloak, the hood of it pulled up and concealing most of her face, and her hand rested on the hilt of her slender sword.

"I sent for a healer," Gaspar said.

"I'm sure we can get one of the enchanters to help," Gavin said.

"Maybe." Gaspar continued to stroke Desarra's hair. "But I don't know if we need an enchantment or if we need something more here." He settled himself down on his knees and used his free hand to hold one of hers. "We're going to get you the help you need," he murmured to her.

"I'm sorry," Gavin said. "About all of this."

"You think this is your fault?"

"If Tristan is involved, then it is."

Gaspar opened his mouth as if he wanted to say something but clenched it back down and shook his head. "As long as we figure out what he is after, none of that matters."

"He's after me and the egg. Power. Who knows what else?"

Gaspar turned his attention back to Desarra. Gavin waited for a moment, then slipped through the door, back out into the night.

That was what this was about, after all. Tristan was after him, not anyone else. They had been used against him. Wrenlow. Olivia. And now Desarra was injured. The longer he stayed in all of this—the longer he remained in the city—the more likely it was that other people would be used against him.

He touched the dark egg again before tracing his thumb over the piece of paper folded up in his pocket. That was what he had to do—go to Nelar, face Tristan, and get Wrenlow back.

But not quite yet.

He couldn't shake the feeling that there was some reason that Tristan had gone after Wrenlow. Doing so forced Gavin out of the city, and he couldn't help thinking that was exactly what Tristan wanted. In leaving Yoran, Gavin would be abandoning it—and whatever Tristan was after.

If it was the dark egg, then Gavin would secure it before leaving. He didn't dare bring it with him. If something happened to him while he was gone, he couldn't stand the idea that he would be responsible for someone else acquiring it and potentially releasing that dangerous magic upon the world.

But if there was some other reason...

Tristan had known about the sorcerers' lairs. That thought kept coming back to Gavin. This wasn't about enchantments. There were some of those in the lairs, but there was something more too. Maybe whatever it was had been tied to understanding how the dark egg worked, but was that all it was? There had been the dead sorcerer, but Tristan wouldn't have needed proof that the dark egg worked.

Which suggested to Gavin that there was something else here. And maybe not even in the lairs. It could simply be within the city.

Yoran was important. It had to be, considering all the magic that Gavin had encountered in his time here. There was too much power that had flared through here for it to just be a coincidence.

And until he had Wrenlow back, Gavin wasn't sure he would be able to figure out that reason.

He made his way through the city and entered the tunnels to one of the old sorcerers' lairs, watching for any signs of glowing in his El'aras dagger as he went. He needed rest, and then it would be time for him to go.

Before anybody else got hurt.

He reached the connecting corridor that brought him to the cavern beneath Cyran's home. As soon as he opened the door, he glanced behind him, worried about what he might uncover. But there was no movement in the shadows, nothing to suggest that the strange women who had attacked him were there again.

Once he stepped inside, Gavin closed the door, sealing

it tight again. He paced around the room for a moment, trying to work free the issues that he had, debating what he needed to do. To get to Wrenlow, he was going to have to sneak out of the city, get to Tristan, and complete whatever job Tristan had for him.

That's what this was, after all. A test.

Complete the test, get the prize, and then move on.

This time, rather than sleep or food, as was often the case with Tristan, the prize was his friend. And likely Olivia too. That meant Gavin had to do whatever he could to get to them, to ensure he completed the task Tristan asked of him so that he could keep his friend alive.

He needed to clear his head.

There was only one way to do that. It was late enough—and dark enough—that he didn't want to venture back out into the city again. He would use this time to work through some of his training and prepare for whatever he might need to do in order to defeat Tristan. That was what it would come down to. Gavin had to be ready, but he also knew that his old mentor had learned a few new tactics. Maybe he should've been training more with others in the meantime.

He stopped at the table and set the piece of paper down, then removed everything else from his pockets. He didn't want any temptation to use the enchantments he had.

Over the last few weeks, Gavin had started to rely on them far more than he ever had before. When he navigated in the darkness, he'd even come to depend on the enchantment that lightened everything, which was a danger. He hadn't even realized he'd been doing it.

He knew better than that, which was why he had to get back to the basics of his training. For all of Tristan's faults—and Gavin now believed that his old mentor had many of them—he had trained Gavin well.

Gavin was a fighter. He knew over a dozen fighting styles and had mastered all of them. He was unrivaled.

Other than Tristan.

He stepped into the center of the chamber, setting his hands on either side of him, and he positioned himself in the fighting stance. He focused on his breathing, letting it come slowly, building as it did, and then began to flow through the movements. Gavin cycled through every single fighting style that he knew, and as he transitioned from one to the next, he ignored the feeling of power within him. He wasn't going to get caught up in trying to summon the core reserves. The only purpose of that would be to distract him from what he needed to do, and Gavin couldn't be dependent on anything other than his own skill. Much like everything else, his core reserves could fade, and he could end up relying on that energy, only to find it missing when he needed it.

He had to focus only on his skill, nothing else. Not that core magic. Not any enchantments. Not even weapons. Nothing other than what he could have with him.

He danced through the movements, letting his mind go blank. As he flowed through the fighting styles, he started to envision Tristan across from him. He had to visualize what Tristan would do; the way Tristan would oppose his moves. And if he could come up with that, then Gavin thought he might be able to find a way to overpower him.

It would take his focus. And yet, there was something distracting about concentrating in that way. There was something off, as if imagining Tristan across from him transported Gavin to a time when he doubted himself—something he had not done since he'd stopped training with Tristan. After leaving Tristan, Gavin had come to view himself as a fighter, a warrior, but he also viewed himself as a person of his own unique principle. Now it was as if Tristan was trying to manipulate him back into working on his behalf, the way he had wanted Gavin to serve all that time ago.

Gavin finished moving through all of the patterns he knew. A sheen of sweat covered his body, and his breathing took a moment to steady.

None of it had helped, really, other than to remind him of the fighting techniques he had memorized long ago. The real benefit would've been in sparring and proving himself against somebody else. But in this case, Gavin didn't have any reason to prove himself against anyone—he didn't have anybody he *could* prove himself against.

A faint chill washed over him. He looked up toward the door. That sense was familiar—and it was definitely magical. Strange that he would be so attuned to it now, but there was no doubt in his mind of what he detected.

He darted over to the table and grabbed for the dagger, then changed his mind and picked up his sword. Inside this room, the sword might be more valuable, especially as he could navigate around here with the sword and use it to keep spacing for himself.

Gavin approached the door, thinking that maybe it was the same strange women who had attacked him before. As he neared, he thought he heard something on the other side.

He started to call upon the core reserves within him, thankful he hadn't used them during his practice, which meant he still had strength left. Then again, if he needed something more, he had the sh'rasn powder on the table that would replenish his reserves.

He decided not to use that energy—there was a danger in doing so that he wasn't sure he wanted to use unless needed. Besides, in this place, he didn't think that anybody could sneak in on him quite as easily. There should be a measure of protection here, which Gavin could take advantage of.

A knock came at the door, and Gavin frowned.

What kind of attacker knocked?

Somebody who wasn't here to hurt him.

Gavin stayed ready with the sword and pressed his hand up against the door. As he pushed power through it, he pulled the door open.

Gaspar waited for him on the other side. "Are you going to just stand there dripping, or are you going to let me in?"

"What are you doing here?"

Gaspar grunted. "You think no one knew where you were?"

"I figured you had some idea," Gavin said.

"Some." Gaspar shook his head, then looked down the length of the tunnel before turning his attention back to Gavin. "You aren't so hard to follow, boy. I started keeping track of you when you stopped going to the Dragon. Figured I ought to know if you decided to leave."

"I told you and Davel that I intend to protect the city."

"You did," Gaspar said. "But you go about it in your own sort of way, and how are we supposed to know what you intend to do to protect the city?" He offered a hint of a grin. "Now, are you going to let me in, or do you just plan to stand there looking goofy and dripping." He took a deep breath and wrinkled his nose. "And you stink."

"Great."

Gaspar pushed through him, and Gavin stepped off to the side, letting him in. He closed the door and sealed it again, then turned to Gaspar. In the darkness, he couldn't make out anything more than a shadow.

"You were just fighting in the dark?" Gaspar asked.

"Practicing," Gavin said.

"Why?"

"I needed to clear my head."

"Clear it like you cleared out of Desarra's home?"

"I wasn't needed there," Gavin said. "And I think she would've been happier with me gone."

"What makes you think that? She didn't send you away, did she?"

"That's not funny, Gaspar."

"She's fine, boy. Imogen brought a healer, and we got her awake. She's at Jessica's place now. I'm not exactly sure what happened to her, and neither is she, to be honest. She doesn't remember a whole lot. Somebody went to her home and knocked her out. When she came around, well, that's when we were there."

"Did she know anything about Wrenlow and Olivia?"

"No, other than that they had been there."

"So Tristan took them from Desarra's home?"

That didn't make sense. Gavin wouldn't expect Tristan to break into someone's home.

But then, it probably wasn't Tristan who had pulled the job. He would've had somebody else do it. Tristan had someone attack Gavin, and then another person had brought Gavin the message about what had happened to Wrenlow, so it only made sense that he would've hired somebody else to take Wrenlow and Olivia.

"Did she remember anything else?" he asked.

"What's there for her to remember? Somebody attacked her, and that's about it. She don't remember much of that, and I don't expect her to either. Not with what she went through. At this point, you just have to get past it." Gaspar stopped on the other side of the table and grabbed the lantern, quickly lighting it and casting the room in a faint glow. "Unless you intended to take off. Is that what you're going to do, boy?"

"I've got to do the job if I want to get them back. I'm the reason this is all happening, Gaspar. I'm the reason that Tristan is even attacking."

"That might be true, but that don't mean you got to do this by yourself."

"You don't want me around. You've made that clear."

"Well, I can't deny that you've been a pain in my ass, but you *have* done a few good things in the city."

Gavin sighed. "I'm the reason Cyran was here. I'm the reason the Mistress of Vines came."

"And you're also the reason the constables aren't chasing down enchanters any longer. Gods, you might even be responsible for getting me back with Desarra." Gaspar shook his head. "Not that I'd ever really give you credit for that. But it's not all bad. Not like anything is all bad. There's always a little bit of good if you dig deep enough."

"I know Tristan," Gavin said.

"You told me. You might not think you've shared a whole lot, but in the time you've been in Yoran, you've talked about him endlessly. Almost too much, if I'm honest—at least, that was what I would've said before he decided to make himself known. Now that he has, now that he's targeted people we care about, it changes things, don't it?"

"I need to do this by myself," Gavin said.

"Is that what he would expect out of you?"

"Yes."

"Even more reason for you not to do it like that, then, isn't it?"

Gavin grunted. "If anybody else comes with me and tries to get involved in this, I know what Tristan is going to do."

"You think this man is some sort of super powerful person, but he can be beaten, just like anybody can be beaten."

"I have enough experience with him to know just what he's capable of."

"Capable, bah!" Gaspar waved his hand. "I've seen what you can do, so I'm not terribly worried."

Gavin started to smile. He didn't know if that was an insult or a compliment. Either way, it still made him laugh.

"That kid wanted to be involved," Gaspar went on. "He's been trying to get involved ever since you came to the city, or haven't you noticed?"

"I've noticed," Gavin said. "To be honest, I resisted training him for the longest time. I knew he wouldn't be able to handle some of the things I have to."

"Why did you think he had to handle the same things you do?"

"I suppose he doesn't."

"Exactly. You got a kid who can dig into things better than anybody else I ever met." Gaspar rapped his knuckles on the table. "Don't tell him I said that."

"Look at you, getting soft. Ever since you got a woman—or got your woman back, I should say—the edge within you is gone."

"I still got plenty of edge," Gaspar said, flourishing his knives and spinning them for a moment before pocketing them again. "It's just something Jessica pointed out to me."

"What's that?"

"She reminded me of what it was like when I was working with the constables. Strange she'd be the one to point that out, but she wasn't wrong. I had a team I could rely on. You know what that was like?"

"I've never had a team," Gavin said.

"Obviously, otherwise you wouldn't have snuck off by yourself."

"So I'm saying. I could never have a team. I was trained to do things on my own."

"You think that makes you stronger or weaker?"

Gavin stared at him, and he shook his head. "I know what it did."

"Do you? You know that it made you more powerful, or do you think that it somehow made you less? By forcing you to dig into things that you wouldn't be able to do otherwise, I can't help but wonder whether this did make you more independent but also more isolated. It was easier to control. Who was going to come for you if something happened?"

"He was teaching me how to get out of anything that may come for me."

"By forcing you to rely on him. That's an interesting tactic, you realize."

"I'm not so sure it was any sort of tactic," Gavin said.

"Not a fair one, that's for damn sure," Gaspar said. "When I was working with the constables, there was one thing they taught us. There weren't a lot of good messages from that time, and after what happened with Desarra"—he shot Gavin a hard look, practically daring him to say something—"I got out. I wanted to get out. I wanted to get away, and yet I recognized that there was something that I missed by leaving."

"The other constables?"

"I missed knowing that somebody else was there if I

needed them. I missed knowing that if something were to happen, there would be another person to have my back."

"Which is why you brought in Imogen."

Gaspar shrugged. "Imogen just sort of found me. And she's been reliable." He smiled and shook his head. "I've tried bringing others in, but no one really clicked." He looked up at Gavin, meeting his gaze. "Until you, boy. Can't say we've always gotten along. Can't say we always will. But you have the right intention, and that's what matters."

With Imogen, it was her discretion. With Gavin, it was his intention.

"I suppose I should be thanking you?"

"Don't go getting sappy on me," Gaspar said. "I'm just trying to tell you that you've got a team, if you are willing to take it."

"And?"

"And one of our team is missing." Gaspar held his gaze on Gavin. "When I was in the constables, what do you think I would've done if one of my team was missing?"

"I don't know." With what Gavin knew of Davel Chan and the other constables, it was hard for him to even guess. They seemed to have some ties to each other, but there was also the possibility that they didn't completely count on one another.

"I would go after them with whatever thunder I could. And I would make sure that the bastard responsible knew better the next time."

Gavin sighed. "You have no idea what you've signed up for."

"Probably not," Gaspar said. "But I'm telling you that I'm willing to do it."

Gavin looked around the room. "Tristan must've had somebody following me here. He sent them down, and I don't know if it was to try to keep me from getting past them or to target me once I got here. It's got to be about that egg." He pointed to it, though Gaspar seemed leery of picking it up. "She called it something else, though."

"Distract. Divide. Defeat. Good strategy. Now what are you going to do about it?"

"Get Wrenlow. Protect the egg. Protect the city. And defeat Tristan."

"Sounds good. Now. If we are going after him, then we need to do it. And you don't have to go alone. I'm coming with you, and so is Imogen. You have your team, and we will go and get our other team member. I'm not going into this blind, boy. I know dangers when I see them, and though I might not be able to see them in this case, I can at least feel them."

"It's good you recognize this isn't going to be easy."

"Not at all," Gaspar said. "But like I said before, you aren't going to have to do it yourself. Now, if you're not going to run off on your own, I'm going to have a few words with Imogen, get back to the Dragon, and then make my own preparations. You had better make yours." He swept his gaze around the chamber. "If this man is as dangerous as you think, then we need to do something that will surprise him. Something he won't expect."

"I'm not sure what that's going to be," Gavin said.

"That's why it's unexpected. Figure out what he

wouldn't think you would do, and then be ready to do it." He tapped his hand on the table again, pushed past Gavin, and then paused for Gavin to open the door. Once Gaspar had disappeared through the tunnels, Gavin sealed the door closed once again.

He had a team. That was one thing Tristan wouldn't expect.

But considering that Tristan had abducted Wrenlow, maybe he *had* figured that out. What was worse, Tristan may have been capitalizing on it, which meant that Gavin would have to find another advantage.

He just didn't know what that was going to be.

CHAPTER TEN

The streets were dark, and Gavin couldn't sleep. He had gathered everything he thought he might need out of the lair, including the sh'rasn powder and the few enchantments he had. Since he had not wanted to rely on enchantments, he hadn't acquired as many as others would have. And now, he ventured through the darkened streets, trying to come up with answers.

He was going to have to return to the Dragon. To Gaspar, to Imogen—to his team. That was something Gaspar had been right about. Even though Tristan had taken Wrenlow, he wouldn't have expected Gavin to work with the rest of their team. Tristan viewed relying on others as a weakness, something he wouldn't have wanted Gavin to do. In Gavin's mind, that was a flaw on Tristan's part.

There was something else that Gavin needed to do, another resource he had—one more thing Gaspar had been right about. Not that Gavin would ever tell Gaspar he was right about anything, but in this case, Gaspar had proven himself to have some sage advice.

Protect the egg.

Protect the city.

There *was* something he could do while his attention was divided. Tristan might not even expect it. Anything to distract would be useful.

He snuck through the streets, staying in the shadows, but his mind raced as he tried to go at a reasonable pace. He needed to get to Zella and the other enchanters to see what useful enchantments they might have.

Near one intersection, Gavin caught sight of three constables on patrol. He ducked back against the building, watching them as they marched along the street. They moved steadily, whispering to each other and generally unmindful of any danger. Then again, he wasn't any danger to them now. When he had first come to Yoran, Gavin had been more concerned about coming across the constables. Now that he had an agreement with Davel Chan, running into the constables was merely an inconvenience, not anything that left him worried the way it once had.

In some ways, that was almost disappointing to him. It was nice having that feeling of working alone. But now that he had essentially allied himself with the entire city, he didn't have to fear maneuvering in Yoran at all. And anything he did would be on behalf of the city.

Perhaps I have more of a team than I gave credit to before.

That could be why Tristan was trying to force him out

of the city. It was something to consider, anyway. In order to bring down Tristan—or at least to capture him and try to figure out what he was after—Gavin was going to have to take advantage of his resources. *All* of his resources.

Gavin turned a corner. In the distance, the building he still referred to as the Captain's fortress rose ahead. It was separated from the nearby homes by a large lawn and a massive wall that secured it. The enchanters had moved into the fortress and claimed it as their own. It was here that he would find Zella. This time, Gavin would come directly to her. There was no point in sneaking.

He headed toward the door of the outer gate and felt something. It was a tingling that washed across his skin, letting him know there was magic nearby. He quickly pulled his El'aras sword from the sheath, but the blade was not glowing at all.

Nontraditional magic.

Then again, in the recent time he'd spent in the city, there had been plenty of nontraditional types of magic and more than a few different attacks that he'd come to worry about. Gavin pressed up against one of the buildings and focused on watching for any shadows that might be slipping along the road.

It seemed too much of a coincidence that somebody would find him here, which suggested that he had been followed.

Zella *should* be relatively safe in the fortress. With everything else that Gavin had been through, there was no reason for her to be in any danger here. No reason other than the fact that she had pitted herself against the sorcerers, along with the Fates, who still wanted to control the city.

Gavin waited for a few more moments, and when he was convinced there was nothing happening in the street, he started forward again.

And then he froze.

This time, he knew he wasn't imagining the magic he felt. He reached for the sword, and a flurry of shadowy movement darted toward him, coming from all around.

Gavin wasn't sure what it was, only that he could feel some sense of energy that started to circle him, as if trying to loop around him in a pattern. It reminded him of the attack in the tunnels beneath the sorcerer's lair, so he guessed it was something similar.

He unsheathed the sword and whipped it around, using it to try to carve through any sense of magic he detected. He turned in place, holding on to the power within him, and readied for the attack.

The gate to the compound opened, and a young face that he recognized poked out. Mekel looked to be fifteen, with hollowed eyes and a bit of growth on his chin, though Gavin knew them to be about the same age.

"Get back!" Gavin shouted.

Mekel frowned and eyed the sword, then pulled the door closed.

Balls.

Now that the enchanters had revealed their presence, he was going to have to act quickly. He needed to protect them to ensure that this attacker wouldn't pose any danger to them. Either that, or give the enchanters time to prepare their own defenses.

The pressure continued to squeeze him, reminding him of how the Mistress of Vines had trapped him and used her magic to hold him in place. Gavin could feel the pressure constricting around him.

He knew he could force his way out from it. But not yet. He needed to draw the attacker in, mostly so that he could see what she was doing and what she was planning.

He didn't have to wait that long.

As that power continued to constrict around him, he found his arms forced down to his sides so that he couldn't even bring the sword up. The energy flowing through him, though, gave him hope. Gavin maintained that connection, holding on to his core reserves and trapping that energy within him.

Gavin felt someone move near him and turned his head, but he found that he could only turn it a little bit without attempting to break free of whatever this power was that was holding him. Until he knew what was going on, Gavin wanted to draw them in even more, to see if there was anything he might learn.

"You're the one who attacked me near my chamber," Gavin said through clenched teeth.

Though his voice didn't carry, he hoped Gaspar would at least hear. If nothing else, Gaspar had proved that the enchantment still worked, so Gavin had to use that. Maybe Imogen would come. Together they could handle a sorcerer.

With the power he felt around him, Gavin didn't think

he was going to have that much time to hold out. Either he was going to have to overwhelm the sorceress, or he was going to find himself on the wrong end of whatever she might do to him.

She strode down the street quickly and stopped in front of him. When he had seen her in the cavern, he hadn't been able to get a good look at her. There had been a darkness about her; something that seemed to shroud her. She was dressed in a dark leather jacket and pants, with a shimmering cloak hanging around her. Flaming red hair poked out from beneath the hood.

"Where is the *t'ranth?*" she asked.

The dark egg. That was what it had to be.

"You're not getting it." He flicked his gaze down to the stone ring on her finger. He knew he hadn't imagined it before. "I don't have a *t'ranth.*" All of this was wasting precious time. Why send her after him if he already had Wrenlow?

Gaspar missed one. Distract. Divide. Defeat.

He left out delay.

It would buy Tristan the time he wanted to do whatever he planned with Wrenlow. *That* was why.

"I know it's here," she said. "You're making this harder than it needs to be. Just hand it over and—"

"Listen," Gavin said, anger filling him. "If he wants the damn egg, he's going to have to come for it himself. I'll use it against him. You let him know that!"

She looked behind her for a moment before turning to Gavin. "The what?"

Irritation filled him again. She worked with Tristan.

She had to. Now he was ready to be done with this so he could find Wrenlow.

Gavin focused on his core reserves, ready to explode outward with it. He needed to draw her in close enough that he could question her and so that she could feel the effects of his power as the Chain Breaker.

As she approached, though, power started to constrict around him again.

Would I even be able to do it?

This power felt somewhat different than what the Mistress of Vines used around him. Whereas she'd used thick, almost physical manifestations of vines around him, the power wrapping around him now was invisible—and considerable. He started to have a difficult time breathing.

"We don't have to do it this way. All I need is the *t'ranth*. I know you have it," she said.

Gavin glowered at her. "I know what he's after. You can tell him that it's fully protected. He's not going to get it from me—and not while he has my friends."

She stood in front of him, and almost too late, Gavin started to worry about the other who had been with her before. She hadn't been alone when she had targeted him last time.

And if there *was* another, equally powerful and able to use this sort of power, Gavin didn't know if becoming the Chain Breaker would be enough. He focused and then began to press outward with his power. It was more difficult than he expected. Thankfully, he had the sword unsheathed and could use that as a focus.

"A dular?" She stepped toward him. "You're not

escaping from me with *that* kind of power. It's impressive, but not that helpful against me."

Gavin cocked his head to the side, frowning. "Dular" wasn't a term that he'd heard much recently, though it was one he was familiar with. Not so much in Yoran, though.

It meant an enchanter.

That's all she thought him to be?

But she thought the dular to be impressive.

Who is she?

"Not a dular," Gavin said, trying to focus even more of his core reserves into the sword. He needed more time.

Still, he had made this mistake of trying to draw her in. He'd not anticipated that she would be as powerful as she was. She held him easily.

"Who are you?" Gavin asked, needing to distract her. He'd found that sometimes sorcerers could be easily distracted, especially if they wanted to prove how skilled they were. This woman obviously was powerful, and he had a sense that if he could get her talking, he might be able to coax her into a lull so that he could get out of whatever she was trying to do. "What sort of catchy name do you have for yourself? We've had quite a few of your kind come through here. We've had the Apostle. The Mistress of Vines. The Fates." Gavin watched her face as he said each of the names, wondering if she would recognize any of them. If she did, she didn't give any indication of that. "You'll find that Yoran isn't very fond of sorcery."

"And I think your understanding of magic is substandard."

Gavin forced even more of his core magic out from him through the sword, and then the blade began to glow. It had been restricted before, as if there was something that had held him back. But as he forced that power out from him into the blade, the light started to glow brightly all around him.

The sorceress looked down at it, and Gavin jerked. He didn't have much he could do, especially not with the power she had wrapped around him, but he twitched just enough that he managed to break free of some of the bindings she held. The suddenness of it seemed to startle her, and she took a step away from him.

That was the break Gavin needed. He twisted the sword, drawing it through the magical bands she held on him, and suddenly he could move.

The blade continued to glow. Gavin was summoning quite a bit of power through his core reserves, and he worried about how much energy he was sending out from him. He didn't have unlimited stores of that, and eventually he would need to focus that magic, harness it, and find a way to continue pouring it out from him so that he could keep her from whatever she intended.

"That's an interesting trick," she said.

Gavin chuckled. She seemed actually impressed.

Where had Tristan found this one?

He twisted, swinging the blade around toward her, and he struck a barrier that had formed around her. It was the same barrier she had used before, and again there was nothing he could do to get past it.

She stood with her hands pressed out from her sides

toward the ground, as if she needed some contact with the ground to form that barrier.

Gavin smiled to himself. "Where's your friend? She has to be around here somewhere," he said. "That would be the only way you could hold me."

She regarded him strangely. She was powerful, but he had another sense from her. Curiosity. Had Tristan not told her everything about the job?

"What do you mean by that?"

"No single sorcerer has ever been able to hold me before on their own. So, why don't you tell me where they are, and I'll make this easy on you." He flicked his gaze to the side, looking along the street. With the glowing light of his blue blade, he couldn't see much, but there was no sign of anybody else. When he turned back to her, she was still watching him with an odd expression on her face. "You sent her away? You stayed to die?"

"Who said I was going to die?" she said.

Smoke swirled around her.

That's new.

She twisted her fingers in a sorcery pattern, but not one Gavin recognized.

"I'm going to carve right through this barrier. And then we'll see just how powerful your sorcery is."

"If you think that all I have is sorcery, then you're mistaken. And if you think I have to do this alone, you're a fool."

She moved her hands out, and the barrier slammed into Gavin, knocking him back. He went tumbling, crashing into a building on the far side of the street. He hurried to his feet, but the woman had already started forward. She twisted her hands, forming another pattern.

This time, light began to glow from between her fingers, stretching outward. Again, this was no kind of sorcery Gavin had ever seen before.

Smoke swirled around her.

No sorcerer that he'd seen before had that kind of magic.

He rose to his feet and readied the blade. He was already starting to call on power from his core reserves, preparing for the possibility he would need to attack. He had no idea what was going to happen, but he didn't want to get caught off guard by what this woman would do or how she might harm him.

What if I'm wrong?

He'd assumed that she worked with Tristan, but there was another possibility.

Damn. Of course they'd coordinate it when he *had targeted Wrenlow.*

"Let me guess. You're working with one of the Fates. They were pretty angry the last time they were here, especially as I managed to exile them from the city. They'll want the *t'ranth* too." He cocked his head, watching her. He was ready for any sort of sorcery she might throw at him. "They believed they were untouchable. But no one is."

Which meant either way, she had to be after the dark egg, the way of controlling the semarrl. He'd been waiting for the Fates to send someone after it, but he would've expected more magic than he had been confronted with so far.

Which suggested that this was only the beginning.

"You don't have any way of controlling it. You might think you do, but you don't." She strode toward him, and there was energy coming off of her.

Gavin held his hands up and braced himself for whatever she was going to do, but he couldn't fight back. Not nearly as well as he needed to.

The source of magic slammed into him.

She was *powerful*. She had magic that seemed to rival that of the Fates.

"You still haven't told me who you are," he said, searching along the street to look for the other. If he could figure out where she had come from and where the other was, he could target her as well. For now, he needed to delay.

But it wasn't just that. He needed something more. As much as he hated it, there was a reason he'd come here in the first place. It was time for him to use his enchantments.

He slipped his hand into his pocket, grabbing the new bracelet Olivia had made for him. It had a limited store of power within it, but it was one Gavin hadn't tapped into before. With it, he thought he could overwhelm this sorcerer. He had questions, and she was going to provide the answers.

He darted forward. The enchantment gave him enhanced speed, and he surprised her by the movement. But she surprised him by how quickly she reacted. She stepped to the side and, twisting her hands, sent out a spiral of red flame that struck him in the chest.

Gavin flew backward but jumped to his feet. His chest hurt, but he would deal with that later. For now, he had to focus.

He tried using his core reserves to push power into the bracelet. As he did, the bracelet vibrated, giving him a sense of the power within it. Gavin was also aware that there was a limitation to how much power was there. He could already feel the energy within the bracelet starting to fade.

Gavin didn't have much time remaining with it. He had to react quickly.

Gavin sped forward, and he slammed his shoulder into the woman, driving her back. She shook herself off and got to her feet, then turned back to him. Another spiraling pattern crashed toward him.

Gavin was ready for it this time, though, having seen it before. Pushing off with his core reserves, he jumped and flipped in the air, coming to land behind her. He brought the sword around, deciding it was better to end this fight —and end her—than to keep dealing with the violence and to keep running the risk that she might overwhelm him. He no longer had the powder Cyran had used on him to suppress magic, so he wasn't going to be able to stop her otherwise.

She surged energy into a translucent barrier that flowed up from the ground and prevented him from attacking.

Gavin grunted. "Balls."

He dropped, swinging his leg and twisting the blade to try to carve underneath the barrier she'd formed. But the sword seemed to slip past it, missing completely.

She had enough strength to stop him from getting past her barriers?

Impressive.

He focused on the core reserves one more time. Gavin slammed the blade again, battering at her barrier. Sparks flew where the blade struck, and she turned to him, completely calm and relaxed, as if unmindful of the fact that she was facing off against one of the world's most terrifying assassins.

His strength continued to fade, much like his speed from the enchantment. He didn't have much of a chance left. Gavin darted back and grabbed some of the sh'rasn powder from his pocket, hurriedly taking a mouthful of it. Normally it needed to be mixed within liquid, but he didn't have time for that.

Suddenly, the strength surged within him. He took a deep breath, then jumped forward, driving the sword out from him and using that to power past whatever barrier she might have around her. He screamed as he did so, slamming the sword into her shield, and then felt the barrier start to fade. Whatever she was doing was finally waning, and he felt he could now get past it.

But then *his* strength faded. He had used too much—far too much—and as he held on to that power and energy, he realized he wasn't going to be able to last much longer.

He shot back, and strength started to leak in. The

sword's glow flickered, and she looked up at him, her expression unchanged.

"I don't want to have to kill you, but you're not giving me much choice," she said to him. "I really have to have the *t'ranth*. It's not safe for you to use it. I'm sorry."

Sorry?

What was strange to Gavin was that she sounded as if she truly were.

With that, she started toward him, the bands of power she had used before starting to loop once more around him. This time, Gavin knew there would be nothing he could do to escape from it.

He'd already spent every bit of power within him, and she was too strong.

CHAPTER ELEVEN

Gavin tried to move, but even as he attempted to escape from her, he found he could not. He focused on the power within him, trying to call for some energy there—to find some power that existed—but he knew that it was gone. If he could get into the sh'rasn powder again, maybe he would be able to draw on enough to help him, but Gavin didn't think there would be any way for him to do so. He could feel that energy within him fading more rapidly than before, as if she were somehow siphoning it from him.

He realized that he was losing strength more quickly now because he was trying to force even more power out from himself. Gavin was attempting to break free, but he knew he wasn't going to be able to.

He was stuck.

She would win.

"Tell me how to—"

She didn't get the chance to finish.

The ground suddenly rumbled. The band of power looping around him surged for just a moment, but then it disappeared. It trembled as it collapsed, that energy sweeping out of him, no longer holding him the same way it had before.

Gavin glanced over. A colossal stone golem lumbered toward him, this one shaped like a giant man.

Mekel.

The door to the gate was closed, but Gavin caught sight of a face looking out from the top of the wall. The enchanters were helping.

Normally, Gavin would've said that he didn't need their help and that he wanted to protect *them*, but not in this case. He should have gone to them in the first place, but at least they recognized his need.

The ground trembled again, and a stone wolf started forward. This one was enormous, larger than a horse, and it prowled toward the sorcerer. Then another thundering sound came, this one from behind him, and Gavin turned to see what looked like a goat, of all things.

"A goat?" Gavin mouthed to Mekel.

The creatures stalked forward, and the sorcerer sent one of her spiraling power blasts at the stone giant, but it simply caused part of the stone to fragment. The golem continued moving toward her.

"They have more of them," Gavin said, looking over to her and gripping his sword. He grabbed another mouthful of powder and felt a surge of his core reserves coming back to him. He would only have a little time left with that, but hopefully enough that he could keep her from succeeding. "Just wait. I'm a little surprised he brought out the goat. That one is lethal."

He looked over to the wolf, thinking that maybe it would be more terrifying, but it just prowled toward her. The sorceress turned in place, sending blast after blast outward, targeting each of the stone golems. But they kept coming at her.

Gavin finally felt the knot of fear unwind within him. It was a strange thing for him to be afraid of anything. That was one thing that Tristan had beaten out of him. He didn't fear death, so why would he be afraid now?

It was something to consider later, but he knew he didn't really need to spend too much time thinking about it. Gavin thought that he understood what it was and why he would feel that way. He wasn't afraid for himself—he feared what would happen to Wrenlow if he failed, what would happen to his friends if Tristan decided to come for them.

Gavin had to be their shield. He had to be their assassin.

He had to be their Chain Breaker.

He darted toward the woman, and she spun, but she'd already been using power. Every magical being had limitations in the amount of power they could hold on to, and a sorceress—regardless of how powerful they were—would have those same limitations. Gavin had to take advantage of that, and now that she'd been forcing these blasts at the stone golem, he could get to her. Not only that, but he could also use his own core reserves, augmented by the sh'rasn powder, to carve through her barriers.

Gavin brought the sword back, pushed a bit of power through, and slashed at the barrier. Power crackled. He tried again, with the same result.

He looked at her. "Fates or Tristan. I don't care who you serve. You don't come into my city and attack us."

He brought the sword back again, and she started to twirl her hands. As he swung the blade, a surge of smoke swirled from someplace behind him and wrapped around the woman.

Gavin brought the blade forward and carved through nothing but air.

She was gone.

He staggered forward and collapsed. The stone golems took up positions all around him, as if protecting him. He wouldn't be able to get up. Not easily. He had used too much strength.

It troubled him that the sorceress would fight him here, unless this was Tristan's way of trying to deplete Gavin's reserves before they faced each other. He wouldn't put it past Tristan to use that sort of test to prove that Gavin had no choice but to fight with only his own ability, and not with magic.

I have to find some other way.

The door to the gate opened, and Mekel emerged, followed by two large stone dogs that prowled toward Gavin.

"Can you get up?" Mekel asked.

Gavin took a deep breath, and he forced himself

upward. He didn't have much strength remaining, but hopefully enough to get inside. "I think so."

"Who was that?"

"I didn't get a name."

"We have *another* sorcerer attacking the city?"

Gavin breathed out and leaned on the stone wolf, patting it lightly. "I don't know if the sorceress is here for the city or if she's here for me."

"Why would she be here for you?"

Gavin looked at the street. A stream of smoke still swirled along it, creating a trail. He could almost follow the contours of that trail. Had the sorceress somehow used that smoke to disappear?

"Can we get away from here?" he asked, glancing over to Mekel. "I'd like to get out of the street, and maybe borrow a few enchantments to see if I can strengthen myself."

Mekel nodded, then made a motion with his hand. The other stone golems started to shrink, but the wolf helped Gavin to the entrance of the fortress.

When they reached the door, Gavin glanced behind them out to the wall, but it blocked him from seeing anything more. The enchanters would have the power needed to withstand another attack, so long as Mekel and his golems were here.

He stepped inside the fortress. The home was dark, and he looked around to let his eyes adjust, trying to figure out whether there was anybody here other than Mekel. He couldn't see much, so he reached into his pocket for the sighted enchantment. The darkness faded, revealing a large foyer.

Zella's fortress was different than how the Captain had decorated it. There had been enchantments in the building when he'd occupied it, but Zella had added to it. Different decorations along the wall all looked to be enchanted. Some were carvings of wood or metal, and others were different ceramic designs. Given the patterns on them, Gavin had to believe they were all enchanted—and all powerful.

She hadn't changed everything. The front room was still designed to prevent entry to those who shouldn't come inside. It was the back of the fortress where he expected to find Zella—along with the other enchanters who'd stayed with her.

Mekel closed the door behind them, and he turned to the window. "I got the watch tonight," he explained. "You can go back to her. I'll let the wolf stay with you."

"You'll let it?"

Mekel shrugged. "I could shrink him down again if you'd prefer."

Gavin continued to rest his hand on the wolf, and he shook his head. "No, I would prefer to keep the wolf with me, if that's all right by you."

Mekel nodded, and the two stone dogs stayed by him, as if they were keeping watch alongside him.

Gavin paused for a second, and the wolf paused with him. He looked back to Mekel. "You've grown in your control."

"Now that we can work openly, I've started to experiment," Mekel said. "I always had to be careful with these before." He motioned to the two dogs. "If they were discovered, the constables would..." He shrugged. "You know how it went."

"I do."

"She knows you're here," Mekel said.

Gavin breathed out, petting the wolf on the back. "Thank you for your help."

"It's because of you that we're like this."

Gavin looked back at Mekel, who was still staring out the window, standing guard. "Like what? Still on edge?"

"Not completely on edge," Mekel said. "Well, not like we once were. At least now we can practice openly. We don't have to worry about the constables."

"Just the Fates," Gavin said.

"They haven't come back."

"Not that we've been able to detect."

"The constables haven't seen anything either."

He'd suspected that Mekel would have contacts within the constables, and this confirmed it. "Thank you," Gavin said again.

He reached a pair of doors thrown open, and he stepped inside. Lantern light greeted him. He took off the enchanted ring and looked into the room, sweeping his gaze around at the others within it.

Zella sat at a table situated off to the side of the room and peered up at him when he entered. She had long raven-black hair and matching dark eyes, with youthful features that had been preserved through the curse the enchanters had encountered when they had forced magic into the jade egg. There were two others in the room with her. Gavin knew the stocky man, Irison, who had a shorn head and an earring in one ear. He sat at the table with Zella, working a knife along a length of wood, carving out what Gavin could only imagine was another enchantment. It was so different from the way the constables used the jade egg to create enchantments.

The last person in the room was a small child, curled up near the fire with a book opened up in front of her. She could only have been eight or nine.

He headed over to the table and sat in the chair across from Zella. "Who's she?"

Zella looked up at him before turning her attention to the girl. "She's a young enchanter we discovered. Now that we can navigate more openly in the city, we've finally been able to identify others who have potential."

"Could you not do that before?"

"Anything we tried before ran the risk of the constables claiming them." She shook her head. "And when they did, they were banished from the city."

"It might've been best for them," Gavin said.

"Perhaps." Zella nodded to Irison. "We continue to look, though. We believe that we can find others."

"And what happens if you can't?"

"Then we can't."

Gavin leaned back, fatigue still washing through him. He hadn't given much thought to the fact that there would have to be others who had magical potential within the city, but it made sense. Even though magic had been outlawed before, there would still be those who developed potential, including enchanters, as well as some with the ability to practice sorcery.

There had once been a sorcery school in Yoran. That alone would be enough reason to bring those with potential into the city.

"Did the Sorcerers' Society claim those who had potential before?" he asked.

She shrugged. "Some of them, but not all. Some were taken by more dangerous factions."

"What dangerous factions?"

"You've traveled the world, Gavin. You know the sort that exist out in the world."

Gavin supposed he did. He had certainly encountered enough of them before, and he certainly knew there were plenty of people who would take advantage of anyone who had magical potential and force them to serve.

Wasn't that exactly what Tristan had done?

"Mekel tells me there was another sorcerer attack," she said, turning her attention back to the book in front of her.

Gavin glanced over at the book, trying to see what was on the pages, but he couldn't tell much of anything. "I think the sorceress attacked *me*. Not the city."

"So you don't believe this to be the Fates?"

"Not this time," Gavin said. He would need to tell her that the sorceress seemed to have skill and power enough to rival the Fates, but maybe not yet. "She's after something she called a *t'ranth*."

Zella shook her head. "I have not heard it."

"Great. Then I have a question for you."

"You need enchantments."

Gavin shrugged. "That too. But I need information."

She closed the book and settled her hands on the table. "Gaspar sent word."

"That sneaky thief," he muttered.

"You didn't think he would?"

"I think he's cleverer than I give him credit for."

"He's a thief, Gavin."

"Yes, and he had been a constable, but…"

As far as Gavin knew, Gaspar had never used many enchantments before. He had never needed them before, but then again, the city had not allowed him to possess any. He hadn't been able to use them, even if he had a way of accessing them. Maybe that was the fact of the matter, more than anything else.

"I need enchantments. We're going to have to leave the city to save Wrenlow from my old mentor."

"I'm sorry," Zella said.

"You're sorry about the situation? Or that you can't provide any enchantments?"

Zella frowned and tilted her head. "You have our collection at your disposal."

That was considerable, given that it included everything the Captain had stolen from the enchanters over the years.

"Tell me what you need, and you can take anything." She shook her head as Gavin started to smile. "Within reason, of course. Some of the items that we create are particular to the enchanter, as you've seen." She glanced toward the door.

The wolf remained seated in front of the door as if keeping watch.

"Any enchantment can be triggered by anyone with the right potential," Gavin said. "And even someone without the right potential can trigger the right enchantment."

That was one of the advantages of enchantments. They allowed anybody with the right connection to magic—whether or not they understood what it was—to trigger it. There were even some that didn't take a touch of magic to be activated. Typically, only sorcerers could create them, and they were incredibly valuable.

"We aren't nearly as skilled as some of the enchanters you might find in other places."

"Dular," Gavin said.

He'd finally remembered where he'd heard the term dular—in Nelar, just like where he'd have to go for Tristan. Though the city was not too far from here, he had not been there in quite some time. It was a place that valued enchantments, unlike other cities. Stranger still, it did not banish those who had the right kind of magic. They welcomed it, much like they welcomed the magic of the dular.

"Where have you heard that term?" Zella asked.

"Not here. Well, not until recently," he added. "The sorceress who attacked me used that term." That gave Gavin an idea about where she came from—at least, enough of an idea that he could recognize it, and maybe even use that to help him figure out where she was from.

"It's an unusual term," Zella said. "We prefer the term

'enchanters' here, especially because it doesn't carry any connotation with it."

"I didn't realize 'dular' did."

"Perhaps not, though there are more than a few people with our particular set of abilities who believe that it weakens us when someone uses a term we did not choose for ourselves." She glanced over to Irison, who nodded once. "They think to diminish us because we are not sorcerers."

"I've seen enchanters with power that exceeds some sorcerers I've dealt with," Gavin said.

"You have, but not everybody has that same benefit, and not everybody has the same beliefs as you do, Gavin Lorren."

"She's dangerous," he said, shaking his head.

"It seems to me it's not danger that troubles you."

Gavin smiled. That was true enough. "I've faced dangerous people before, so you're probably right. I think what bothers me is something I saw on her. A ring. I've seen one like it before, though it's been years."

"A ring? That could be a simple enchantment."

He nodded. "You're probably right, but this is stone and smooth. And it's similar to one I was supposed to get years ago."

Zella stiffened and sat up, looking over to Gavin. "What do you mean, a stone ring?"

"Just that. She was wearing a stone ring."

"Oh no," she whispered.

"What is it?"

"A Toral," she said softly. "And somebody we shouldn't

have in the city. The protections here should have prevented her from entering."

"I don't get the sense that the type of magic she used is the same kind you have, nor is it the same as other sorcerers have." He tapped the El'aras dagger. "This blade doesn't glow the way that it does around you when you use your magic."

"Then she *must* be a Toral," she said. "She's dangerous, Gavin. But then, I suspect you know that. Do you know what she's after?"

"She said a *t'ranth*. I think it's the dark egg." He hesitated. This would be asking even more from her. "That's the other favor I have of you. I need you to keep a particular enchantment as secured as you can make it."

She frowned. "It will be dangerous for that to be here."

"It's safer here than anywhere else in the city."

Zella squeezed her eyes shut. "You have done so much for us." She nodded. "I will do this. There is a place only I can access. I hope that will be satisfactory?"

"That's probably for the best. I don't want anyone to be tempted."

She nodded. "When we get your enchantments, I will place it in a secured vault."

"Thank you." He relaxed. The egg would be safe. Mekel had proven the enchantments could deflect the woman. And Tristan couldn't get in here. Not with all the enchanters protecting it. "What can you tell me about a Toral?"

"You haven't experienced them before?"

He frowned. "I've seen a ring like that before. I was

even tasked with stealing one from somebody once, but I've never known what it meant."

"If you've seen that type of ring and came away with it, then you have done something unheard of that no one else has accomplished. You separated a Toral from their source of power."

"The ring is the source of the power?"

Zella nodded. "I don't know much about it. None who are not Toral—or Sul'toral, their masters—know much about it. It's just spoken about in rumors."

"How is it that you know anything about this, then?"

"When we were dealing with the attack on the city all those years ago, we were looking for ways to defend ourselves. Somebody suggested calling one of the Toral to come and help."

"Are they like that? Are they like the sorcerers you used?"

"No," Zella said. "And those who were wiser recognized that, so they knew better than to do so. But that didn't change the fact that others believed that the Toral might offer us a measure of safety that we wouldn't have otherwise."

Gavin thought about what he had dealt with when facing the sorceress. "So, if I separate her from the ring, I can separate her from her power."

"Maybe. But most of the Toral have other ways of using power."

"Sorcery," Gavin said, and Zella nodded. "So she *was* a sorceress as well."

"Probably, based on what you have described. And that

particular combination of magic is dangerous. We can't withstand that in the city."

It was even more reason for Gavin to leave, which meant that he might actually be helping the city by taking Tristan's job and fulfilling that obligation. It was a strange thing to think about, and stranger still to realize he might need to take the job in order to keep something worse from happening.

Another test, probably.

"What else do you know about them?" he asked.

"I just know that you don't want to tangle with one."

"Well, I've survived twice now."

"Yes, but look at you," she said.

Gavin frowned. "What's that supposed to mean?"

"It means you look exhausted, Gavin."

He *was* exhausted. He'd been sitting and talking with Zella, and he had managed to ignore some of the fatigue, but there were limits to how long he could do so. Eventually, that fatigue would continue to overwhelm him, and he would reach a point where he couldn't tolerate anything more.

"I had to tap into more of my potential than I have in a while," he said.

"That's dangerous. I don't know anything about your magic." There was a hint in her tone that suggested she knew more than she let on, which wouldn't surprise Gavin.

Zella had an obligation to the other enchanters. She worked on their behalf, which made her feel as if she had to do everything in her power to help defend them, protect them, and ensure that they did not face the dangers in the city without support. She had been used to leading them, and Gavin still needed for her to do that.

"But you need to be careful when you draw upon that much magic," Zella continued. "Each person has a limit to how much power they can summon. Magic is part of the natural order of things, and most enchanters, along with sorcerers, come to recognize the limitations they have. But you are something different, aren't you?"

"I don't exactly know." That wasn't completely true, but he didn't know how much she knew about him.

"I worry about the city in your absence. I think even Davel will worry, though he would never say that."

"How about this: you provide me with an enchantment that allows us to communicate, and if you need me, I'll return. I think you and the others will be able to protect the city in my absence, but I'm here for you."

That wasn't what Gavin wanted to do, but what choice did he have? What was his friend's life against the potential danger that might be incurred in Yoran if a person of that kind of magic continued to run loose? Gavin might want to save Wrenlow and Olivia, but if the Toral continued to target the city while looking for him, he wouldn't have much of a choice but to come back.

"I'll hold you to it," she said.

Gavin got to his feet. He leaned on the chair for a moment, wobbling in place, and then forced a smile. "Maybe before I gather some of your enchantments, you wouldn't mind if I rested?"

Zella frowned at him. "You want to rest here?"

"Only for a few hours. Please don't let me sleep any longer than that."

"How long would you sleep otherwise?"

"Normally, not long. With what I did…" Gavin shrugged. "The last time, I slept for three days."

Her eyes widened. "I will give you until morning. Is that long enough?"

"That is. Thank you."

She guided him over toward the fire, and the little girl looked up at him and smiled. She was folding the paper from the book into different shapes, including ones that looked like a crane, a bird, and, surprisingly, a dragon.

"Alana, Gavin here needs to take a nap. Do you mind?"

She nodded. "I will make sure he's safe."

"Thank you," Gavin said, lowering himself to the ground and resting his head. Fatigue worked its way through him, and as he closed his eyes, he noticed the girl setting the paper animals around him. He smiled to himself. Hopefully, they were enchantments that would protect him. Regardless, he was in a place that he thought he could rest safely, where he didn't have to fear awakening to another attack.

The only things he had to fear when he fell asleep were dreams of Tristan and what he might do to Gavin when he finally caught up to him. If only the girl had a way to protect him from those…

CHAPTER TWELVE

Gavin awoke refreshed, and he found the room mostly empty. No sign of the girl, no sign of Irison, only Zella still sitting at the table, reading the book in front of her.

He sat up and looked around. The paper animals that Alana had placed around him were still there. The fire had burned down to glowing embers. The air smelled of the smoke and the warmth, and there was a hint of something else. Some floral fragrance, though Gavin couldn't quite place it.

As he stirred, Zella looked over to him, closing the book again. "I thought you were going to sleep for several days."

"How long has it been?"

"Only a few hours." She got to her feet. "How do you feel?"

"Tired," Gavin said. "But given everything I've gone through, that's not altogether surprising."

"I would very much like to know more about your particular kind of magic," she said.

"I don't know if I can tell you more about it. I'm not even sure about any of it."

Gavin didn't know enough to share anything with her. Not that he didn't trust Zella. At least, that wasn't entirely it. He trusted her somewhat—enough that he'd come here looking for her enchantments and had borrowed her help to defeat the sorcerer. But he wasn't sure about revealing that he was part El'aras. Gavin didn't know what that meant for him yet.

She watched him. "I suppose you will be wanting to borrow enchantments now. And place that dark egg into the vault."

"When I can," he said. He got to his feet and looked over to the door. Surprisingly, the stone wolf was still there, and it watched Gavin, as if it had been waiting for him.

"Mekel said you could take him with you."

"I don't imagine I'll be able to shrink the wolf, will I?"

Zella shrugged. "I can't say whether or not you will be able to, to be honest. The wolf, such as you call it, is only connected to you in this form."

"That's unfortunate," Gavin said.

"Perhaps, but you might find that there is a benefit to it."

"What benefit is that?"

"The wolf does not grow tired."

"Why would that be a benefit... I see." He realized what she was getting at. What would it be like, riding a stone wolf? "I might need two others, then."

"Who else is going with you?"

"Gaspar and Imogen."

"It seems to me you're bringing a capable team," Zella said.

"That's my hope," he said.

She motioned for him to follow, and she tapped on a section of the wall he hadn't noticed in his tired state. A door opened, and she stepped through. Gavin paused at the entrance and looked back at the stone wolf, which was still watching him.

The door led down, and Gavin studied it for a moment. It hadn't been there before.

"A new way of reaching the storeroom?" he asked.

"We thought a few modifications were in order when we took this place over."

"It's still the same storeroom, though."

"Perhaps." Zella tipped her head toward the wolf. "You can leave him there."

"I'm not sure I can," Gavin said.

"He will not go anywhere. Mekel has instructed him to stay with you and protect you."

"If I'm going down there, then is he really protecting me?"

"More than you can imagine," she said.

Gavin followed her into the other room, and as soon as he did, the door closed behind him. It had to be another enchantment, but it was a skillfully made one.

There was only a stream of light along the floor, a pale blue that glowed softly and radiated upward, giving enough light for him to see his way forward but not so much to illuminate everything. She stopped at another wall, and she pressed her hand on it.

"Everything here is enchanted?" Gavin asked.

"Everything that matters," Zella said.

The door came open, and he followed her inside. As before, the door closed right behind them, sealing them in once more. A massive table occupied the center of the room, laden with hundreds of different enchantments set upon it. Rows of shelves lined the walls, and much like the table, various enchantments filled them as well.

She held her hand out, and he withdrew the dark egg.

"There's something unpleasant about it," she said. "I know it was in this place for years, but I wish we would have destroyed it."

"Maybe it should stay here anyway. It deters the Fates."

He hadn't wanted to trust anyone else with it, but the enchanters' safety depended upon it.

"We would never use it."

Gavin smiled tightly. "They don't have to know that."

She pressed her hand on a section of the wall that started to glow, revealing a deep opening. She slid the dark egg inside, then closed it again, sealing it off. Finally, she nodded to herself. "That will hold it. None will know it's here. Now. What would you prefer to take with you?" she asked. "I'll see if I have anything that might be useful to you."

It was a strange relief to unburden himself from the egg.

It would be safe.

Now he could focus on Wrenlow.

Find him.

Stop Tristan.

Deal with the Toral.

There were thousands of enchantments within the Captain's storeroom, items that had been taken from the enchanters over years, and possibly even accumulated during the war. So many of them had originally belonged to the enchanters that Gavin hadn't objected when they'd wanted to reclaim them, especially given what they had experienced in Yoran over the years. He'd waited for Davel to protest their taking over the Captain's fortress, but so far, he had not. Perhaps Davel even understood what the enchanters had lost.

"You know what everything here does?" he asked.

"I know well enough."

"Don't let Davel Chan see this."

"He won't," Zella said softly.

"I won't tell him, if that is your concern."

"I did not think that you would," she replied.

There was a bit of heat in her voice, and Gavin realized that, for however much the constables and enchanters might be working together, there was still some distrust between them. With everything they had gone through over the years, he wasn't terribly surprised that they would still be wary of each other. The enchanters probably distrusted the constables more than the other way around.

Gavin looked along the shelves and the table, then frowned. "I could use several enchantments for speed and strength."

She nodded to him. She headed along the table and stopped in front of one section, gathering several small items. Only one of them looked like the bracelet Gavin used.

He still wore it, even though it had been spent. Gavin wondered if Olivia might be able to replenish its power. The bracelet seemed fitted to his wrist. He was familiar with how it interacted with him.

"These will be effective," she said, handing him a stack of what looked like stones.

He took them and examined one, noticing a pattern delicately carved into the stone. Similar patterns were etched into the others.

"Much like the other enchantments Olivia gave you," Zella said, "you will find that there are limitations to how long the power works. They will drain faster the more you borrow from them."

"I think I borrowed from it too fast last night," Gavin said.

"How so?"

"I felt it vibrating."

Zella glanced down at his wrist, and she pressed her lips together into a frown. "You felt it vibrating?" When he nodded, she looked down at the table. "That is an unusual reaction for an enchantment. Then again, I suppose you know that, though."

"I didn't. Not really," Gavin said.

She frowned again. "Well, it is, and you will find that it might not be completely spent if it was vibrating. It might have been that you were trying to draw upon it in a way that caused it to react poorly."

Gavin furrowed his brow. What would he have done to cause that? Maybe it was the way he had been trying to push power out from his core reserves and trying to summon more power than what the bracelet was able to give him. If so, there might be a limit to how much of the enchantment he could even use.

"What else would you like?" she asked.

"I've seen some constables with impenetrable skin."

Zella nodded. "A useful enchantment."

"I think it might be just as useful to Gaspar as it would be to me."

She looked over. "Not all of these are for you?"

"I have trained not to use enchantments," Gavin said.

"Just because you can use one doesn't mean you become dependent on it."

"I'm afraid what Tristan wants out of me is to demonstrate that I don't need them."

"You believe this is all some part of your training?" Zella asked.

"Not anymore," Gavin said. "But I know Tristan, and I know what he intends. I suppose I should say I know *why* he would do what he intends. He still views me as the child I was when I first went to him."

"I would like to hear that story sometime."

"There's not much to it," Gavin said. "I went to him after my parents were gone. He claimed me—claimed to save me."

"You no longer think he did."

"After what I've learned?" Gavin shook his head. "I don't even know anymore. I'm a fighter because of him, I'm the person I am because of him, and I might even be able to reach for magic because of him."

That was the strangest part of all of it. Why would Tristan have wanted Gavin to be able to access magic? There seemed to be no reason for him to help with that or encourage that connection to magic, yet Gavin had little doubt that was what had happened.

"I had just started learning to control my connection to magic when the war started," Zella said. "So many of us had the same thing happen."

"I know," Gavin said.

She sighed. "You've heard, but that's not the same as knowing. No one can know unless they've lived it."

"I've seen similar fighting in other places."

"It was awful," she whispered. She looked away and scanned the table. "But it made us stronger. In its own sick and twisted way, we all came away stronger. I wonder if we would've developed our abilities as much as we did otherwise."

"Mekel seems even more powerful now that you can work openly," Gavin said.

"He is. Others are like that as well. It is unusual, though." She frowned as she shifted some of the enchantments around on the table, lifting one and closing her eyes for a moment before setting it back down and moving on to another. "It is not typical for people to grow more potent with their abilities over time. At least, not quite as dramatically as he has."

"Do you think it just has to do with him practicing?" That was what Mekel had believed, and it made a certain sort of sense to Gavin, so he would've expected that.

"Perhaps that is all it is," she said, shaking her head.

"You're worried," Gavin said, watching her. He should have noticed that before. When he had first come here, he had been distracted by his own fatigue.

"I'm concerned I don't understand what is taking place," she said. "And that there are those of my people—and they *are* my people, regardless of what you might try to tell me—who have decided to work so openly with the constables."

Gavin stepped around the table toward her. "First of all, I would never claim that they weren't your people. You did everything in your power to protect them, and that makes them your people. And second of all, I think some of them are working with the constables in order to ensure that they are protected, at least in a certain way. Besides, aren't you still visiting with Davel from time to time?"

He wasn't entirely sure how much Zella would admit to when it came to her actions with the constables. Perhaps none at all, though he thought she needed to at least acknowledge that she had been working with Davel in questioning her mother.

"My mother hasn't shared anything useful with me," Zella said, turning away.

"You aren't going to be able to forgive her."

"Should I?" Zella looked up, hurt flaring in her eyes. "I lived all these years thinking that she sacrificed herself to protect our people, but she was responsible for what happened to us. She is to blame."

Gavin didn't know what to say, and he certainly didn't think that he could come up with anything to ease her mind. It wasn't his responsibility, anyway. "I understand."

She looked over. "Do you?"

"I understand how learning that someone you cared about betrayed you can be hurtful. I've had it happen a time or two."

"I suppose you have," Zella murmured. She glanced down at the table and grabbed an item from it. "Here. This is what you were asking for."

"I see," he said.

Gavin wished that he had the opportunity to test it, but he feared spending the power from them before he had a chance to work with them. And he feared letting anyone else come to rely on them.

"How certain are you that these will work?" he asked.

She arched a brow at him. "You don't trust me?"

"I trust you," Gavin said. "I'm just concerned about depending on these when it comes down to what we might face."

"You know what my ability is," she said.

Gavin nodded. "I do."

"Then you should know that I can tell you what each

of these does. Trust me, Gavin. I wouldn't send you with anything dangerous, or useless."

He grunted. "Useless enchantments would be dangerous."

"I know."

Zella made her way around the table. She stopped a few other places and closed her eyes each time, focusing as if to probe for power. By the time she worked her way all along the table, then back, she had a stack of items that she handed to Gavin. She started working through the shelves as well. When she was done, she glanced at the enchantments he held.

"You're going to need something to carry that with," Zella said.

"I feel like I'm asking too much of you."

"Maybe." She smiled slightly. "But perhaps not. You *are* the one responsible for freeing all of this, after all."

That wasn't entirely true, but he wasn't going to argue with her about those details now. She motioned for him to wait a moment, and then she headed out of the room.

He walked around the table. The enchantments were all different shapes and sizes. Some of them were tiny, little larger than the pebbles she had given him, each of them with strange symbols carved into the surface. The symbols were what gave the enchantment power, though he had no idea how they were formed. The enchanters never shared that secret, only that it was some part of the magic they possessed. Gavin didn't know if the power they used made a difference either. He had no idea about enchantments, only that they were sometimes useful, and other times not.

He found another carving that reminded him of the one that Mekel had made, only this one looked like a detailed figure of a man. Long arms swept toward the ground, and what appeared to be fangs protruded from his mouth. Gavin picked it up and twisted it in place, feeling a strange twinging as he held on to it.

"I wouldn't use that one," a voice said.

Gavin looked over to see Alana coming into the room. She was small, yet she strode around the table and touched some of the items before moving onward.

"I'm surprised she let you in here," Alana said.

"I needed some enchantments for what we have to do."

"She says you're our protector."

"I'm not so sure about that," Gavin said.

"You don't want to help?"

"I've tried," he said.

"She tells me I wouldn't be able to make my shapes without you."

"What do your shapes do?"

Alana smiled. "Those are *my* protectors." She stopped, lifted one of the enchantments, and wrinkled her nose as she looked at it. "Some of these are ugly. At least, I think so. Don't tell Mekel I said that."

"I won't," Gavin said, returning her smile.

"I like my protectors better. They're prettier, don't you think?"

"I think so. I especially liked the dragon you made."

"You recognized it?" Alana asked.

"I've seen other ones, though none quite so skillfully made."

"You've seen dragons?" She set down the enchantment and settled both hands on the table, looking across it at Gavin. "I didn't know that anybody had seen any dragons."

"Not quite like that," he said. "But I've seen other carvings."

"Oh. Enchantments."

"That's all dragons are."

"There have to be real ones," she said. "I've seen them in books."

Gavin shrugged. "Sometimes things are nothing more than stories."

"Not everything, though," she insisted. "Some things that people think are stories are real. And they are even better than we believed."

Gavin just smiled. He wasn't going to argue with Alana and tell her that in all of his travels, he had never even come close to seeing a dragon. And he wasn't going to tell her that there were stories of dragons in different lands, but in each place, the dragons looked different. In some, dragons looked like the paper shape she had made—something like a bird, though more massive, and supposedly able to breathe fire. In others, dragons slithered along the ground, and whether they had stunted wings or no wings at all didn't change the fact that they were little more than serpents. There were other places that claimed that dragons were a kind of magic, and that was one Gavin found easier to believe.

"What are you doing in here?" Zella asked, stepping

into the room and looking over to Alana. "You're supposed to be sleeping."

"I felt you down here," Alana said.

"You felt my presence?" Gavin asked.

"Not you. Well, maybe you," she said with a giggle. "I felt both of you. I wanted to make sure it was safe."

"You know you don't have to protect this place." Zella leaned down and wiggled a finger at her. "Now get to bed before I have to make you."

Alana giggled again. "I'm sorry, Zella. I'll try to get some sleep, but knowing you're down here is too exciting."

"Why is it exciting?" Gavin asked.

"Because she let somebody else come." She started to turn but paused, pulling the paper dragon out of her pocket and handing it to Gavin. "Take this. If you're our protector, then this can be *your* protector."

Gavin smiled. The dragon fit in the palm of his hand, and she had folded it up so that it could be flattened outward. Was this an enchantment at all? Maybe it was just her way of entertaining herself.

"Thank you," he said.

She flashed a grin and hurried off down the hall.

Zella shook her head. "That one is going to be trouble. Especially as her magic develops."

"She's still working on it?"

Zella's brow darkened for just a moment. "It's sort of like what is happening with Mekel. It's strange that he's growing stronger, whereas Alana has found that her magic is developing in ways we don't even understand."

"Why do you think that is?"

She sighed. "We don't know, and I don't know that we really can. All we can do is try to support her as she progresses with her magic and try to help her understand what it means for her."

Gavin held the paper dragon, turning it in his hand. "It's skillfully made."

"Most of hers are. She works with paper, similar to how Mekel works with stone. That's why I've tried to keep them together."

"You think she can learn from him?"

"I know she can. It's a matter of whether or not he's willing to teach. Unfortunately, he tends to be stubborn, and though we tried to encourage him to be willing to work with her, it's not always easy. He's one of those who's had a difficult time with his connection to magic, along with his understanding of his place in the city. But then, even though that's changed now, he finds he's still struggling, much like many of our people are. That's the challenge I have bringing them back together."

"It seems you're dealing with quite a tough situation."

"I am." Zella pulled a leather satchel out and began to set the enchantments inside. "You'll need to organize these so that you can reach for them however is most convenient for you. I can't tell you how you will need to use them, but I can assure you that all of these will work the way you want them to."

"There's still one more I need," he said.

She paused. "That's right. You did promise to return to the city if needed."

Zella handed him a small ring, which he took and examined. It appeared to be some sort of communication enchantment, but he didn't know how it worked. It only needed to permit her to reach him, though.

"If your enchantments aren't enough"—and given what he'd seen of them, he had a hard time thinking that could be the case—"go to Davel Chan," Gavin said, and the corners of her mouth twitched. "I know you don't necessarily want to work with him, but he understands how to maximize the enchantments. He can work with them well enough to ensure your people are safe if the Toral returns."

She took a deep breath, nodding slowly. "I suppose I can do that. I would prefer not to, though."

She motioned for him to follow, and Gavin walked with her out of the room of enchantments, the door closing quickly behind them. They returned to the room with the hearth, the table, and the stone wolf.

Gavin nodded to the wolf. "Are you ready to go on a journey?"

The wolf stretched, lowering his head slightly. It looked almost alive.

Had he not known it was an enchantment, he could imagine it howling at him. Maybe because it was enchanted it could speak to him, though probably not. At this point, he had to be thankful that the wolf would even come with him.

Zella stood in the doorway. "Travel safe, Gavin. Find your friend. Then please return to the city. We will keep the egg protected until you return."

"Even if I don't, you will be protected."

She smiled tightly. "Perhaps, but we will not be safe without the Chain Breaker."

Gavin shook his head. Not only was he going to have to protect those within the Dragon like Jessica and figure out a way to rescue Wrenlow and Olivia, but now he was being asked to defend the enchanters too?

He supposed that was on him, though. It was because of him that they had stepped back into the light of the city and begun to operate more openly. It was because of him that they'd risked themselves when it came to the constables. He owed them, and he supposed he should offer them whatever protection he could.

He looked down at the stone wolf and stared at it. Was this going to be his fate? Would he stay in the city indefinitely?

He clutched the satchel of enchantments against him and stepped through the door, the wolf accompanying him. Mekel was still at the window standing guard. The two stone dogs remained near him.

"She says you need two more?" Mekel asked.

"I do," Gavin said, glancing over to the stone wolf. "Large enough that they can be ridden."

"How far do you need to travel?"

"Several days from the city," Gavin said.

Mekel nodded and leaned down, fumbling with something before handing Gavin two sculptures. One was another wolf, and the other resembled it but had a larger head and a longer, slender tail. "Tap on these to activate them. I'm afraid you won't be able to shrink them back down once you've activated them, so once you enlarge them, the power of the enchantment will be fully active."

"Will they protect us the same way as the others did?"

"Of course. All you have to do is ask."

"And the wolf?"

Mekel looked over. "He seems to like you. I told him it was okay to go with you."

Gavin smiled. "I suppose I need to thank you as well."

"Thank me when you get back."

CHAPTER THIRTEEN

Gavin found Davel Chan just inside the prison. The lead constable stared down the hallway with his arms crossed over his chest and his fingers twitching, as if tracing out a pattern. His mouth pinched into a tight line that Gavin could barely make out in the pale light that illuminated the hallway.

"I heard you would be here," Gavin said.

He'd considered telling him about the location of the dark egg but had decided against it. Davel didn't need to know. If the enchantments worked as he hoped, the Toral wouldn't be able to detect it any longer.

Davel didn't look over. "Did you come to question her?"

Gavin shook his head. "I doubt she knows anything that will be of much use to me."

"She was close to the Triad. She hasn't said much about them, other than acknowledging their desire to defeat the

Fates." He looked over. "I've been wondering what might've happened had they succeeded."

"They didn't," Gavin said.

He was pushing for information about the egg, Gavin suspected.

"I can still wonder." Davel straightened and wiped his hands on his pants. "It doesn't do any good to question what might've been. All that matters is moving forward."

"Maybe in an attack, but for those of us who want to learn from the past, we need to understand it so that we don't repeat it."

"Do you really think that's a possibility?" Gavin said.

Davel took a deep breath, then let it out slowly. "I would've said no, but with everything that we have encountered in the city…" He shook his head, and he frowned at Gavin. "I imagine you know that we experienced another attack."

Gavin tried to keep his face neutral. "When?"

"Earlier today. My men took care of it."

"Only constables? Or were there—"

"My men took care of it," Davel repeated.

Gavin smiled to himself. It was a good thing that he had begun to take advantage of the enchanters. Eventually, he hoped that even Davel would come to grips with his use of magic. That is, if he could even believe that he had any. So far, Davel had denied the truth that Gavin saw clearly.

"That's why I'm here. Not because of the attack. I didn't realize that there had been one," he admitted. There was no point in keeping that from Davel. Otherwise, if he began to suspect Gavin, they would end up arguing again. They needed to work together, not against each other.

"Because I'm leaving. I wanted to ensure that the city was protected before I go."

"It's about time."

Gavin chuckled. "I intend to return."

"We can take care of ourselves."

"You can if you keep working with the enchanters."

"Yes. And we will," Davel said.

Hopefully, that would be enough. Hopefully.

Gavin still didn't know what to do with the dark egg while he was gone. The lairs were protected—at least, as much as he could make them. He had placed a few of Zella's other protections around the chamber, wanting to keep it secured from even the enchanters if they decided to try to break into it. He didn't think they would, but both Davel and Zella knew of those spaces. And given the connection they had to the Triad, he couldn't put it past them to attempt to see if they could find out something more about it.

"I'm not here to argue with you," Gavin said. "I just wanted to let you know that I will be gone."

"You don't need to inform me of your decisions."

"I might not, but I still feel as if I have an obligation to the city. I did promise to help protect it from the Fates."

Davel turned to him, and he nodded slowly. "I can't say that we are fully prepared to deflect one of their attacks—yet. I have something in mind, but it will take time to bring that to fruition."

Gavin wanted him to explain more, but he could tell that Davel had no intention of doing so.

"How long will you be gone?"

"Not long, I hope. I also let Zella know that I would be leaving." He tapped his pocket. "She gave me an enchantment that will allow her to communicate with me if there are any troubles."

"She doesn't need to reach out to you if there are issues."

"Until the two of you are working together better, I think this makes sense."

"I'm trying," Davel said.

"It's not just you," Gavin said. "I saw it in the barracks. Some of your constables aren't completely convinced that you should have welcomed the enchanters."

"I'm using them, aren't I?"

"That's just it," Gavin said. "You're using them. Maybe you should be doing something more than that."

They were a team, but until all of them felt like they were a part of it, Gavin wondered if they would be able to act the way they needed to.

"Did she put you up to this?" Davel asked.

Gavin grunted. "No. I think if she knew I was here, she would be irritated with me."

"Good." Davel turned and strode down the hallway, heading toward the cell that contained the Keeper.

Gavin followed. Zella's mother, the Keeper, sat with her back against the wall, her head bent forward, and her arms wrapped around her legs. She didn't look up as they approached, though Gavin detected a faint twinge of power, barely more than that. Just enough that suggested she was trying to pull on magic.

"She's going to reveal the weaknesses that we need," Davel said.

"And if she doesn't?"

Davel glanced over. "Then she stays."

Could that be the issue between him and Zella? Gavin didn't think so. From what he had seen from Zella, she didn't want a relationship with her mother. She was too angry with her about what she had done.

But she probably didn't like the idea that the constables had her mother imprisoned.

"Keep trying to get through to her," Gavin suggested.

Davel grunted. "Travel safe."

Gavin looked through the bars of the cell once more. Would there be anything he could learn from her? Maybe in time.

For now…

He headed out of the barracks, through the darkened city at this early morning hour, and met Gaspar and Imogen on the outskirts of the city. Three stone creatures waited.

Gaspar had a pack slung over his shoulder, and Imogen had a similar one, with her sword sheathed at her side. Both were dressed for traveling.

"About time you showed up, boy. I don't want to be gone too long. Desarra has recovered, but…"

"I understand," Gavin said.

"She told me to go," Gaspar said, shaking his head.

"Wanted me to do what I could to find her sister for her." He looked up. "You're going to do that, aren't you?"

"Of course I am," Gavin said. "But I had to make sure the city would be protected in my absence. I gave the dark egg to Zella. If the sorcerer returns, she shouldn't even be able to find it."

Gaspar grumbled, and he looked as if he wanted to say something to argue with Gavin, but he bit his tongue. He slid onto the back of his stone wolf.

Imogen climbed onto her creature, which had a larger head and was bigger than the other two. The image brought a smile to Gavin's face. Even her wolf looked more ferocious than theirs.

"Nelar won't be too far from here. If the message is right"—and Gavin thought he knew *exactly* what the message implied—"then I know where we need to go. It's just outside the city. We get this done, then we get Wrenlow and Olivia back."

"I guess we get to see how quickly these things go," Gaspar said. He tapped on the stone wolf, and the creature lurched forward.

Gavin did the same, and the wolf lunged after Gaspar, streaking across the ground. There was a lumbering movement that was somehow fluid. The wolf's fur was dense, though obviously stone, which made it difficult for him to grip. Wind whipped around him, and everything blurred past. They hadn't gone long when he felt a tingling that left him with an energy that sparked along his skin.

He tensed, and the wolf seemed to realize what was

going on. He looked over to the others and tapped on the wolf again. The creature came to a stop, twisting its head to look at him with eyes that were surprisingly lifelike. Gavin couldn't shake the strange energy that he felt.

The forest stretched past him, and when he turned, he couldn't see Yoran behind them anymore. The air shifted again, as if there was a crackling sort of power here.

Gavin reached for his sword. As soon as he did, something blasted toward him. He turned with the unsheathed sword, twisted his hands, and jerked forward. The blade managed to catch the attack.

It felt as if he was carving through magic. Could it be the same strange attacker that had come at him in Yoran? Why would she have come out here to fight him?

He jumped free of the wolf, which let out a strange, creaking howl. If he was going to have to fight, Gavin wanted to be ready and didn't want to have his hands constricted in any way.

He spun in place but didn't see anything. Daylight had started to break, and the clouds that had obscured the sun before had parted, revealing the bright morning sky. It didn't fit his sudden anxiety.

Gavin turned in place. Each time that he did, he could feel the strange sensation.

"Boy?"

He looked over and realized that Gaspar and Imogen had returned.

"I'm not exactly sure what's going on," Gavin said. "I can feel something, but I don't know what it is, and…"

He had no idea what was bothering him, only that

there was something pushing in on him. The distinct cold of magic.

The sorceress?

Imogen jumped free of her stone creature, her sword unsheathed in a single movement, and she set her back against his.

Gaspar grunted. "I suppose I should be ready."

He climbed down from his stone golem, and with a flourish, a pair of knives appeared in his hands. He had several bracelets on either wrist and three rings on each hand. With that many enchantments, Gaspar would be incredibly well protected. Hopefully, protected enough that he wouldn't have to worry about a sorcery attack. If it was the woman who had targeted Gavin in the street, then it might even be enough to overwhelm that kind of magic.

Gavin turned, waiting. He felt nothing.

He looked back toward Yoran.

"What was it?" Gaspar asked.

Gavin clenched his jaw. "That's just it. I'm not entirely sure. Power, I'm certain, but…"

"There are plenty of different kinds of power in the world," Gaspar said.

Gavin arched a brow at him. "Is that something you have experience with?"

"I didn't meet Imogen in Yoran, if that's what you're asking."

Gavin glanced over to Imogen. He wasn't sure what he had been asking, but he was surprised that Gaspar would reveal that. Especially as he had made a point of keeping details of their friendship from Gavin whenever he'd asked.

"I don't like leaving Yoran like this," Gavin muttered.

He sheathed his sword and made his way over to the stone wolf.

"They can manage," Gaspar said.

"I know they can. At least, they can manage *now*."

Thankfully, they should be able to withstand any sort of attack from a typical sorcerer while he was gone, so long as the enchanters and the constables still worked together.

Gavin breathed out, frustrated. "I don't feel anything else."

He climbed onto the wolf, and they started moving again. This time, Gavin kept them at a slower pace, unwilling to push nearly as hard as he had before. He wanted to hurry to rescue Wrenlow as quickly as possible, but not so fast that he overlooked his obligation to Yoran.

While traveling, he detected several other strange feelings along his skin. Most of them were faint, though when they did pick up, he could feel a tingle of energy that left him unsettled. He didn't know how many of them he needed to be concerned about. Maybe none.

The road they took led them along the edge of the forest, occasionally plunging through the trees before veering back out. A rolling hillside looped off to the east, with flowers dotting the meadow. As evening drew long, he glanced to the sky. They still had some time before they reached the city.

They hadn't been pushing the stone creatures. Gavin

had no idea what they could do if they were pushed to go faster.

He looked at the others. "We should make camp."

Gaspar grunted, and they traveled until they reached a small stream cutting through the forest. It seemed as good a place as any for them to rest for the evening. The stone creatures sat motionless as soon as they climbed off their backs.

Gavin tapped on the wolf and leaned toward it. "Can you keep an eye on us?"

As soon as he spoke, the wolf let out its strange mournful howl and turned, looking out toward the forest. All of the creatures were incredibly impressive.

"I'm starting to wonder if we should've asked for more of these," Gavin said.

"For travel, or because you like the way they look?" Gaspar asked. He whispered something to his wolf, and it turned and stared through the trees as well.

Imogen patted hers on the side and stroked the head, as if petting the fur. Gavin smiled to himself.

"From the sound of it, some of the enchanters are getting more powerful," Gavin explained.

"Without any restrictions to using their magic, they are able to do so more openly, and I suspect there are some who have never really stretched themselves," Gaspar said. "It was the intended effect."

"It might've been intended, but it still wasn't right."

Gaspar nodded. "Given what I've seen of you, I'm surprised that you're defending the enchanters."

"Me too."

Imogen moved to the center of the stone creatures, gathered some branches, and made a small fire. She walked to the side of the clearing and crouched, her hands pressed together in front of her and her eyes closed.

This was the most time that Gavin had ever spent with her. He had fought alongside her and knew her to be incredibly skilled, but he had never spent an entire day with her before.

"What is she doing?" he asked.

"Clearing her mind," Gaspar said, glancing in her direction before turning back to Gavin. "She does that at least once a day, sometimes twice."

It looked like the way Gavin would pause and focus, trying to get his mind ready for a fight. Maybe she was doing something similar.

"How long have the two of you been together?"

Gaspar shook his head. "We're not going through that, boy."

"Is there a reason for secrecy?"

Gaspar tilted his head to Imogen. "Not my story to tell. It's hers."

That was something Gavin understood. And appreciated. If it were him, he would want the opportunity to reveal his story, and not have somebody choose on his behalf.

"Is it tied to Jalash?" Gavin tried to sound casual, but doubted he was. When it came to Gaspar, he wasn't nearly as deceptive as he'd like to be.

"You saw that, did you?"

Gavin looked over. "You're not denying it?"

"What's to deny? Imogen has something she's looking for. We're using all the resources we have to find it."

Gavin grunted. "Not all of them."

He pulled a packet of dried jerky from his pocket and began chewing. If they were going to have to fight, he had to be as ready as possible. He didn't want to be surprised, and he wanted to be as refreshed as needed, which meant that he would need to have a full stomach.

"I suppose that's true," Gaspar said. "I'll talk to her."

Gavin started to smile. "Really?"

"Can't say she'll agree to it. Imogen can be secretive."

"No kidding."

"But if we're going to work together, maybe it's time we bring you in on everything."

The way he said it left Gavin thinking there was *much* more to what they would have to bring him in on. And he couldn't help but feel as if they should have before.

Perhaps it was the same with him. He had needed their help from the beginning, but he hadn't always been forthright with them. *A team.* That meant they had to work together.

Gavin had never really had a team. Just those he took on jobs with him. Having one now would be to his advantage—and it would be something Tristan wouldn't expect. He'd trained Gavin to work alone.

He sat back, studying Imogen. She got to her feet, and she moved out of the clearing.

"Where is she going?" Gavin asked.

"I find it best to leave her alone."

Gavin frowned and got to his feet, starting toward where Imogen was going.

Gaspar reached for him. "She's not going to care for it."

"We're working together," Gavin said, shaking him off.

He followed Imogen and found her in another small clearing, her sword unsheathed, flowing through movements. It was no different than how he practiced alone, and knowing her exquisite sword skill, he wasn't at all surprised that she would practice like this. She swept her blade through a quick arc and turned to him, hilt held in both hands, the blade perfectly still in front of her.

"I'm sorry," he said.

Imogen sheathed her blade in a flurry. "I need to remain sharp."

"We could spar."

She arched a brow. "I'm not sure that sparring with the Chain Breaker would do me any good. Or you."

Gavin smiled. Having seen her move with the blade, he had little doubt that he would be challenged, at least some. "You might be surprised. I don't have to fight hand-to-hand with you. We could find a couple of lengths of wood and treat them like practice staves."

She glanced over to him, her gaze drifting down to the hilt of his sword. "Must we?"

She flashed a hint of a smile and darted forward. The movement was sudden, a fluid glide, and she stood before him. Gavin unsheathed his blade in a heartbeat and brought it up to block. Imogen twisted her blade in a swirl of movements.

Gavin had known she would be incredibly skilled. He

had seen her fight, dealing with sorcery and not struggling with it.

But sparring with her…

It was exhilarating.

They moved in a dance, their blades playing off each other. Every time Gavin thought he had the advantage, she slipped beneath his defense, and he had to deflect. He avoided using his core reserves. He didn't want to draw on any magic to face her. Plus, it was far more rewarding to do without it.

He held back. Gavin could call on his core reserves, but he didn't want to use them against her, thinking that doing so amounted to cheating, in a sense. He noticed the pattern to her movements, and it was a pattern that he could follow, but he'd need time to study it so that he could master the technique. Thankfully, Tristan *had* trained him to learn patterns quickly.

Strangely, he had the sense that *she* held back as well.

It was enough to make him push harder—but he didn't, not wanting to do so when they might have to fight the next day. Still, she pushed him harder than he would have expected while holding back.

And then she stepped back, lowering her blade. She bowed her head, and with that, she strode away. Gavin turned to watch her and realized that Gaspar was standing there.

"How did that go?" Gaspar asked.

"She's incredible," Gavin said.

Gaspar grunted. "I think she was holding back."

Gavin had done so, and he had come to suspect that

she had as well. Gaspar knowing the same shouldn't surprise him, though somehow it did.

He started to smile.

"What is it now, boy?"

"Just that I think I misjudged her."

"Most do." Gaspar nodded toward the clearing. "Time to get some rest. The wolves took off, so I wonder if they picked up on anything."

Gavin frowned. The wolves had left? They were set to protect them. If he and the others didn't have the wolves, they also wouldn't have any way of getting to Nelar quickly.

He followed Gaspar and nodded to Imogen, who was sitting in the clearing.

As he did, the stone wolves returned, prowling with their steady movements.

If the wolves had needed to leave to protect them, Gavin doubted that any of them were going to be getting much sleep this evening.

CHAPTER FOURTEEN

The wolf raced across the ground, moving far faster than Gavin had ever gone, even by horseback. What was even better was that the wolf didn't tire or slow, which made it easier for them to keep up pace. He pressed down on the stone, still feeling like there should be fur as it looked so lifelike.

They'd had a fitful night. No other attack had come, but the wolves would dart off every so often, leaving them. The sounds of their odd howls had called out in the night. It had been surprisingly soothing. When they'd howled, Gavin had stirred. Thankfully, he didn't need much sleep, but he worried about the others. He didn't know what had drawn the golems off to protect them, and the stone creatures couldn't speak to share. Gavin had to hope they *were* offering protection and not just disappearing for another reason.

He wanted to be out of the forest. He wanted to find Wrenlow and get back to Yoran as quickly as possible.

He looked over to Gaspar, who sat astride his own creature, which galloped alongside Gavin. Imogen rode slightly behind. Nobody spoke, which would've been difficult to do on the racing stone animals, with the way they sped across the ground and chewed up the distance.

His backside ached from sitting on top of the wolf, and his arms throbbed from how he had to grip the creature, essentially holding on to his neck as the only option. Every loping step left him hurting more. Though Gavin had been a bit doubtful when Mekel and Zella had called it a *him*, he decided that it had to be true. No woman would treat him so poorly.

They hadn't gone but half a day before they reached the outskirts of Nelar. The wolves started to slow.

Gavin looked over to Gaspar, shaking his head. "We shouldn't be here already." Had they ridden hard the day before, they could have made it in a single day. That seemed impossible.

"These damn things are moving at three times the speed of any horse I've ever ridden on," Gaspar said.

"Faster," Imogen said softly.

She didn't look nearly as distressed as Gavin or Gaspar, just as though she was more amused than anything else by how they'd been traveling.

"Regardless of that," Gavin said, "we still need to keep moving."

"Keep moving?" Gaspar patted the creature on its side, and it stopped. He slipped off the wolf's back. "I don't know if I can ride this thing anymore. My ass hurts like I've been bounced around by—"

"A mountain?" Gavin asked.

"Pretty much," Gaspar said, then looked over to Imogen. "How are you holding up? You barely have any ass to begin with."

A tight smile crossed her face. "I can manage."

Gaspar grunted. "Women always make it look easy."

"I want to get through this," Gavin said.

"We got here quickly."

Gaspar peered around, and Gavin did the same. In the distance, Nelar rose ahead of them. It was a walled city of stacked white stone, unlike Yoran, and a few towers soared above it. Several massive homes near the center stretched taller than the surrounding structures. No one else traveled toward the city.

"We're not going in," Gavin said. "When the letter indicated that I had to come to Nelar, I knew," Gavin said softly.

He had brought the letter with him, though he doubted that it would make any difference. It was merely a missive on where to find Tristan, and probably had little to do with Wrenlow. Nothing that would make much difference in the long run, anyway.

"Remind me where we have to go," Gaspar said. "I know this place means something to you. Or did."

Gavin sighed as he pointed to the north. Past the outskirts of the city, the forest stretched much like it did around Yoran. The trees were not quite as leafy, mostly pine, and many towered above the ground. The forest also carried with it a certain energy. Beyond would be El'aras lands, though he had never traveled that far before.

"He brought me out here. Used me."

"I'm sorry, boy."

Gavin looked over to Gaspar. He actually seemed to mean it.

"There's a house nestled into the forest," Gavin went on, not wanting to get caught up in what he experienced all those years ago. They *had* defined him, but they no longer did. He would find Tristan. And stop him. "That's where he's going to be."

"If we follow what he wants you to do, we aren't going to surprise him."

"I don't know if we can surprise Tristan."

"You've got a way." When Gavin looked over to him, Gaspar shrugged. "Us. Your team. He's not going to expect you having this kind of help."

Gavin chuckled to himself, sliding off the wolf's back, and he looked out toward the forest. The wolf turned to him, and he patted him on the side. Gavin closed his eyes for a moment, remembering what it had been like when he had gone there with Tristan all that time ago. How nervous he had been, how uncomfortable he had felt, and how unsure he'd been that there'd be any way for him to complete the job.

Why would he have had that dream and then be given this job? The timing of it was so suspect to Gavin, which was part of the reason it bothered him so much.

"All of this is a message."

"You said it was a test," Imogen said. A darkness surged behind her eyes. "I've had tests like that."

She didn't talk much, and when she did, it left him with more questions than not.

"I'd like to know about your tests," he said.

"My people are raised as fighters," Imogen said softly. "We learn the blade early." She glanced down at the hilt of her sword, and Gavin didn't dare breathe or speak. He wanted Imogen to share, especially as he knew so little about her or her people. "Testing yourself against others is considered a rite of passage. It is how you progress from the earliest stages of knowledge to higher levels of skill."

"When do you learn to fight sorcery?"

He didn't know if she would answer. She'd never spoken about it before, though had acknowledged that she had the ability to handle that kind of power.

"From the beginning."

"Why?" Gavin asked.

She looked up at him, holding his gaze. "Coming from you, I find that question surprising."

"What do you mean, coming from me?"

"I should think that if anyone understood the dangers sorcery has caused this world, it would be you."

Gavin frowned. Could she really hate sorcery that much?

He supposed she could, but she had hidden her dislike well. She had fought alongside him, her sword a useful tool in the battles they had faced together, but he had never known that she had been raised to combat sorcery. Gavin supposed it made a certain sort of sense.

Gaspar grunted. "I just want to get this job over with so that we can go back."

"Are you worried about Desarra leaving you?" Gavin asked.

Gaspar snorted. "Do you think I have a hard time keeping her satisfied?"

"You're getting older."

"And you're getting slower. Let's get going. You said there's a house in the forest?"

Gavin nodded. "That's what the letter indicated." Gavin pulled out the letter and handed it to Gaspar. "It says the city and the year. That's it."

"You would remember that so well?"

"It was a job I didn't do as well as I should have," Gavin answered.

He started forward, the wolf following him, and knew that Gaspar and Imogen would hurry to keep up.

He reached the outskirts of the forest and walked among the trees. It wasn't far by foot, though it was a long way when injured. Gavin was still tired and wished he had more time to rest and recuperate his core reserves, but at least he wasn't hurt this time. He had enough strength that he didn't have to fear he wouldn't be able to keep up and keep going. Gavin stared through the trees, and every so often, he found his hand drifting over to the stone wolf's back, wanting to reassure himself. He kept his El'aras dagger unsheathed but saw no indication of magic.

The enchantment remained in his ear, and he waited for it to crackle and make noise to indicate some sign of Wrenlow, but so far there had been nothing.

"How deep into the forest do we have to go?" Gaspar asked, sweeping around one of the trees.

There wasn't much undergrowth here. The pine trees left the forest littered with needles, and the aroma filled Gavin's nostrils, though it was not unpleasant. It struck a memory for him, and he remembered everything he had gone through at that time.

"Not much farther," Gavin whispered.

The afternoon sun sent shadows streaking across the forest floor by the time they reached the clearing. He tapped the stone wolf on the back, and the creature paused at the edge of the clearing the way Gavin had once paused with Tristan. He looked at Gavin, waiting.

The paint on the shutters of the quaint wooden house had faded over time. Grass and weeds grew unchecked around the home, but it still looked cozy. Comfortable. No smoke drifted from the chimney. A trampled path led to the doorway, suggesting that others had been here recently.

"Here?" Gaspar murmured.

Gavin nodded. "This is it."

"Why do you think he would've brought Wrenlow out here?"

"I don't know."

"Well, if we're going to be out here, we might as well go and see what they've been doing."

Gavin breathed out a slow sigh as he stared at the house, but he doubted that he could do anything other than keep moving. He stepped forward, and as soon as he did, the skin along his arms grew tight and started to tingle, leaving him awash with an uncomfortable sensation.

He held his hand out, but it was too late.

Gaspar grunted and became frozen in place.

"Magic," Gavin said, glancing off to the side where Imogen was still making her way through the forest, staying a few steps behind them. She hadn't stepped forward through the strange, shimmering barrier that created the power that had enveloped him.

She unsheathed her sword. In the fading daylight, it seemed to glow.

That had to be his imagination. Why would her blade be glowing?

"You need to get me free, boy," Gaspar said. "We're going to do this together."

Gavin focused on his core reserves, and instead of only using that, he decided to try something different. He grabbed one of the enchantments for strength and pushed a connection through it. He took a step. It felt like he was plunging through mud, but he was able to move.

"He's trying to deplete my magic," Gavin said.

"All of this is to weaken you?"

"All of this is to try to draw me out." Gavin looked over to the house. Would Wrenlow even be there? It was worthwhile for him to find out, but if he was there, Gavin didn't know if he would be able to do anything.

"Try using your enchantments," Gavin said.

He turned and backed toward Gaspar, trying to focus on the power within him and attempting to use as much as he could to reach Gaspar. But Gavin didn't know how he was going to be able to free him once he got to him. Removing that power around Gaspar was going to be difficult, if not impossible. The old thief would have to find a way to fight through it himself.

"There's some sort of magical trigger here," Gavin said. "I don't know what it is, but we have to figure it out." He glanced over to Imogen, who stood among the trees. "Do you think you can figure out what's holding us?"

She nodded.

Gavin turned back to Gaspar. "Imogen is going to help you."

"Dammit, boy, don't you go leaving me here."

"I'm not leaving you," Gavin said. "I'm just going to see if Wrenlow is inside."

"We're a team," Gaspar snapped. "That's how we pull this off. That's how we surprise him."

Gavin stopped. He took a deep breath, and he looked back. "You're right. We're a team." He continued pushing on power through the enchantment, using as much energy as he could to force himself forward, trudging through the mud that made it so that he could barely move.

He reached Gaspar and looked around him. Gavin didn't see anything that looked like it was holding him in place, but he could certainly feel whatever it was that had him trapped. He was all too aware of it.

"Do you have any magic of your own?" Gavin asked.

He had questioned Gaspar about it before, especially after having learned of the constables and their magic, but he had never really pushed Gaspar. He didn't know if

Gaspar had magic, and if he did, whether Gaspar even knew. Davel certainly didn't believe that he had magic, even now that he worked around it as often as he did. If he chose to accept that, he would learn to use it. If he chose otherwise…

Gaspar stared at him and shook his head. "You know I don't."

"Then you're going to have to draw upon heavy enchantments."

"I'm not as opposed to that as some people are," Gaspar said.

"If they fade…"

"If they fade, they fade."

Gavin reached into the pouch and pulled out several different enchantments. He handed Gaspar three for speed, two for strength, and one for the impermeable skin. Then he moved away.

Gaspar clenched his jaw for a moment, and then took a step. Then another.

"Dammit," Gaspar muttered. "Not going to be able to sneak around with these kinds of enchantments, now are we?"

"I think that's the point," Gavin said.

"You don't have to seem so happy about it."

"This isn't my happy face," Gavin said. "This is me recognizing that Tristan is trying to weaken us. When the enchantments fade, I have only one other way to get through this."

"Then let's hope the enchantments don't fade," Gaspar said.

They crept toward the house. Gavin moved slowly, intentionally drawing upon the enchantment. The longer he did that and the more he pulled on power through the enchantment, the harder it was going to be for him to move if his enchantments faded.

If this was a test, there was a real danger in how Tristan might be forcing Gavin to expend all of his enchanted power just to get through here. Gavin might not be able to do anything other than what he'd already done.

And then he'd be forced to summon his core reserves.

They finally reached the house. Gavin had no idea where Imogen had snuck off to. She was somewhere circling around the forest, looking for whatever power was limiting them, but she still had not returned.

"Do you have any way of reaching Imogen?" he asked.

Gaspar nodded. He flicked his fingers, and Gavin glanced down, realizing he was tapping on something. An enchantment? She must have had one as well, some way for them to communicate.

"You could have shared that little secret with me," Gavin said.

He reached the door, which looked different compared to what it had before. Maybe that was time or age or experience. When Gavin was younger, this had been one of the last tests he'd needed before working on his own. Retrieving the ring had been a test, one of many that Tristan had forced him through, but a test nonetheless. And Gavin had passed. Injured, barely able to walk, and yet he had still succeeded.

Until he had lost the ring.

Maybe that was what bothered Tristan. Gavin had failed. He hadn't failed Tristan too many times, or as fully as this, but Tristan had become angry each time. And occasionally violent.

Gavin pushed on the door, and it opened softly. Invisible power exploded outward in a blast. He was tossed back, and he tried to roll, landing on his shoulder. He knew immediately that it had been dislocated. He looked up, seeing Gaspar already crawling to his feet.

The old thief was quicker than Gavin had expected, but then again, he also hadn't absorbed nearly as much of the force as Gavin had. Or had he?

He smiled tightly. It was not just that he had absorbed some of the force. Gavin also had not used his enchantments the way he should've.

Dark swirls of pungent magic streamed out from the inside of the house and solidified into tall, slender figures who surrounded them.

Gavin recognized them, and they moved with a strange fluidity that was drawn from the magic they summoned. He'd faced the summoners of Vuthyl before. They had magic, though it was different than that of sorcerers. Tristan had wanted him to know how deadly they were. At the time, even Tristan had warned him against confronting them too openly. He had advised Gavin to approach with caution and to avoid endangering himself unnecessarily.

And they should not have been anywhere near here.

The power it would have taken to get them here had to be considerable.

He already knew the type of fighting style they were going to use. Gavin dipped his hand in the pouch, ignoring the pain and the fact that he was going to have to jam his shoulder back into place before he finished this fight. But for now, he pulled on the power of three speed enchantments, along with two for strength and the one that made his skin impervious.

Gavin bounced up, pushing against the magic that worked around him and tried to confine him by squeezing down upon him. It was powerful, considerable magic, but he could feel his enchantments working.

He darted forward and reached what appeared to be a dark cloud, a low-level type of magic. Similar to an enchantment, this was a pungent radiated power that reminded Gavin of rotten fruit coming off of the Vuthyl that allowed them to create darkness around them. It was effective, but only against people who couldn't fight in the dark.

Gavin could.

He slammed his injured shoulder into the first of the figures he saw in the darkness, forcing it back into place. A muted cry escaped his lips as he tried to ignore the surge of pain that flowed through him. He gritted his teeth and spun toward the next person, dropping and waiting for the small movement, the faint hint of wind.

It was little more than that, little more than a whisper. But there was something.

Gavin could hear breathing.

He crouched low and then brought his fist up, careening into the next attacker's chin. He spun around, using the power within himself to focus on the next person. He couldn't feel any other movement, nothing but the energy that was here, and yet there was something that he thought he needed.

That power was there.

Gavin darted forward. He swept his leg around and knocked one of the others down.

He slipped.

Fighting like this was exhilarating. It was difficult, especially with this power that tried to slow everything around him, but using the enchantments made Gavin feel free.

"I need your help, boy," Gaspar muttered through the enchantment.

Gavin twisted and kicked outward, striking one of the Vuthyl attackers in the back, and then jumped forward. He could feel something and began to spin when he smelled Gaspar's distinct cologne. It was better than the stench of the Vuthyl magic.

"You shouldn't have been wearing your perfume today," Gavin whispered through the enchantment.

"Figured you might need to be able to find me, and it's better to cover up your stench," Gaspar replied.

"That's not mine. Besides, you just needed to cover up the old man smell."

"You've fought these people before?" Gaspar asked.

"I have," Gavin said. "They tend to be challenging."

He ducked, and something whistled over his head.

Gavin jumped, lunging forward and bringing his elbow out, which cracked into a forehead. The figure went down.

"I really need for Imogen to take down the enchantments around us."

"She's trying," Gaspar said. "Give her time. You've got to trust her."

Gavin dropped again and then spun. He twisted his heels and collided with another attacker, catching him in the midsection. He brought his knee up, forcing it into the man's face.

He landed and waited in the dark, but he didn't see any others. The darkness started to dissipate, the smell going with them, and he could gradually start to see more of the house. The attackers had been forced away.

The front door remained open, though, and that was where Gavin needed to get.

"What other surprises do you think he has in there?" Gaspar asked.

"Well, I wouldn't be terribly shocked if Tristan has another dozen or more men."

"All hired? Or all trained by him?"

Gavin frowned. "You know what, this is a bit unusual for him. Typically, he only sends those he's trained himself against others. I'm a little surprised he would actually hire so many."

First in the city, then the warehouse, and now with the people of Vuthyl? Gavin had believed it was Tristan, but maybe he had it wrong.

He looked over to the doorway. "Tell Imogen I'm going in."

"Can't you just wait until she gets the barriers down?" Gaspar said.

"I feel something coming."

There was the cold wash of magic.

Gavin tapped on the enchantment. "We only have a little time before the enchantments fade. If I'm not fast enough, we'll end up facing Tristan without any enchantments."

"And you're worried about that?"

"I've used quite of bit of my special magic. If we don't have enchantments…"

Gavin reached the door. Another pair of people came out. One had dark hair, black, with pale skin. The other…

Red hair.

The sorceress. And not just any sorceress—the Toral.

That was the magic he'd felt.

"You," Gavin said.

He hadn't expected her to be here. The fact that she was, that she had come to attack, meant that he had made a mistake. He thought she was after the *t'ranth*, which he believed to be the dark egg, but he didn't have it on him now.

What was she after then?

Him?

No. When she'd gone to the lair in Yoran, she'd been after something.

T'ranth.

"Did you take them? Is this because of you?"

"What's because of me?" she snapped.

Gavin turned his attention back to the door, but then glanced toward Gaspar. He had a limited amount of time remaining. Only long enough for the enchantment to linger, and as soon as that faded...

Gavin had to be ready for the enchantments to stop working, and then he would have to call upon the core reserves within him. Only then would he be able to do anything more.

He lunged toward her, pulling out his sword, but he was too slow. He slammed into her barrier, and sparks shimmered across it. The other dark-haired woman stormed away from the house, blood dripping from her hands. What sort of fight had she gotten into?

She headed toward Gaspar, smoke swirling away from her.

"Gaspar!" Gavin yelled.

"I've got it," he said.

"She's got some sort of magic. I don't know—"

Gavin didn't get a chance to finish. The Toral came toward him, and she was filled with terrible energy. He needed to summon as much magic as he could.

There was only one way he could do it.

Gavin focused, calling on the core reserves. And he had to do it quickly. Suddenly, he jerked forward. Some restriction around him had faded. Imogen had broken through the magic.

Gavin smiled. "I guess it's just between the two of us," he said to the woman. "I hope you're ready to dance."

She stepped toward him, holding her hands in front of

her, and power began to spiral between them, even more than it had when he had faced her outside the Captain's fortress.

Shit.

It looked as if she was more than ready to dance.

In fact, it seemed as if she was ready to destroy him.

So much for coming out here and getting Wrenlow.

He thought that they would have time, that they could stay ahead of her, that they could find Tristan. But now he had to just hope they could just stay alive.

CHAPTER FIFTEEN

Gavin darted forward, filled with power and energy, and prepared for the possibility that she was going to be able to counter everything he did. He also knew he had fared poorly against her twice before.

The first time, she hadn't known what he could do, and the second time, he hadn't known what she could do. Yet, in both times, he still didn't know whether there was anything he could do to stop her.

He tried to ready himself. Thankfully, he was already filled with power, and Imogen had managed to remove the barrier that slowed them. None of it seemed to affect this woman, though. Which suggested that she had been the one responsible for it.

Given what he had seen of her and the power she possessed, he should've expected that she was the one using her strange brand of magic to capture them.

She attempted to create the same loops of power

around him as she had the last time. Gavin reacted, not giving her the opportunity, and he focused his energy and tried to explode outward.

She was ready for it. It was as if she knew exactly what he was going to do—which she probably did. Gavin strained, trying to call on even more power, but even as he did, he could feel something pushing against him.

Her magic once again. This time, in this place, he was aware of something more that came with it.

It wasn't just her magic. It was that strange smoke he had seen before. The smoke circled around him, looping in a way that made it difficult for Gavin to do anything other than stand in place. Somehow, he was going to have to figure out how to get past her and break through that smoke. He took a moment, nothing more than that, to glance behind him toward the dark-haired woman.

"I need you to mitigate that power," Gavin whispered through the enchantment. He had no idea whether Gaspar would even be able to react, but he heard a grunt in response.

Gavin darted forward and slammed into her, then crashed past her. He rolled into the room, which had two chairs. Nothing else.

Anger filled him—followed by a crushing disappointment.

No sign of Wrenlow. No sign of Olivia.

They were supposed to be here.

Wasn't that the point of all of this? Where's my friend?

Gavin tried not to think about what Tristan had done with them—and why he treated this as some sort of a game. He'd played too many of Tristan's games in his life. He was done with that now.

Find Wrenlow.

Gavin cried out, and in a fury, he summoned more power. He tried to call upon everything within him that he could, letting that power and magic flow up from deep inside.

He swung the dagger and unsheathed the sword at the same time. With the two El'aras blades, Gavin lunged outward. He could feel something, some aspect of her power attempting to push backward against him, and he let out another cry. He kicked as she started wrapping power around him again and held him to the ground.

"I'm going to need somebody's help," Gavin said.

He didn't hear anything in response.

"Gaspar?"

If Gaspar couldn't get there, then maybe Imogen could. One of them. Somebody had to help.

Gavin called upon energy, trying to fill himself with as much of the core reserves as he could. Still, there wasn't enough.

She stormed toward him. "We felt your presence. I don't know what you think you're doing coming to Nelar to attack me with the *t'ranth* but you'll fail. The same way others have tried and failed."

Gavin had no idea what she was talking about.

Now wasn't the time for a long conversation.

"What did Tristan send you here for?"

She faltered a moment. "Send me?"

He focused on his core reserves once again, and he

forced more power out from him. It was enough to get himself free, and he tumbled off to the side, landing on his back. He rolled over and realized he wasn't alone in the room.

There were five bodies lying near him. None of them moved. Who had done that?

He scrambled to his feet and looked over to her. She stormed toward him, power flowing out from her the way that it had ever since she had been coming toward him.

"Since you're here, you might as well give me the *t'ranth*," she said.

"You're not getting it. It's too dangerous." He had no intention of telling her where the egg was. If that was what the *t'ranth* was. Besides, he didn't want anyone to release the semarrl again—though he might need them to stop her. She was *powerful*.

She lifted him.

It seemed so easy the way she did it, leaving him feeling helpless and unable to fight back. He tried to push outward, to hold on to the power within him, but he couldn't. There was only so much he could do, only so much effort he could use. Even as he tried, he recognized there was simply not enough strength within him to counter her kind of magic.

If there was one thing Gavin had learned in his time fighting others, it was that there were always magical forces beyond his ability. He could train with his own skill, and he could master techniques to become the best fighter he could possibly be, but there was always somebody with more powerful magic. It was why he had long avoided dealing with those with magic.

But in this case, he was distinctly aware of just how outmatched he was.

When he had dealt with the Mistress of Vines, Gavin had felt as if he was able to handle her, so much as such a thing could be handled. But with this, he didn't feel as if there *was* any way for him to overcome it. She was simply too powerful.

But he had to fight. He had to struggle. And as much as he failed, he would have to keep trying again. Wrenlow depended on him.

"Where are my friends?" Gavin choked out. He was hanging in the air, suspended by her power. Though he knew how foolish it was for him to demand answers, he was determined to get free.

"Who?"

It was the first moment of confusion she'd shown.

"Them." He pointed to the two chairs, and she turned.

It was just enough of a lapse that he could spin. He jerked free, managing to break some of the bindings around him, and he had his arms free. Gavin started to focus on the core reserves, trying to call more up through him, but he wasn't going to have time.

He grabbed the sh'rasn powder from his pouch and dumped a mouthful in. He didn't have a lot remaining. Either he was going to run out of it entirely, or he would have to ask the El'aras for more. Even if he called, there was no guarantee the El'aras would even answer.

The energy flooded into him, and he was filled with

warmth. The feeling came from the magic within him, but also from something else. It came from the powder.

He kicked, shredding through the resistance she had wrapped around him. He wouldn't be able to summon this power for long, so he knew he would need to act quickly enough to break through her hold, though he didn't know what it would entail. He darted toward her and stabbed with the sword, hitting her barrier.

"That's the only reason I'm here. I don't care what you're after—you're not getting it—but I *am* getting my friends back. Wherever you've taken them—"

"I have not taken anyone. I don't care what you might have heard—I'm not using dark magic." She glanced to the door. "How is it out there?"

There was a whisper of smoke, and Gavin didn't know if that was an answer or not.

More confusion struck him.

She knew something. She kept turning up in the same places as him.

Dark magic?

He didn't know what that meant.

"You're working with Tristan. I want my friends back."

It was her turn to look confused, and as she neared the door, she glanced out. Gavin tried to surge forward, attempting to use as much power as he could to break through what she was doing, but he felt her barrier reemerge.

She was powerful and skilled, and he wasn't able to surprise her with anything he did. She glanced over to him, and he frowned.

"Please," he said.

He shouldn't beg, especially not somebody who served Tristan, but what choice did he have? He needed to find Wrenlow. Gavin was convinced he could. He had to capture this woman, though he didn't know if such a thing was even possible. The Toral magic she had access to was beyond what he could even fathom.

He rushed forward, holding on to the energy within him. Something shifted. Her magic shimmered and then solidified, throwing him back.

Gavin crashed into the far side of the room. He started to get up, and the woman watched him for a moment.

"You really don't know about the *t'ranth*, do you?" She sighed, looking toward the door again. "I'm going to kill that man," she muttered. Turning to Gavin, she said, "I don't have them." She stepped outside. Smoke swirled up and around her. Tension that had been in her face faded as she disappeared.

Gavin got to his feet slowly, which took everything within him, and he headed to the door. Imogen held her sword over a fallen figure.

Gaspar.

He didn't have a chance to think through what the Toral had said to him, the confusion she'd shown, or the comment about killing someone.

If she meant Wrenlow...

The strange thing was that he didn't think she did.

Which meant he didn't have the full story.

What if the *t'ranth* wasn't the egg?

Or maybe she didn't want to use it, but wanted to keep it from Tristan—or the Fates?

She was powerful, and Zella had warned him that Toral often used dangerous magic, so he had to be careful with that line of thinking.

Gavin raced over to Gaspar and looked around the clearing. "What happened?"

"They were too much for us," she whispered.

"They?"

"The creature we faced."

"How was that even possible?" he asked.

"I don't know," she said.

Imogen sounded worried in a way that Gavin had rarely seen from her. Whatever had happened, whatever she had dealt with, had been too much for her.

Gaspar lay motionless, reminding Gavin of what had happened to Desarra. It was the result of power, but what kind? That was an answer he didn't have, and he wasn't sure that he was going to get it. Not from Gaspar's unconscious state.

Gavin looked at Imogen. "We need to get him to Nelar. We might be able to get him the help he needs."

"There won't be time," she said.

"There will be."

He wasn't losing Gaspar.

This was his team. That was what Gaspar had kept reminding him.

He wouldn't let anyone fall.

Gavin placed his hands under Gaspar to scoop him off the ground. His hands came away wet, and he rolled

Gaspar over and examined his back. Blood stained his clothing, and he continued to bleed heavily.

Gavin frowned and picked Gaspar back up. "Hold on."

He started jogging. From somewhere in the forest, the stone creatures reappeared and started to follow them. Gavin looked over to see Imogen running alongside him as well.

"Why didn't the stone creatures help us?" he asked.

"They couldn't get through the protections," she said. "I tried to lower the barriers quickly, but they were deceptively challenging."

"How so?"

Imogen glared at him. "Is now the time?"

Gavin turned his attention straight ahead. "No," he said. Now definitely wasn't the time. All he needed to do was keep moving. "There will be several different kinds of healers in the city."

"How well do you know this place?" she asked.

"A little bit," Gavin said. "It's been a while since I've been there, though."

He jogged, knowing he couldn't go too quickly and run the risk of burning off his energy, especially with as much power as he'd already drawn upon to fight. He had to keep moving, but he could already feel his strength fading.

"Do you want me to take him?" Imogen asked.

"No," Gavin said.

"I know what you did in there."

"Do you?"

"I know well enough."

The strange part was that Gavin was certain she *did* know. He had no idea how she did, or whether he'd ever know what she had learned about him, but he wasn't sure it even mattered. "I will carry him," he said. "Besides, at this point, you might be the better one to fight if it comes down to it."

She looked over, then she nodded. Under other circumstances, Gavin would've loved to have an opportunity to talk with her, to figure out more about her and her power, but now was simply not the time.

It felt like an eternity before they reached the edge of the forest and made it to the city. Gaspar still hadn't awoken—not that Gavin expected him to. There had been enough blood loss that Gavin was surprised that Gaspar hadn't perished, but this was Gaspar. The old thief was stubborn.

As they approached the city border, a squat stone building with a low surrounding wall greeted them.

"There," Gavin said.

"What is it?" she asked.

"A sorcery outpost."

She frowned. "Are you sure?"

"Look at the markings."

The building was a pale stone, and there were runic markings all over the structure. They were signs of sorcery, or perhaps writing that came from an even earlier time. Approaching as they did, Gavin could feel the energy of the building itself push on him, as if trying to raise his awareness. In the daylight, the stone of the building and the wall surrounding it seemed to gleam.

"He won't like this," she said.

"I'm sure he won't," Gavin agreed. "I'm not sure he has much choice in the matter."

And any run-of-the-mill healer might not be enough. What Gaspar needed was *real* healing, somebody who understood and could get him through what had happened.

Imogen pushed the gate open, and Gavin hurried up the path and kicked on the door to knock. He looked over at Imogen, who was watching intently. She had sheathed her sword, but there was a certain danger radiating from her.

When the door finally came open, a young face looked out at them. He had dark brown hair, a long jawline, and a serious expression on his face. "I'm sorry, but we are—"

Gavin pushed past him, ignoring the young sorcerer's protests. "We need healing. This man has been hurt."

"You realize where you are?" the sorcerer asked.

Gavin looked up at him. He was of half a mind to pummel him, but that was just his frustration getting to him. "I do, which means we're someplace we can get some healing. Are you not capable of doing that?"

The sorcerer studied him. "Bring him down here."

He motioned to a hall leading off the main entrance, and Gavin followed him. The sorcerer opened the door to a large room, as large as Gavin's sleeping quarters at the Dragon had been. A bed occupied one wall, a row of cabinets another. A washbasin filled with water sat on a table next to the bed. Gavin lowered Gaspar down to the bed.

"Can you tell me what happened?" the sorcerer asked.

"Not really," Gavin said.

"Why not?"

"Well, because I didn't see it." He looked over at Imogen, and she shook her head. "Neither of us did. All I know is that he got injured. And you're going to fix him."

"You don't demand healing from a member of the Sorcerers' Society."

Gavin turned to him and unsheathed the El'aras dagger. "I will damn well do what I please. And you will heal my friend. Otherwise, we're going to see how much your magic can be used on healing *you*. Unless you don't want to find out, you're going to do everything in your power to ensure that he comes through this. Do you understand?"

To the sorcerer's credit, he flicked his gaze to the blade, but he didn't flinch. Maybe threatening him wasn't going to be the most effective strategy. Gavin wasn't about to negotiate. Not when it came to Gaspar's life. Not when his blood was on Gavin's hands. Literally.

"Stand over by the wall," the sorcerer instructed.

"If you do anything other than try to heal him—"

"I will do all I can. Now, stand off to the side."

Gavin nodded to Imogen, and they took their place in front of the door. At least this way nobody could jump in and surprise them.

The healer went to work. He held his hands out, running them over Gaspar's body as he mumbled something under his breath.

"I don't know what happened back there," Gavin said. "I don't even know why they left."

"It was sudden," Imogen said quietly. "I was not expecting that, but they finished their attack, and then they just vanished."

The Toral had made a point of telling him that she had not taken Wrenlow and Olivia. She was after something she thought he had, but she hadn't killed him when she had the chance.

"Something doesn't quite fit together," he said.

"You have been telling us that for a while."

"All of this…" Gavin shook his head. "I thought it had to do with Tristan and everything he was doing, but I'm no longer certain."

"This was where you said we were supposed to go," Imogen said.

"Because that's where I thought we *were* supposed to go."

"And now?"

"And now I don't know," he said. "Now I wonder if, perhaps, we were played all along."

And if they were, why? Until he had better answers, he was going to have to stay here in order to keep Gaspar alive, but then what? Now that they had lost their only lead, Gavin didn't know if there was anything more that they could do.

He watched the sorcerer as he continued to work on Gaspar.

It was times like these when Gavin wished he had a better understanding of magic and that there was some way for him to know just what they were doing. But he had to rely on the sorcerer to do the right thing.

"Do you think they left us because of what you said?" Imogen asked.

Gavin furrowed his brow. "To be honest, I don't really even know what happened there or whether there was anything they would have done differently."

"Differently?" She cocked her head to the side. "I'm not asking about differently. I'm asking whether you think anything was done as the result of what you said."

Gavin shook his head. "I asked why they took Wrenlow and Olivia. That was it."

"And they did not?"

"Why are you asking?"

"Because something was odd," she said.

"Other than the entire attack?" Gavin asked.

"The attack. What happened with Gaspar. And what preceded all of it."

Gavin frowned. "There was something strange, now that you mention it. When I got inside the home, some men had already been taken out."

"Taken out?"

Gavin nodded slowly as he thought about what he remembered. "The other attackers were outside, and they started on us as soon as we arrived, but the ones inside..."

They were dead.

"You took care of them?" Imogen asked. Gavin nodded, and Imogen's eyes tightened. "I am surprised you brought him here."

"To a sorcerer?"

"To the city."

"Would the two of you be quiet?" the sorcerer asked.

Gavin glowered at him. Meeting a sorcerer with an arrogant attitude was not surprising. "We'll be quiet, just as long as you can guarantee you will help him."

"I'm doing everything in my power to help him. And you must do everything in your power to leave me alone while I'm working. Now, if you don't mind, I would like a little quiet."

Gavin grunted, and he leaned against the door. He had no choice but to wait. Imogen watched the sorcerer, and Gavin couldn't tell whether she was irritated or amused.

Until they had answers, he had to be patient.

He was skilled in many areas. Patience was not one of them.

CHAPTER SIXTEEN

The healer had left, and Gavin and Imogen stood on the far side of the room, resting against the counter. As far as Gavin could tell, Gaspar was as well as the healer could make him, breathing regularly, though his eyes were closed. He didn't even know if the man was conscious.

"We could take him from here," Imogen said.

Gavin looked over at her. She had her attention focused on the door and appeared as if she wanted to grab her sword and be ready to attack anyone who came inside the healing room. She remained tense, with an edge about her as though she was ready to scream.

"Where would we go?" he asked.

"Anywhere but here," she said.

"He's going to have to ride the stone creature back."

"And you don't think he can do that?"

"I'm not sure he will be able to in his current state."

Until Gaspar recovered fully, Gavin wasn't sure that there would be any way for him to get back on his feet.

"He could use an enchantment," she said. "We are in Nelar, after all."

Gavin nodded. They were, which still surprised him, especially considering that the Toral had mentioned the term "dular." He hadn't given enough thought to that word over the years. After the conversation with Zella and hearing the way she had described her views on dular versus enchanters, Gavin started to question whether he should feel differently.

"You know, I don't know anything about you," Gavin said to Imogen.

She turned her attention to him, regarding him for a moment before flicking her gaze to Gaspar. "He's not shared anything with you?"

"Not about you, no. Other than to say he appreciates your discretion."

She smiled slightly. Even that seemed mysterious. "I suppose he does."

"You aren't from Yoran," Gavin said. He glanced toward the door before turning back to Imogen. "You recognized something about the people who attacked us."

"Not about all of them. I recognized something about one of the attackers. I have seen her kind before."

"The Toral?" Gavin asked.

"The one with the black hair."

"She had some sort of power as well." Gavin remembered the way the blood had dripped from her hands and the smoke had streamed around her. "What was it?"

"Something that has not been seen in this part of the world in quite some time."

"A type of magic? Or…"

"Or," Imogen said.

Gavin grunted. "I was attacked by somebody like you. Back in Yoran, in the warehouse. There was an attack, but…" He shrugged, remembering the way the woman had jumped on him and the speed with which she had moved. "I don't really know what to make of it. She was quick, strong, and yet she didn't use a sword the way you do."

"Then she's not Leier."

That's where she's from.

Gavin had heard of the Leier, but never known any. They were all fabulous swordsmen—or women. Tristan had made an offhanded comment to him about training with them, but nothing had ever come of it.

"I've been wondering why you're with Gaspar." He wanted to ask about the man he'd seen her with from Jalash, but that could come later. When he had more answers.

"Gaspar offered his help finding something important to me. That is all."

"Is it anything I could help with?"

Her brow furrowed, and for a moment, darkness flittered across her eyes. "It's something I need to do myself. I don't know if you can understand, but there are things important to my people. Tasks that we take upon ourselves. This is mine."

Gavin decided not to push, though it didn't change his

curiosity. "If you change your mind, I'm here for you." He started laughing. "I thought he kept you around to help him pull jobs."

"There is no need. Gaspar does not require my assistance for his assignments."

"Assignments? I think Gaspar has jobs, not what I would call assignments."

"You can call them what you want," she said.

Gavin smirked, but she just stared at him. Finally, he shrugged. "I suppose, then, that I should thank you for coming along."

"You can only thank me when this is all over."

"I would still like to thank you. You didn't have to come."

"I find it interesting," she said. "You've brought an intriguing type of power within the city. I must admit that when it first appeared, I did not care for it, but…" She smiled. "I have found myself fascinated by what I've experienced."

"Most people would be terrified by it."

"I am not most people."

"No," Gavin said. "I suppose you are not."

Imogen watched him and then turned to look at Gaspar. "He is coming awake."

Gavin glanced toward Gaspar and realized that she was right. He had opened his eyes. Surprising relief swept through Gavin. He really hadn't wanted to lose Gaspar—not that he'd tell the old man.

"Damn," Gaspar mumbled.

"What?" Gavin asked. "Did you hope you would die?"

"No. I was hoping I wouldn't have to see you again." He looked over to Imogen, his brow furrowing. He cocked his head to the side as he watched her, and Gavin realized that he was tapping on something.

His enchantment.

"You can go ahead and say it," Gavin said. "Either that, or you can tell me to go so that you can say whatever you want to say."

"I need to have words with Imogen. Is that what you want me to tell you? It would be nice if you'd give us a few moments," Gaspar said.

Gavin grunted. "Well, since you asked so nicely, maybe I will."

He pulled open the door and paused. He hadn't expected to be left alone inside the Sorcerers' Society outpost, but here he was. Should he leave the outpost entirely? There were so few sorcerers he had any interest in spending time around. In this case, Gavin believed this sorcerer was helpful, but he worried about what he would end up owing.

He waited in the hallway for a moment. The door next to him opened, and Gavin looked over to see the healer step out into the hall.

The sorcerer frowned at him. "You mentioned Toral."

Gavin tilted his head to the side, studying him. "Did I?"

"You do not have to deny it. I could hear you."

"The walls are stone," Gavin said.

"And I placed an enchantment," the sorcerer said, shrugging. "Consider me curious as to what happened. Since you decided to intimidate me, I wanted to know."

Gavin smiled. He couldn't help but feel a little impressed that the sorcerer was willing to push like that, especially with Gavin's threat. Few had the stones to threaten a sorcerer, and usually those who did could back it up.

"You know the Toral?" Gavin asked.

She'd mentioned Nelar was her city.

And she *was* a sorcerer.

This could be *her* outpost.

Gods, but Gavin hadn't even considered it before coming here. He'd been so focused on getting Gaspar help, that he'd not paid any mind to any danger that might be there.

"I know the term," the sorcerer said, though he did so cautiously, watching Gavin.

He had the distinct cold wash of magic feel coming off the sorcerer, and Gavin wondered what power he might be readying to use against him. Little would work. Gavin had rested long enough that his core reserves had recovered.

"I'm curious as to why you do," the sorcerer said.

Gavin shrugged. "Because we faced one. I don't know why, only that there are friends of mine who were abducted, and that's why we're here. Does that make you feel better?"

The sorcerer regarded him, pressing his lips together into a tight frown. "Somewhat," he said, nodding. "Is that why you were injured?"

"I wasn't injured," Gavin said.

"You weren't, but he was." The sorcerer gestured to the

door while tugging on his robe. "I haven't seen anything quite like it before."

"What happened?"

"He had a hole through his chest." The sorcerer waved his hand as Gavin opened his mouth to say something. "Before you start to question me, I don't know anything more, other than that it was perfectly round, as if a projectile had gone through his chest. I didn't have to remove anything, not that you seem to care about that."

"I care," Gavin said.

And he did. Seeing Gaspar near death had been harder than he'd expected on him.

He'd been forced to tamp those feelings down, but hearing the sorcerer talk about what had happened to Gaspar brought that emotion back to him.

All because he'd come with Gavin to find Wrenlow.

"Do you?" the sorcerer asked.

Gavin narrowed his eyes, regarding him. "Will he fully recover?"

"He's awake, isn't he?"

"He is."

"Then he should recover," the man said. "The alternative was that he would have perished by now, but seeing as how he has already come awake, I suspect he will continue to make improvements. It's not always a guarantee, as you likely know."

"I didn't."

"Well, it's not."

Gavin frowned, then nodded. "What do you know about the Toral?"

"Nothing," the sorcerer said.

Gavin watched him for his reaction. He could recognize when someone hid emotions from him, and this man was suppressing his surprise. It was in the way his eyes had widened slightly, his held breath, and the imperceptible step backward, as if to move away from Gavin.

He was hiding something.

"You can deny it, but I can tell you recognize that term. And I know she's from Nelar," Gavin said.

His eyes twitched. This was a man not accustomed to keeping secrets.

"As I told you, I have only heard the term."

"You've more than just heard it."

Gavin didn't have Gaspar's skill with questioning. He didn't even have Wrenlow's way of getting information—a charming sort of friendship that disarmed a person. Nothing at all like how Gavin had to negotiate for intel. Normally, when Gavin wanted answers, he just forced them out of somebody. And in this case, he didn't know what it was going to take for him to find out what he wanted.

"I'm just trying to help my friends. That's all," Gavin said. "So if there's anything you know, anything you might be able to tell me, I would appreciate you sharing."

"Not a threat this time?" The sorcerer smiled tightly. "I've been threatened by others before. I recognize that you meant it."

"I did," Gavin said.

"And I've been around those who know violence. Like you."

Gavin shrugged. "I do."

"Why?"

"That's my training."

"Do you enjoy it?" the man asked. It was a strange question from a sorcerer, stranger still from a healer.

"What's there to enjoy? I take jobs. I fulfill those jobs. Then they're completed."

"Like the man in there."

Gavin tipped his head toward the door. "He's a thief. He's nothing like me."

"You aren't a thief."

Gavin shook his head.

"I see. Then you are a killer." Disdain lingered in the last part of what the sorcerer said.

"Under certain circumstances. Now, since you've questioned me, I would like more information about the Toral. At least, more about what you know."

"I know they have power."

"You're going to have to share more than that," Gavin said.

"I know some can perform sorcery."

"Again, you're going to need to do more than that." Gavin watched him, the way he was trying to keep something from him. "You know this *particular* Toral." He had been trying to figure out what it was and what it meant, but as he looked at this sorcerer, he realized that was the case. "You can admit it."

His shoulders sagged a little. He'd break. Gavin could see that now.

It would take little more than a push.

Would he be willing to push him?

The sorcerer had helped Gaspar—but Gavin still had Wrenlow to help.

The sorcerer kept him from making that choice. "Perhaps I know her."

"Then you can admit your connection to them as well."

The sorcerer frowned. "Not if you intend to do harm to her."

There it was.

That's why the sorcerer had been so evasive. Not just because she came from the city, though that had to be a part of it. "You don't just know her," Gavin said, smiling, "you care about her."

The man straightened, and it seemed that a debate warred behind his eyes. "She's a friend."

Gavin grunted. He was amused by the idea that the Toral would have a friend like this, and he also believed that having a connection like this meant that he should be able to figure out who this person was.

"I need to speak with her. She came after… something. The two of us need to have a conversation." Mostly because he wasn't sure if they'd had a miscommunication so far—or not.

"I'm afraid I won't be able to help with that," the sorcerer said.

"Then I'm afraid the two of us are going to have a very different conversation."

"You intend to threaten me again?"

Gavin narrowed his gaze. "I thought I was doing that now."

"I see."

"I'm sorry, but I *need* to speak with her. It's a matter of life or death. And if I don't find my friend…"

He'd let the healer fill in whose death he meant.

The healer watched Gavin, but he didn't say anything. There was just a darkness in his eyes that lingered, a look that said he wasn't going to say anything more.

Under other circumstances, and if Gaspar hadn't nearly died, Gavin might have actually appreciated the determination from this man. But at this point, in this circumstance, Gavin needed to force him into providing some useful information about this Toral.

"At least tell me how you know her," Gavin said.

"So you can harm her?"

Gavin glanced at the closed door leading to the healing room. "She's the one who attacked us."

"The only reason she would have attacked you is if you had done something worthy of it."

Gavin frowned. "You don't just know who she is. Gods, you know her *well*."

The healer stared at him.

Gavin made a move toward him, but the healer created a spiraling pattern that started at his feet and worked its way up to his head, wrapping a barrier around him. He held his arms out and pressed his hands together as he watched Gavin.

"I have little doubt you can get through this," the sorcerer said. "Seeing as how you've made a point of proving your capabilities, I understand I won't be able to keep you from harming me if that is what you choose, but

I can make it difficult for you—along with your friends—to escape from here. If that is what you prefer, I will do whatever is necessary to ensure my safety, but I have a feeling you won't."

"Don't be too sure," Gavin said.

The sorcerer shook his head. "You need something still, so I don't think you will hurt me." He stood off to the side, though, as if waiting and uncertain whether or not Gavin would harm him.

Rather than attacking, Gavin just grunted. "Who is she?"

"Someone of power."

"I'm aware, but I want to know more about her than that. Who *is* she?"

"I can't reveal that to you."

"You can't, or you won't?" Gavin asked.

The sorcerer watched him and said nothing.

"Then get word to her that I would like to speak to her."

"Why?"

Gavin wanted to threaten the sorcerer, to force him into working with them, but he doubted that was going to be effective. "You can tell her that I have two friends missing and that was why I was there. And you can tell her that I have what she wants." Gavin still had no idea what the *t'ranth* was, but she thought he had it. If she thought he knew what it was... then maybe she'd be willing to talk. At this point, that was all he really wanted.

The healer pressed his lips into a thin line and stared at

Gavin, brow furrowing as confusion flitted across his face. "You have it?"

"I do. Seeing how she was willing to go through such lengths to acquire it, you can let her know that I have it. All she has to do is come and get it."

He knew it was dangerous, but he suspected he was right and just needed to get through to her so he could figure out exactly what she was up to.

The healer shrugged. "I will see what I can do. I can't make any promises. It will take time for me to get word to her. She's not always easily accessible."

Gavin looked over to the door. "We will be here until my friend recovers. And I can assure you, either my equally capable colleague or I will be here waiting, in case you decide to betray us."

"I've helped you. I didn't betray you."

"You helped us because you have no choice in the matter. But if the situation were to change, we want to ensure that you aren't going to do anything to harm my friend."

The healer shook his head.

Gavin slipped past him, feeling the brush of the invisible barrier around him as he returned to the room with Gaspar.

Imogen relaxed only slightly when Gavin came into the room.

He closed the door, looking from Imogen to Gaspar. He had fallen back asleep, which Gavin figured was probably for the best. As injured as he was, rest was going to be the most important thing for him. It was the only way he was going to recover as quickly as he needed to.

"The damn sorcerer knows the Toral," Gavin said to Imogen.

"He told you this?"

"He can hear us talking," Gavin said, sweeping his gaze around the room. The enchantment that the sorcerer placed could be anywhere. Gods, he could have simply put an enchantment on any one of them. "We just have to be careful."

"Then we should go," Imogen said, glancing back over to Gaspar. "We need not remain here."

"Is he well enough to travel?"

She shook her head. "Not yet, but now that he's been healed, it should not take long for him to fully recover."

Gavin leaned against the wall, feeling unsettled. They needed to get moving, to do something, but he didn't know what that would be. He wanted to pace and think, but there wasn't much space in here.

"I'm going to see if I can get some answers in the city," he told Imogen.

He looked at Gaspar before he left. His skin was pale, his eyes closed, and his breathing regular. All were signs that the old thief would recover from this, but Gavin couldn't shake the feeling that he was going to need time —and with everything they had dealt with so far, it didn't feel like time was on their side.

"I'll stay with him," Imogen said.

Gavin stepped back out into the hallway. The healer was gone, though Gavin wasn't surprised. Still, he thought that the healer was probably somewhere nearby, watching or listening, ready to react if they did something to draw his attention. He'd probably place spells on them, so Gavin prepared to respond if it were to come down to that.

Again, he found that he wished he had a better understanding of the magic he possessed and knew how to use it. Then he wouldn't have to worry about exploding it out so wildly. Against the sorcerer and the Toral, he would've had an advantage in trying to use that power while fighting, but so far, he had not been able to focus his magic well enough. The only way he'd used it had been in bursts of power.

He stopped in the entrance hall of the outpost. The tile floor and the stone sculptures were incredibly exquisite, making him think they were probably enchantments, which often took on remarkable detail. He was in a place of sorcerers, so it shouldn't surprise him that they would have these kinds of impressive enchantments. They might be for the protection of the outpost, which would be reason enough for Gavin to be careful.

Could he use something to diminish the enchantments? He shook his head. Not unless it became necessary. For now, he would stay here, and he would let those enchantments protect Gaspar as much as they could. He turned to the door, and when he reached it, he had a feeling of somebody watching him.

He looked over his shoulder, but he didn't see anyone. The only person they'd encountered in the outpost had been the healer. Typically, there were higher-level sorcerers within an outpost. He would've figured that, in a place like this, there would be at least three or four different sorcerers, all of different abilities, ranks, and standings within their society. Something felt off to him, though he wasn't entirely sure what it was or why he should feel that way.

When he stepped out of the outpost, a cool tingling washed over his skin. Some protection faded. Maybe the sorcerer had been telling the truth about making things difficult for them.

He stood on the step, staring out into the city. It was early morning, the sun barely creeping up above the horizon. The air was already intensely humid, making it challenging for him to breathe, though Gavin had learned different techniques to breathe through humidity in order to function well. He took a slow, steady breath, then quickly exhaled and stepped beyond the small wall surrounding the outpost.

He didn't know how to figure out what Tristan had done with Wrenlow, but if he could get the communication enchantment to work…

There was only one way to accomplish that.

Gavin touched the marker in his pocket, turning it from side to side. Would Anna mind? She probably would not, especially as she had provided him with the marker in the first place. But in this case, he worried that what he needed from her was so specific and personal that it might upset her to learn that he wanted it to find his friend and not for anything greater than that. Still, maybe she would be willing to help.

It wasn't just for him. It was because there had been a strange Toral attack.

And knowing what he did of Anna and her willingness to help him in the past, he had to hope that she would see his need and work with him.

Gavin pulled out the marker and studied it for a moment. How long would it take for her to respond? They may not have time to wait. He squeezed his hand around the marker, and he focused on his core reserves. He let out a trickle of energy into the coin and waited.

When there was no answer, Gavin looked over to the city. The last time he had been here had been years ago, and he was a much younger person. He didn't recall much of it, though the city itself looked about as he remembered. Situated to the north of Yoran as it was, there was something different to it. An energy, perhaps, or perhaps it was just the humidity in the air. Many of the pale white stone buildings—those similar to ones found in Yoran—had a strange moss that grew along them, and the air stunk from it.

He headed into the city.

It didn't surprise him that the Sorcerer Society outpost would be at the outskirts of the city. Nelar was a place that had long been ruled by enchanters, or dular, as the people here called them.

He had never known that it was a derogatory term. When he had come here many years ago, he had overheard it and had asked Tristan about it, but he hadn't known that the people wouldn't care for that term. Had Zella not told him, Gavin would not have known.

Everywhere he looked carried the sense of enchantment. He noticed large sprawling symbols on many of the buildings, along with sculptures sitting outside of doorsteps, or decorations hanging from eaves or along rooftops. All of them had complicated symbols worked within them, evidence of an enchantment. The cold washing sense of magic came from many of them.

This was different than Yoran.

There was no attempt to hide the magic, and as he made his way through the city, Gavin looked at buildings with enchantments etched onto the surface, or people who openly carried enchantments, obviously moving with speed or looking around with enchanted eyesight, or probably even enchanted strength.

He reached what looked to be the center of the city. It was a massive courtyard. A large stone sculpture filled the center of the courtyard—likely another enchantment—and there was evidence that fighting had once taken place here. He could see it on the burn marks along one of the walls, as well as the reconstruction of a massive manor house nearby.

Fighting had happened here. And recently.

Knowing there was a Toral within the city, or at least one who had come to the city, left him thinking she probably had been involved. Everything seemed calm now. Whatever had taken place here had been resolved.

There was what the Toral had mentioned to him.

She'd faced other attacks.

She'd protected Nelar.

That had to be what she feared now.

And despite the attack, magic was still used openly.

That was another different thing than in Yoran, though while Nelar appreciated enchantments, he didn't see many members of the Society.

Perhaps they weren't all that different, after all.

Gavin tore his gaze away from the courtyard and started to wander to explore more of the city, when the coin began to vibrate.

CHAPTER SEVENTEEN

Gavin had lost track of how long he'd waited for the coin to work for him.

He'd tried over and again, this time pacing through the city while watching over Gaspar, going in and out of the outpost worried about whether he would fully recover. So far, he had not. He kept waking up, but he didn't react much.

Imogen preferred to stay with Gaspar, and Gavin understood her dedication. Whatever debts she owed Gaspar obviously kept her tied close to him, as if she feared leaving him for too long. Gavin hoped she didn't view Gaspar the way Gavin had once viewed Tristan.

He hurried to the edge of the city, looking at the stone wolves to ensure they were still there and that he and the others had a way to return to Yoran. Gavin had been concerned about leaving the stone creatures behind, not knowing whether there was any way to lose track of them. He had been pleasantly surprised to see that they had remained in place, waiting for them.

When the marker Anna had given him started to vibrate, he pulled it out, squeezed it for a moment, and frowned. He looked around and started to wonder if Anna would be able to find him. The last time she'd responded to the marker, she'd tracked him through the coin, but it had never vibrated quite this strongly.

He moved toward the city, and the vibration eased. Gavin stopped, peering down at the marker, and the vibration started up again.

Is it trying to guide me somewhere?

He circled back toward the creatures, and he rested his hand on the stone wolf. The marker continued to vibrate. The wolf twisted, the gray stone somehow flexible, and looked up at him.

"Do you know where to go?" Gavin asked. The wolf lowered his head. He let out a soft, creaking whine. "You want me to climb on."

He hadn't expected that, but maybe the wolf knew exactly where the El'aras were and how to reach them. He scrambled onto the wolf, grabbing its ears, and they started off. With any other creature, holding on to the ears would be torment, but since it was not really alive, Gavin knew he couldn't hurt the wolf.

He focused on the vibration, though he didn't know if he needed to, as the wolf seemed to know exactly where he was going and trotted ahead. Gavin sat up enough to protect his backside and avoid the jostling.

They reached the boundary of the forest. He should

have known. Of course it would've been at the forest. This *was* Anna, after all. They'd met in the forest the last time he'd summoned her.

As the creature kept moving, Gavin frowned to himself and slipped the El'aras marker back into his pocket while still trying to clutch the wolf's ears. They slowed at the edge of the clearing with the house in the distance, and Gavin climbed off.

He didn't have to wait long.

"Why this place?" Anna asked, stepping out from the trees on the far side of the clearing.

She was as lovely as she had been the last time he'd seen her. Her golden hair flowed in waves past her shoulders, and her crystal blue eyes pierced him with a certain intensity, something knowing about the way she looked at him. Maybe that wasn't anything surprising, given that she was El'aras and Gavin was at least part El'aras, so he shared some of her magic.

"I was going to ask you the same thing," he said, looking around. "Is it just you?"

"Would you prefer others to have come?"

"I'm a little surprised you were willing to come on your own." He wasn't going to press on her delay in getting back to him.

Why now? And why here?

"You should not have been," she said, smiling slightly. "I came as you requested."

Gavin smiled tightly. *Not* exactly *as requested.* "I'm sorry I needed to summon you again. I know that you are busy." Even with that, he wasn't entirely clear what Anna had been doing. Hiding, as far as he knew, like she had been in Yoran. She was the Risen Shard, which mattered to her people, and it meant that she had some fate that she had to prepare for.

"Are you sorry?" she asked.

As he looked across the clearing at her, he realized that was not exactly true. "Maybe I'm only sorry about the reason I had to summon you."

She chuckled, a soft sound that carried across the distance. "And what reason is that, Gavin Lorren?"

"This," he said, tapping on the earpiece for the enchantment. "My friend Wrenlow is missing, and I can't tell if the enchantment has been compromised or if I simply can't get through to him. I've encountered someone who has the ability to mitigate my enchantment."

Anna crossed over to him and stood in the middle of the clearing, where he joined her. She looked slightly up at him. She was tall, much like most of the El'aras were, and her gaze swept over him, holding him in place. She reached out and touched his ear, the feel of her hand warm and pleasant. She closed her eyes for a moment, whispering to herself. As she did, a surge of pressure worked past Gavin before fading.

"What was that?" he asked.

She opened her eyes and stepped back. "That was me testing the enchantment as requested." She cocked her head to the side, then shook it. "There is no deficiency within it. The enchantment works as it ever did."

"I see."

"I can tell that is not the answer you were hoping for."

"I didn't know if the enchantment had faded," Gavin said.

"El'aras enchantments do not fade like others," she replied.

"They don't?"

"If you had come with me, you would have learned that by now."

"You understand why I could not have," Gavin said.

"I understand why you chose not to, not why you could not. It does not take all of my time to make my preparations." She offered a hint of a sad smile and regarded Gavin with it.

Why would she do that?

"I have put it off long enough, and unfortunately, it seems that the time for my preparation has drawn near." Before he had a chance to question what she alluded to, she glanced past him, and her gaze took in the stone wolf. "Interesting creature you have with you."

"Friends of mine provided it for me. Transportation." He seemed like more than that, though Gavin had to remind himself that the wolf was only an enchantment. That was it.

"I imagine it's easier to travel with that than it is to travel by horse."

"Maybe easier and faster, but not more pleasant. My backside…" He grinned, shaking his head. "You don't want to know about how my backside aches from the journey."

Anna chuckled. "I thought your name was the Chain Breaker, not the Saddle Breaker."

Gavin snorted, and he looked over to the house. "You knew."

"Stories of the Chain Breaker have spread even to Yoran."

There was something about the way she said it that suggested more to him. "It's about more than me being the Chain Breaker. What is it?"

She eyed him for a moment. "Hopefully, you never have to know." She forced a smile. "Why this place?"

What was she keeping from him? He wondered, though he knew that he wouldn't be able to force her to share.

He realized the bodies had all been cleaned up. "This was the first time I failed him," Gavin said.

"The first time?"

He shrugged. "I suppose it was the only time I failed Tristan. It was how I knew exactly where to find this place."

"Indeed?"

Gavin turned, crossing his arms as he stared at the building. "He reminded me of my failure from time to time. I think Tristan wanted to make sure I knew I would not be permitted to fail again."

"And you did not," she said.

He shook his head. "I didn't. I feared failing him." It was how he had known Tristan had called him here. It was a message he'd sent. Gavin had gotten that message loud and clear, unlike the enchantment he shared with Wrenlow. "He abducted a friend of mine. Along with somebody special to him."

"I see. And the great Gavin Lorren, the Chain Breaker, came on a job in search of a friend." She cocked her head as she regarded him. "You have changed more than I would've expected."

"I didn't realize you'd expected anything from me."

She smiled again. "Perhaps I misspoke. You have changed."

"You knew I changed. When I was last in Yoran, I couldn't leave because of my commitment to the city."

"And is that different now?"

Gavin shook his head. "Not yet. I'm hopeful I won't be needed there indefinitely..."

Now that he had Davel Chan, the enchanters, and even Gaspar working on behalf of the city, there was an element of protection there he didn't need to provide like he had before. And with that, Gavin had to hope that his friends and the people who had once relied on him would be able to manage without him going forward. Unfortunately, he didn't know if such a thing would even be possible until he removed the threat of Tristan and the Fates.

Though he *could* leave the dark egg in Yoran. There might be others who could use that to push back the Fates. He'd have to consider that, especially given what he'd learned about the egg from the Keeper.

"I've been struggling with what Tristan might want from me," Gavin said.

"Have you come up with any answers?"

"Not yet. And yet I can't shake the feeling there's

something he's after, but it's more than what I've seen so far."

"Perhaps you must ask him."

Gavin grunted. "I've been trying. He tested me in the city. He attacked me, wanting to uncover how much power I had and whether or not I'd be able to fight past the staff masters of Jind."

"That is a very specific test."

Gavin shrugged. "It's because I had not always been successful with their fighting style. He knew it, and he knew I would have needed to work on that without him."

"And he wanted to see whether you have increased your skill in the time you've been away from him."

Gavin nodded. "That's my suspicion."

"Interesting. He has been difficult for us to find."

"What are you trying to do with him?"

"We are trying to determine what he might do next. When we learned he was alive, he had not posed any threat, but that has evolved—much like many things that deal with him have evolved over time."

Gavin pursed his lips. "I think I might be the only one who'll be able to stop him."

"Probably," she said. "But it still raises the question of why he trained you the way he did. Unless he thought he could control you."

"He thought to use me. Isn't that what you said?"

"I'm not so sure I said it or that someone else said it to you. Either way, it fits, does it not?"

Gavin nodded. It did, but it still didn't make complete sense to him. Why would Tristan have trained him all those years to become the fighter and the assassin he had, if Gavin would ultimately be skilled enough to defeat him?

Unless that was never going to be the case.

Until he captured Tristan and had that conversation, he doubted he would know.

"This has been particularly difficult," Gavin said, gesturing to the house. "I think Wrenlow and Olivia were here, but we were too slow. We were caught by a Toral and another woman. A sorceress, or something along that line." He still didn't know what to make of the dark-haired woman, only that she had a strange type of magic that he had never seen before, which had challenged Imogen.

"You faced one of the Toral?" she said, turning to him.

"We did."

"That is odd."

"I think it was more of Tristan's message," he said. "That was part of this job, after all. I was supposed to recover a ring. Now that I've faced the Toral, I understand it was a Toral ring. He wanted me to acquire it for him."

"The Toral have a unique sort of magic," Anna said. "Distinct from others. It is drawn from a greater power, though it takes immense control in order to hold on to it."

"Is that why she was a sorceress?"

With a frown, she turned her attention to the house, and she held her hands out from her. A bluish color began to spiral out from her hands and headed toward the building, washing through it before withdrawing again. It happened quickly, in little more than a blink of an eye. As she used that magic, Gavin felt the way she poured that power out from her, even if he had no idea what she was doing.

Anna glanced over to him. "You could do that, you realize, Gavin Lorren."

"I don't think that I could."

"You underestimate yourself, but you need not. You have the potential. You've already proven you do. All you need is the willingness to utilize that power."

"It's more than just a willingness," Gavin said.

"Are you afraid of it?" she asked.

"Should I not be?"

"It is a part of you, no different than your heart or lungs."

"I can't choose whether or not my heart or lungs work," Gavin said.

"Then perhaps it is a part of you no different than the fighter you have become." She smiled slightly. "That might be the better comparison, after all. You can learn to use it, much like you can learn to become the fighter. It just takes time."

"I'm not so sure that I have the time necessary right now to do that."

"You have chosen not to." She looked over to him and studied him. "There will always be another assignment, Gavin. That is how you were trained, and that is how your mind works. I know men like you, and I know you view yourself as needing to take on the next task, and then the next. You have rarely paused, to continue your own education, since leaving your mentor."

"I find I need to continue my education during my journeys," Gavin said.

"Only you haven't journeyed, have you?" Anna asked.

"What is this about?"

"It is about nothing more than what I have said. You must be challenged. I can see that, unfortunately. It seems that, regardless of what approach we take, fate has something in mind for each of us." She said the last part softly, and when she looked up, she held his gaze. The strange, sad expression lingered in her eyes before she blinked it clear.

"Maybe when we solve this issue with Tristan." Gavin didn't know if he would have the time that he needed even after that, or whether he would still find himself drawn into something else, something more than what he'd already done.

She smiled at him. "Perhaps."

"It would be easier if I didn't have to go to the El'aras lands."

"Easier, but not better for you."

"Why not?" he asked.

"Because you would not be given the opportunity to learn what must be learned. You cannot do that here."

"Why not?"

She chuckled, shaking her head. "So many questions, but you have done nothing to find the answers."

"I've been trying to understand the power I have," he said.

"Let me guess. You use it with bursts of energy."

"Well..."

She laughed again. "It is uncontrolled. When you use it in that way, you have no finesse. You will find you use far more energy than is necessary, and that lack of control becomes detrimental."

"I know," Gavin said. "I've had to use the sh'rasn several times."

"Dangerous," she whispered.

"I understand the consequences."

She watched him, her mouth pressed in a tight frown. "Your training gives you a certain ability to withstand what most would not. It also places you in danger others would not be in. Because of your training, you run the risk of drawing upon more energy from yourself than you should. It puts you in a position where you might overwhelm yourself."

"I know," Gavin said.

"But it also places you in a unique position where you might be able to do more." She shook her head. "Unfortunately, I don't know what to tell you, other than that you must be careful, Gavin Lorren."

"I don't have much choice," he said. "I'm running out of the sh'rasn powder, anyway."

"I might be able to do something about that." She reached underneath her dappled forest-green cloak and pulled out a jar, which she handed to him. "Be careful with it, though. As you've seen, there are limits, even if you know how to push past them."

"I know there are," he said. "Just as I know that I have to find my way beyond them."

"There are some limits that you will not be able to

push past. Not easily. I caution you." She turned her attention back to the house. "I wonder why your mentor would've gone after a Toral ring. He would not have been able to access that power without appropriate training."

"Given Tristan's resources, it's possible he had that training," Gavin said.

Anna frowned. "It is something for me to consider," she said, shaking her head. She turned back to him. "If there is nothing else, I will depart."

"You could help." Gavin reached out and touched her on the wrist. "Find my friend Wrenlow. And Olivia. Help me stop Tristan."

She smiled sadly. "Unfortunately, it was difficult enough for me to slip away as it is. Had you not assisted me with what you had done before, I would not have come, but you have proven your value to my people."

There was something in the way she said "my people" that suggested it was more than just hers, but also his. Gavin didn't feel like the El'aras were his people, but she certainly seemed to.

"And I must be leaving," she said. "It is time for me to return to what I must do, and you must be ready for what you must do."

"What's going on?"

She hesitated, then breathed out slowly. "Perhaps you should know. You may be in danger."

He tensed with immediate concern. "Why is that?"

"The man you know as Cyran escaped. It is the reason I could not get to you before now."

The comment took him off guard, more than he had expected. "How would he have escaped?"

Cyran escaping from the El'aras was more than surprising. It suggested that he might be more powerful than Gavin knew.

"I do not know. There was an attack on the temple where he was held."

Gavin smiled slightly. "Temple?"

"You don't believe the temple would be equipped to hold somebody of his stature?"

"I fear it might be too kind for him," Gavin said. "With everything he's done, I think he deserves something a bit more brutal than that."

"Perhaps he does," she said. "Perhaps we should have been more assertive with holding him. Unfortunately, it is what it is. At this point, he is gone. I doubt he will come after you, even though you are responsible for what happened to him previously."

Gavin wasn't entirely sure if that was true or not. Knowing Cyran as he did—at least, knowing who he'd been before and the kind of person that he'd become—Gavin wouldn't put it past him to come for vengeance. Especially if he knew Gavin was busy trying to fight off the issues Tristan posed for him.

It was one more thing to be concerned about.

"How did he get out? Could Tristan have been responsible?"

"That is what we believe." She seemed irritated. "It was a mistake, more than anything else."

"A mistake?"

"An unfortunate one. He is gone, and I would caution you to be careful."

Gavin patted his pocket where he had slipped the sh'rasn powder. "If he comes, I might need this."

"He is a powerful sorcerer," she said. "Unconventionally trained, and because of that, he will do unexpected things with his power. You must be prepared for that."

"It's personal for him," Gavin said. Cyran had been his friend. He thought the two of them had been close and should have been fighting on the same side. "But I will watch out for him."

She tipped her head to the side, as if listening to something, before she turned her focus back on Gavin. "I must take my leave. I have been gone long enough, and my people have seen to it that I cannot disappear the way I did the last time. They want to ensure that I fulfill my obligations, much like you will need to fulfill yours. You must return."

"I must, must I?"

"I will report if I learn anything of your friend."

Gavin nodded, but he doubted that she would be able to find anything or do anything for him at all at this point. She walked away, and when she reached the edge of the clearing, she disappeared.

Gavin watched for a moment, then headed to the house. He pulled the door open and paused as he envisioned what it had looked like when he had originally gone in there for Tristan's assignment and failed. Then he saw in his mind as the Toral had come through here, destroying everything in her path.

What would Tristan have done had he acquired a ring like that?

Unless he had.

Could that be why the Toral was after me?

He had started to think that she didn't want to harm him, but she thought he had something. There *was* something in Yoran.

Could it be the dark egg?

The idea of Tristan acquiring a ring left him trembling.

It was time to get back to Nelar, to Gaspar, and decide what they were going to do now. Only then could they plan their next steps, but the problem for Gavin was that he didn't know what they needed to do or where they needed to go. The only thing he believed was that they were running out of time to save Wrenlow and Olivia. Whatever Tristan planned would be coming soon.

And since he had already stopped them once, Gavin feared waiting too much longer.

He left the house and paused in front of the stone wolf, resting his hand on top of it for a moment before climbing on. The wolf started off, loping quickly through the forest, as if knowing exactly what Gavin wanted and what he needed. They reached the outskirts of the city, and then he dismounted.

Gavin headed straight toward the outpost. The same feeling of cold washed over his skin as he pulled the door open and stepped inside, enough to warn him that whatever magic he might be able to access would be mitigated. He hurried to the room where Gaspar was recovering.

Gaspar sat on the edge of the bed as Imogen watched the door.

"You're up," Gavin said.

"Damn right, I'm up," Gaspar said. "It's taken you long enough. We can't sit around with Olivia missing—"

"And Wrenlow," he said.

"The kid will be fine. I can't go back to the city and tell Desarra I didn't find her sister." He let out a shaky breath. "Where have you been?"

Gavin tapped on the enchantment in his ear. "I called her. I needed to know whether or not this thing was even working."

"And?"

"And she said it was functioning. She also said that El'aras enchantments don't deplete quite as quickly as other kinds of enchantments."

"You worried about that?"

"I was concerned I wouldn't be able to count on it."

Then again, Gavin shouldn't have been. He should have known that he would have access to the power within the enchantment for as long as he wanted, especially given that it was made by the El'aras. It was different than one made by an enchanter, or even a sorcerer. Both had their own unique skill set, but neither of them had the same power as the El'aras.

"I tried to see if she would help us too," Gavin said.

Gaspar grunted, sliding off the edge of the table. He wobbled there for a moment, clenching his jaw. "And?"

"She said she couldn't."

"Figures. Why would the El'aras get involved in this kind of business?"

Gavin shrugged. "I don't know why they would, but I would've expected for them to have some interest in doing so. They seem to be invested in this for some reason."

Gaspar grunted again. "For some reason? You don't even know the reason? I can tell you why. It's because of you, boy. They want you. They want your power. You just have to figure out what they want from you."

Gavin didn't have the sense that they wanted anything from him, but maybe Gaspar was right. Maybe that was the only reason Anna had been willing to work with him at all. Maybe it was all about something that she thought he could offer, and that was the reason she had been willing to talk and work with him.

But he didn't know.

And maybe it didn't even matter.

"People like that have an agenda, boy. They always do."

"What about you?"

Gaspar leaned toward Gavin. "What agenda do you think I have?"

Gavin breathed out slowly. He knew better than to push Gaspar. "None, I imagine."

"You're damn right, it's none. But that woman and her people were in Yoran for a reason. They left after you came. Don't you find that interesting?"

Gaspar wasn't wrong. Anna had been vague with him about what she had been doing and her reasons for leaving. She'd been hiding in Yoran for a while before he'd found her, at least as far as he knew, but what if it was about something more?

"I will push for more information when this is over. Will that work?"

"It's going to have to, isn't it?"

Gavin chuckled and eyed him. "Are you well enough to get going?"

"As well as I can."

"Then we need to keep looking. I have to find Wrenlow and—"

"We are going back to Yoran," Imogen said. "Nelar has its own unrest. While you were gone, I overheard the healer talking to someone."

"The Toral?"

"I'm not sure. From what I have heard, several buildings have burned."

"I saw that, but I think it was a while ago." He suspected the Toral was even involved in some way, though he didn't know the details.

"We're leaving," Gaspar said.

Gavin wanted to argue, but it didn't make sense for him to. It was time for them to return. He didn't have any way to pursue Wrenlow or to know where Tristan would've taken him. They needed to get back to the city and regroup, then they could figure out what needed to be done.

He sighed. "Fine. Do you think you can handle the journey back on your stone wolf?"

"I can handle it," Gaspar said.

There was a flicker in his eyes, just a moment, but it

was enough that Gavin wondered if perhaps Gaspar wasn't nearly as confident as he wanted to portray.

And Gavin understood. He wasn't looking forward to the ride either. Partly because he felt that returning to Yoran was nothing more than a setback, but partly because he simply didn't want to ride on the stone wolf all the way back to the city.

"When do you want to leave?" Gavin asked Gaspar.

"Now," Imogen said.

Gavin frowned, but he had the good sense not to argue with her. There was no point in doing so, not when he had no reason to believe that they could—or should—stay here.

So he nodded. "Let me pay the sorcerer, and then we can go."

CHAPTER EIGHTEEN

Gavin found the sorcerer sitting in an alcove in the entrance to the outpost. He was dressed in a crimson robe, with the half-moon crest of the Sorcerers' Society embroidered on the left chest. His hair drooped into his face, but he looked up the moment Gavin appeared. His eyes flashed with irritation.

"Did you come to threaten me again?" he asked.

"No," Gavin said, looking around the outpost and once again feeling like it was strangely empty. As he had before, he believed there should be other sorcerers working in the outpost, but there were none. He couldn't help but feel that there was something he was missing.

The sorcerer folded a book closed, reminding him of Wrenlow.

"I came to pay you for your service," Gavin said.

The sorcerer raised an eyebrow. "You're actually going to pay?"

"I pay my debt."

"I see. Well, for the service you were offered, the price is typically set at a standard rate of one silver per day. Along with supplies, and a flat rate of five gold—"

Gavin leaned forward and rested his hands on the desk, fixing the sorcerer with a hard gaze. "There is no flat rate. We both know that. Sorcerers get to determine their own fees. Even those within the society." Gavin regarded him, trying to put as much intensity and darkness into his stare as he could. "I have experience around sorcerers, so I know what you can do, and I know what you can choose. In this case, you can choose whether you want to try to put one past me, or whether you would like to charge a fair rate."

"I am only stating the fee for the outpost," the sorcerer said.

"Then the outpost is overcharging." Gavin leaned back. "Is that because you don't care to heal dular?"

The sorcerer shook his head. "It has nothing to do with the dular. Why, when the attack came, I was there helping them…" He sighed. "It doesn't matter. Pay what you think you should, and we'll call it even. Is that what you want to hear?"

The attack had involved the dular and the Society together?

That was a story he'd love to hear.

Imogen was right. It was *time for them to get moving.*

"I'm not beyond the means of paying," Gavin said. He fished into his pocket and glanced inside the pouch of coins. *Do I really want to argue with the sorcerer about the value of his services?*

Gavin certainly had no problem negotiating for his own fee, and when he had been hired by Davel Chan, he had earned far more coin than he had acquired in quite some time. It was enough that Gavin would've been able to travel anywhere, set up for a period of time, and not worry about finding payment.

"Here," he said, dropping the pouch on the counter. "We will call that even."

The sorcerer didn't lift the pouch. "If you believe so."

Gavin tapped the table. "If you find your Toral friend, I would like to speak with her. That's all. I just want to have a conversation so I can find out what she knows about the man she's working for."

The sorcerer frowned for a moment but then nodded. "I told you that I will see what I can do. As long as you leave and stay out of the city."

"I don't intend to return for a while." Gavin chuckled. "And if I do, I can assure you that you won't see me."

He headed down the hall and greeted Gaspar as he came out of the room, walking slowly but moving more quickly the longer he was on his feet. Imogen stayed at his side, one hand on the hilt of her sword and her gaze flicking all around her, as if she expected one of the sorcerers to jump out at them at any moment.

It was enough to make Gavin smile, but he knew better than to grin at her. She was too dangerous.

They reached the desk with the sorcerer again, who had gotten to his feet and held the pouch open in front of him. "This is too much. I thought you said you weren't going to pay the flat fee and the daily rate and the—"

"I paid you what I think your services were worth. And if, for whatever reason, you decide you can share what I asked with your Toral friend, then so be it."

Gavin had no idea whether the man would do that, but since he had threatened the sorcerer, he figured he should at least leave on better terms. What did it matter if he offered a few more coins than what the services *should* have cost? Gaspar lived, after all.

"I don't need your bribe," the sorcerer said. He hefted the pouch and tossed it back at Gavin.

Gavin caught it in midair, then slammed it back down on the table. "It wasn't a bribe. It was payment for services rendered. You saved my friend, and that has value. Now, if you decide you want to do something to save my other friends, tell your Toral friend to find me. She'll know how."

Gavin turned his back on the man, guiding Gaspar out of the outpost and into the street. The sun was starting to set, which made it a terrible time for them to leave, but he understood Gaspar's desire to get out of the city.

"Do you really think it's wise for you to anger a sorcerer?" Gaspar said. "Don't you think you've had enough trouble with sorcerers in the past?"

"This one helped you," Gavin replied.

"He did, but was it because he had no choice?" Imogen muttered.

"Partly," Gavin said. "But I'm not going to feel bad about that either. He helped. That's all that matters."

They carefully made their way to the edge of the city, slower than Gavin would've preferred, but he had to give

Gaspar the chance to walk on his own. There was a part of him that was tempted to tease him, but he knew better than to do that. Especially given everything that had happened so far and how Gaspar wouldn't take the teasing all that well. When they neared the outskirts, the stone creatures came toward them, as if they had been summoned.

Gavin looked over at Gaspar. "Are you ready for your ride back?"

The old thief shook his head. "I would rather do anything else." He glanced over at Imogen, who fixed him with a glare. "But it seems I'm being told we need to return."

"We do," she said.

"Fine," Gaspar said. "And if I bleed internally while we're jostled by these damn stone wolves, then it's on you."

"You won't bleed," Imogen said. "Unless I shove my sword in your back."

Gaspar chuckled as he climbed onto the wolf. "You wouldn't do that."

"Try me."

They headed off, the stone creatures racing with the strange gait they had. As they hurried across the ground, following the road stretched between Nelar and Yoran, Gavin tried to settle onto the creature's back and get as comfortable as he could. There wasn't any way for him to really relax at this point, though.

He looked over to see Gaspar clutching his stone wolf, arms wrapped around it and legs strapped on either side.

He had his jaw clenched and his face worked in concentration. The intensity in his eyes told Gavin all he needed to know about how hard this was on him and just how much he struggled.

Gavin had to be cautious with him and get Gaspar back as quickly as they could. They stopped to camp, no one speaking much, other than Gaspar and Imogen sitting off to the side of the campfire, murmuring to each other. Gavin glanced over, and there was a part of him that wished they would include him in their conversation, but he understood their reluctance to do so.

They awoke early. Gaspar was moving less gingerly, and they climbed atop their stone golems and began the rest of their journey back to Yoran.

It was late by the time they reached the outskirts of the city. Yoran was mostly dark, though there were enough flickering lights in some windows for Gavin to see by. He had been tempted to reach for his enchantment to augment his eyesight a half a dozen times along the road but had refused to do it.

He followed the others into the city, and when they reached the Dragon, Gaspar climbed down from his wolf. Imogen did as well.

"Are you coming in?" Gaspar asked.

Gavin looked at the tavern entrance. "Not yet. I need to make my own preparations."

"For what?"

"For whatever might come. This isn't over, and until I understand what it's about, I don't know what we need to do."

And maybe there was nothing he needed to do. Maybe this was only about figuring out whatever the Toral was after, providing it to her, and getting Wrenlow and Olivia back.

If she was friends with the sorcerer at the outpost, then maybe she wasn't entirely bad. Regardless of working with Tristan.

I had worked with Tristan.

He would have to barter with her, and that was something he thought he could do. He didn't know whether he would be effective or whether she would even be responsive to it, but he had to try.

Gaspar glanced over to him, frowning. "We're going to find the kid."

"I know," Gavin said.

"And we're going to find Olivia."

"I know."

Gavin climbed off the stone wolf, which followed him as he walked around the city, watching him as much as it watched the city. *The damn thing thinks to protect me.* He swept his gaze from side to side, trying to decide what he needed to do, but he was tired and knew that he should probably just return to the sorcerer's lair.

His mind worked through what was going on here, the same way it had been doing ever since he had been attacked. Gavin had been trying to guess what the Toral was after. He had no idea what it was and whether there would be any way for him to figure it out without her telling him explicitly.

Gavin turned the corner and made a decision.

Cyran. The Mistress of Vines. The Fates.

All had been tied to a magic that had been exiled from the city years before.

Maybe there was something else in the city. Something more than the dark egg.

Now that Cyran was free, would he come back?

There would have to be a reason. It *could* be the dark egg, but that hadn't been what he'd been after when he'd been here before. None of the jobs Cyran had demanded he pull had been tied to that. They'd seemed almost as if they were a way to test his capabilities.

The same way Tristan had tested me recently.

Despite his claims otherwise, Cyran *had* taken after Tristan in many ways.

Why Yoran?

He had gone to the one beneath Cyran's home, so he knew what was there. In fact, he knew it so well that he knew there wasn't anything he would find. It was his sleeping location and nothing more. But there had to be something in one of the other lairs.

He hadn't visited them nearly as often as he should have. Gavin headed through the city. Every now and then, he paused and looked along the street. He had lost track of how late in the night it was, though he knew it was well past midnight. It was a time when he should be sleeping, and the city was thankfully quiet and empty. He passed a few patrols of constables, but he ignored them as he made his way to the first building. It was situated on the outskirts of Yoran, on the opposite side of the city from Cyran's home.

He had tried to figure out why the Triad would have the lairs situated the way that they were. They were not centrally located within the city. None of them were terribly fancy, for that matter. They were simple constructs, and other than the structure beneath them, Gavin would consider them unremarkable. It surprised him that any sorcerer would be willing to accept such an ordinary abode. There was more to them than he knew. Older, as well. They might even be tied to the El'aras, since he knew they had once lived in these lands.

It was one more thing he had to investigate when he had time. And it was one more thing that suggested that the city itself was the reason there had been as much of a magical presence as there had been, even though sorcery had been outlawed and banished twenty years ago.

He stepped inside the building, slipping the enchantment that enhanced his eyesight on his finger. He looked around but didn't see anything—empty, much like it always was.

He found the trapdoor beneath the carpet in the back room, much like it was in Cyran's home. Gavin opened the trapdoor and climbed down the ladder, lowering the door again. He stood there for a moment, focusing on the darkness and the energy around him. He couldn't feel anything and didn't see anything, so he started down the tunnel.

There had to be something here that Cyran had been after. That was what had started all of this.

And then Tristan had come.

If Gavin was right, Tristan had helped Cyran escape

from captivity. Which meant they were still working together.

Could it all be about the Toral ring?

Gavin hadn't seen one in the city, other than the one worn by the Toral who had attacked him. He reached the chamber off the tunnel and used a bit of his core reserves to trigger it to open. He peered inside for a moment and could feel some energy, but there was nothing else. It was strange for him to be aware of the energy that was here, as if there was something he was supposed to find. Maybe it was simply his own connection to magic, and that somehow pressed on him in a way that gave him a tie to the power here.

Gavin was aware of that residual sort of energy rolling against him, something that had lingered here. He had never been quite as alerted to it before. It was as though leaving the city and returning had changed his sensitivity to it.

Or maybe speaking with Anna again had changed it.

He made his way through the chamber, sweeping his gaze around everything. It was empty, having been cleared of anything magical in the time he'd been here. There had been a few different enchantments, none of them useful—at least not to him—and some furniture, but nothing else. Certainly no magical artifacts like he had found in other places throughout the city.

Gavin stopped and ran his finger along the hilt of the El'aras sword. That was the only unusual thing he had found in all the places he had visited. And that had been in the lair beneath Cyran's home. Gavin unsheathed the sword, looking at the blade.

The blade was significant because it had its own magical enchantment built within it. It summoned the power of the El'aras and allowed Gavin to concentrate that power to push it out from him. But that would not have value to a sorcerer.

The sword wasn't what Cyran—or Tristan—had been after. And it certainly wasn't what the Toral was after. She had not attempted to take the sword from him during their fighting.

He wasn't going to find answers here. He headed back out of the chamber and sealed the door closed once again, then made his way back out onto the street.

What do I need to do?

If they were going to face the Toral, and if he was ultimately going to face Tristan, Gavin needed more enchantments. He didn't want to wake Zella at this time of night, but she would have somebody watching. Perhaps it would even be Mekel.

The stone wolf took up his position alongside him again, tracking him through the streets, and Gavin smiled to himself. The wolf had stayed outside the home, placing himself so that he looked like a sculpture. Now, with the wolf following him around the city, it would look unusual to anybody who saw them.

Gavin would have to figure out some way to shrink the wolf back down when he wasn't needed. Then again, there would come a point where the wolf would expend all of his power and fade. At that point…

He didn't know what would happen, only that it was an enchantment, so the power within it would eventually fail. Much like every enchantment did.

He was surprised by how sad it left him feeling.

Gavin made his way toward the Captain's fortress, sweeping his gaze all around him. He didn't see anybody watching him, but he also knew that he might not even notice if they were. They would likely have some enchanted mechanism to be able to observe him.

Energy crackled in the air, and he paused.

Magic.

He unsheathed the sword and held it out, but the blade didn't glow.

Could the Toral be here?

Stone crumbled along the street, and Gavin paused, crouching down next to it.

As he held his hand out to it, there was a distinct sense of magic emanating from it. Power. This had been an enchantment.

Could it have been one of Mekel's?

Zella hadn't sent word to him. He had the enchantment she'd given him, so why not alert him if there was a need?

Could they have come for the dark egg?

Zella would definitely have sent word if that were the case.

This was something else.

Not about the egg, but perhaps a different attack.

He crept forward. Another crumbled enchantment.

It was large, and like the first, made completely out of stone.

He could feel the magic coming off it, energy that radiated outward, and there was considerable power within it.

Gavin shivered.

There had been an attack here.

And he had been gone.

He moved carefully along the edge of the street, staying in the shadows, but he didn't see anything. He couldn't shake the feeling that there was some sensation there, though, which left his skin tingling and tight. He had come to recognize how magic felt against his core reserves. It felt as if a rope brushed against his awareness, as if some power was trying to push in on him and force him to react.

By the time he reached the fortress, he still hadn't encountered anything.

The home was dark, and Gavin approached slowly. He made his way through the gate and reached the main entry, where he held his hand out, focusing on the power within him. As he probed for any energy that was there, he didn't detect anything.

He pushed open the door. There was a bit of resistance, but Gavin channeled his core reserves into it and then blasted it open.

The entry was empty, which was unusual. *Where were the enchanters? Shouldn't someone be standing guard?* He headed through the outer chamber to the next door, then felt something nearby.

He spun, looking to see if there was anybody else

there. The only thing that he noticed was what he felt. Power, nothing else.

Gavin pushed his core reserves into this door, but that wasn't going to be enough. He unsheathed the El'aras dagger and slid it into the lock while focusing his magic into it. The door resisted him at first, but finally, the lock opened.

He pulled the door open. The next room was empty as well.

Something had happened.

Where was Zella? Where were the others?

They should be here. They should *all* be here.

The enchanters were gone.

Gavin headed into the room slowly. He turned in place and looked around. He thought about Zella, Alana, and even Irison. Something had happened that had worried them enough that they had either left or…

Gavin didn't know.

We hadn't been gone that long, had we?

A couple of days. Nothing more than that, but certainly long enough that something could have taken place here. He needed to go to Davel Chan and find out what he might know.

He headed toward the storeroom, but it remained sealed shut.

There was no sign that anyone had forced their way in.

Which *had* to mean the dark egg was still safe.

Someone had been here. He was sure of that.

Gavin left the fortress and walked back into the street, starting toward the constables' building. As he neared the barracks, there was more activity than there had been in other parts of the city. Groups of people came and went. Constables, most of them. Some were enchanters that he identified by the sheer number of enchantments they wore. He noticed a few limping. One of the constables had a bandage around his head.

He hurried forward, wanting to reach Davel to question him about what had taken place while he was gone.

He never had the chance.

A voice crackled in his ear. "Gavin?"

He froze. "Wrenlow?"

CHAPTER NINETEEN

Gavin's heart hammered in his chest as he approached the Dragon, unable to believe that Wrenlow would still be alive, especially after everything that had happened. How had he ended up back in the city, and back in the Dragon, of all places?

He reached the tavern and pulled open the door. Wrenlow was sitting at one of the tables, watching the door, and he got to his feet as soon as Gavin came in. He wobbled for a moment before sinking back down. His dark hair looked lank, and there was a hollowness to his eyes that hadn't been there before, but he was still Wrenlow.

Olivia sat next to him. Her brown hair was damp, as if she had recently bathed. She stared at the table with her head bent forward, and Gavin noticed a series of enchantments along one wrist and another pair around her neck.

With that many enchantments, he couldn't help but wonder how they had managed to be subdued.

She didn't get up.

Gavin swept his gaze around the tavern, worried that this may be some sort of a trap and that Tristan might be trying to play some game with Gavin, but he didn't see anything to suggest that Tristan was involved. Though he wouldn't put it past his old mentor to do that.

"You don't have to worry," Wrenlow said.

"What do you mean?"

"He's not here."

Wrenlow sunk back down into the chair, and Gavin approached.

Gaspar leaned on the wall, his elbows propped against it, like he was trying to look better than he was. Imogen remained near the hearth, one hand still on the hilt of her sword, as if ready to attack.

Maybe she was.

"How did you get back here?" Gavin asked.

"We were rescued. Then broke free," Wrenlow said, looking to Olivia. He smiled slightly. "It's my fault that this happened. We were out in the street."

"What do you mean you were out in the street?" Gavin asked, taking a seat across from them.

"Well, when we were captured. We were out in the street. They caught us there."

"Who did?"

"I don't even know," Wrenlow replied. "I didn't see them. It happened so quickly…" He shook his head. "I know you would be disappointed in me, Gavin, and I should have been able to protect myself better than I had. But even with the enchantments, I wasn't fast enough."

"That happens sometimes."

"Not to you."

"But you aren't me," Gavin said. "You shouldn't be expected to do the same things as I can do."

"But you've been working with me. You've been training me, so I won't be surprised by anyone."

"And there's only so much I can prepare you for," Gavin said.

Jessica sat at another table, folding a stack of towels in front of her, and she nodded to him. Her chestnut hair was pulled back with a ribbon, and her eyes were drawn, worry etched in them.

He'd brought trouble to the Dragon again. Gavin didn't want to keep bringing danger or keep causing problems for the people here. All he wanted to do was to ensure that his friends were safe, but every time he tried to do the right thing, he ended up leaving them in a worse situation than they were in before.

And now…

"What can you tell me about what happened while you were away?" Gavin asked.

"I can tell you about the abduction," Wrenlow said, looking over to Olivia before turning his attention back to Gavin. He leaned forward, rested his elbows on the table, and rubbed his eyes. "I should have known better. I should have known we were just seeing the start of all of it."

"We didn't know," Gavin said.

"We didn't, but that doesn't mean we shouldn't have

known. And then I brought Olivia into it. I wasn't even trying to do that. I was trying to keep her safe, but…"

"It's not your fault," Olivia said softly. She looked over at Gavin. "He tried. You'd be proud of him. He fought the first one. He was moving fast."

"Because of the enchantment you made for me," Wrenlow said.

"But you were using the power within it the right way." She smiled at him. "And you should be proud of what you did."

"I would've been prouder had nothing happened to you."

"You have to let it go."

Wrenlow opened his mouth, and Gavin reached forward and took Wrenlow's arm. "The two of you need to stop arguing," he said. "What happened after you were taken?"

"I don't know. We were blindfolded and placed in the back of a cart."

"Together?" Gavin asked.

"No. We were separated, though every so often, we'd be placed near enough to each other that I knew she was still there."

"You didn't see anything," Gavin said. He leaned back and looked over to Gaspar and Imogen before turning his attention to Wrenlow again. "Do you remember anything about when you were brought to that house?"

"I don't remember a house," Wrenlow said. "We might've been in one, but it was difficult to keep track of everything. The cart seemed to move pretty regularly, and we were blindfolded the whole time. I tried to use more enchantments, but they confiscated all of them."

"Even your El'aras enchantment?"

"They didn't seem to care about that one," Wrenlow said. "It didn't work, though. I tried to get a hold of you over and over again, but it was like there was some sort of interference. I've never seen anything quite like it before, but then again, I don't know nearly as much about enchantments as Olivia. There was a night when we were placed near each other, and I asked her about it. She said that maybe somebody had a particular enchantment that allowed them to interfere with others." Wrenlow shrugged. "I'm not surprised, though. Given what we've seen about other enchantments, it would make sense that somebody would have the ability to disrupt others, wouldn't they?"

Gavin didn't know, and given what they had gone through with the others and how much trouble they'd dealt with, he figured he should have been looking into it before. He would have to ask Zella about it, if he could figure out where she had gone.

"What happened with your rescue?" Gavin asked.

"It wasn't so much a rescue as it was that we were let go," Wrenlow said. "I don't even know what to make of it. We were in one of the wagons—at least, I was. I think Olivia was as well." She nodded. "And when the wagon stopped, there was a strange sound. It sounded like fighting, though it was quiet. Muted. When it was done, I was worried something had happened, or maybe you were there, but then there was nothing. It took me a while to realize I could get out of the box, and when I did, we were at the edge of the city, of all places."

"You were?" Gavin asked.

"Right. So Olivia and I came back to the Dragon."

Gavin looked over to Gaspar. "Something's not fitting right here."

"No," the old thief said.

"Why would Tristan have released you?" Gavin asked.

"I didn't see Tristan. At least, I don't think I did. You've described him enough times that I think I'd recognize him. I didn't even hear what I *think* he'd sound like. They gave us food and water, but we never saw anybody's faces."

"What else can you tell me?"

"Magic," Olivia said.

Gavin looked over to her, frowning.

She stared at her hands. "There was magic there. I don't know if it was enchantments or sorcery, but there was a considerable amount of it. I tried to create enchantments, but I couldn't do anything when I attempted to. It was as if they had some way of preventing me."

That was odd. But then, maybe it wasn't. They had been dealing with a sorcerer who also had Toral powers.

That had to be what it was. She had Wrenlow and Olivia all along.

Why would she have released them, though? And why would she deny having them?

Gavin leaned back and crossed his arms over his chest, frowning. "I don't like this."

"No," Gaspar said. He pushed off the wall and hobbled

over to the table, sinking down and taking a seat. He clenched his jaw with each movement, as if he were in complete agony.

Gavin worried that Gaspar might've recovered well enough to return to the city, but he wasn't well by any means. Imogen watched Gaspar too. Gavin could see the concern etched in her eyes. She never took her hand off the hilt of her sword, appearing ready to attack anyone who might be responsible for harming Gaspar again.

"We need to figure out what's here. And I think that means the Toral," Gavin said. "I'm less and less convinced that she really wants to hurt me. She could have done so many times." He hated admitting it, but she was more powerful than him. Maybe as powerful as one of the Fates. He'd used his core reserves and still failed. "I don't know what she's after, and have no idea what this *t'ranth* is, but we need to learn so that we can decide how to approach her."

With what he'd learned in Nelar, it *was* about approaching her. Not attacking.

"That's a dangerous gambit," Gaspar said.

"What do you mean 'Toral'?" Wrenlow asked.

Gavin filled him in on what they had been dealing with, then looked over to Gaspar. "I went to find Zella when I left you both, and the fortress was empty. I think the egg is still there. At least, the storeroom is protected."

Gaspar glanced over at Imogen, who nodded. She slipped out of the tavern, saying nothing more. "We need to know what's happening to the enchanters," Gaspar said by way of explaining himself.

"Zella would have sent word if there was real trouble."

Gavin stared at Wrenlow, then Olivia. He felt his mind trying to work through everything to process what was going on, but he was struggling with it. Pieces didn't fit together the way he needed them to.

"I started off going on the belief that the Toral is working with Tristan," Gavin said to Gaspar. "I'm less convinced. Now I'm starting to figure out what she's really after. If it's not the dark egg, then what brought her to the city?"

"Could she have been after you?" Gaspar asked.

It had been him each time they'd encountered her. That might be what it was about. She might have been tracking him, but they didn't know why.

She'd believed there was something.

T'ranth.

"And there's also the sorcerer who helped us," Gaspar said.

"You had a sorcerer help you?" Wrenlow asked.

Gavin glanced at Gaspar, realizing that he hadn't told Wrenlow about that. "A sorcerer helped heal Gaspar, and he knows the Toral. I have a feeling he knows her well enough that he wanted to protect her. That's not the kind of person who wants to hurt others."

He didn't know what kind of person that made her. And that was the problem.

Gaspar frowned at Gavin. "Let's play this out. If the Toral isn't involved with Tristan, we still need to figure out what this *t'ranth* is. And whether you have it."

"Not just that, but she mentioned dark magic. I don't

have anything other than the egg that has dark magic. And she wasn't after the egg in Nelar."

But she'd detected Gavin.

What *did* he have?

Enchantments. El'aras weapons. His own magic.

None of that was dark.

Could there be something else in the city that I'd grabbed?

Yoran had become a nexus of magic ever since he'd come, and it had drawn Cyran here for a reason. The only other thing he had was the sword, but that was El'aras made too.

Gavin looked down at the blade sheathed at his side. "The only thing I can think of is the sword, which was in Cyran's home. And yet, when I faced her, she would have seen the sword, and she didn't try to take it from me."

"I've never heard of the Toral before now," Wrenlow said.

"Neither have I," Gaspar said.

"Zella had heard of them. And Anna."

"Sounds like you have some planning to do," Jessica said, then got to her feet. "Let me know if you need anything *I* can offer." She headed into the kitchen and disappeared.

Gavin was going to have to deal with their situation at some point. He needed to know whether the two of them could stay friends at least. That was what she claimed she wanted, though there was a part of Gavin that suspected she didn't really want to just be friends. Still, she had allowed him to return to the Dragon, and she hadn't pushed him away, which she absolutely could have done.

He didn't know, though.

"So, you have two magical beings who know about this Toral, but they don't know anything useful about her," Gaspar said.

He'd told Gaspar about Cyran's escape, and now he shared it with Wrenlow. "I think Anna knew more, but she didn't share," Gavin replied. "She said that the Toral access a different kind of magic than enchanters and sorcerers. If it was El'aras magic, I figured she would have said something. The more I think about it, the more I start to wonder whether or not this Toral was working against us directly. I don't know what she was after, but there was something she wanted, and she hesitated when we mentioned that Wrenlow and Olivia had been taken."

It was that hesitation that Gavin needed to understand.

And there was one way that he could.

"We have to get a message to her."

"You tried that already," Gaspar said. "Before we left, you'd told her sorcerer friend you needed to speak with her."

"I did," Gavin said. "But this is different. That was about trying to get word to her so she could release Wrenlow and Olivia. But if she wasn't responsible for their captivity, then I don't know whether there's anything more we need to do with that."

"There's something I can show you," Wrenlow said, standing. "I don't know if it will help, but it can't hurt, right?"

"Why don't the two of you stay here," Gavin said to

Olivia and Gaspar. He looked over to the door leading to the kitchen. "I'm sure Jessica wouldn't mind."

"She'll be fine. You just have to give her time," Gaspar said, nodding toward the kitchen.

Gavin smiled to himself. There were times when it felt like he and Jessica *were* fine, but others when he questioned if they could be. "I know."

"We'll be safe here. For now." Gaspar nodded to him. "Take care of the kid."

Wrenlow frowned at him. "I'm not—"

Gavin stood and shoved him toward the door.

The darkness of the city swallowed them. Gavin started moving quickly through the street, holding on to the power within him. He had to be prepared for the possibility there might be somebody after them. He hadn't used his core reserves all that much recently, so he thought he had enough power just in case.

"Where were you released?" he asked.

"That's what you need to see." Wrenlow hurried forward, moving faster than Gavin thought he should.

"Would you slow down?" Gavin asked.

"We need to finish this so I can get back to Olivia."

"She's not going anywhere."

"Not yet, but she still needs me. I'm going to help you with this, then get back to her, and I want to…"

"I understand," Gavin said.

"I know that you do. You…" Wrenlow shook his head. "I shouldn't say anything."

"No, go ahead. What is it?"

"You just don't know what it's like to have somebody

that you care about," Wrenlow said. "You've isolated yourself. All this time, you've barely let yourself be close to anybody. I mean, I might be the only one you truly care about. Even with Jessica, you never got so close that anything would ever come of it."

"I went after you," Gavin said.

"I know, and I thank you," Wrenlow said. "But we both know you've been wanting to leave the city for a while. Even after the last attack, you stayed because you felt like you had to, but not because you wanted to."

"I stayed because I was needed."

"What if you weren't necessarily needed?" Wrenlow asked. "Didn't you say that Davel Chan has been creating enchantments? And then the enchanters are here, all of them more powerful now. And with you having removed the threat of magic…"

"What are you saying?"

"I guess I'm saying that maybe you don't have any reason to be here. And maybe you don't really care about the city."

"I care," Gavin said.

"You care because you think you have to. You think that's what I want from you, but"—Wrenlow took a deep breath and let out a sigh—"I guess what I want is for you to figure out what *you* want, Gavin."

"You know what I want."

Even as he said it, Gavin knew it wasn't true. *He* didn't even know what he really wanted.

But he knew he needed answers. About himself. About

his magic and how he could use it. Gavin wanted to know why Tristan had trained him to learn magic.

What reason did he have for it?

Wrenlow turned his head away and looked into the distance. "It's not far from here."

They continued down the street and passed a series of shops until they reached a road that led away from the city. It was on the south side of Yoran, far enough from where they had been that Gavin wouldn't have been able to find this place without looking for it distinctly.

"This was where they released you?"

"This is where we were when we broke out." Wrenlow paused. There was a pile of scrap wood nearby, and he nodded to it. "Those are the remains of the wagons."

"The remains? What did you do, tear it apart?"

"When it seemed like nobody was coming, I started kicking," Wrenlow said. "I needed to get out, and as soon as I did, I started breaking Olivia free. I knew we were in Yoran, and I was hopeful that we would come across the constables, but none of them came."

"Wagons wouldn't draw the constables' attention," Gavin said.

"Wagons may not, but the thumping from inside as I was battering my way out should have drawn it."

"I can talk to Davel for you."

"That's not what I'm saying," Wrenlow said. "Once we knew we were in Yoran, we weren't as concerned."

Gavin made his way around the remains of the wagon. The wood had been stripped free, shattered, and there were a few darkened footprints that he could just make out. Not so much that he could tell how many people had come through here, though.

He took a deep breath and looked up at Wrenlow, thinking of his journal entry. Wrenlow wanted to make Gavin proud. And he did. He'd changed so much from the inquisitive but frightened young man Gavin had found. "I'm proud of you."

"Why? Because I let myself get captured and barely survived it?"

"But you did survive it," Gavin said. "Others might have panicked. You, on the other hand, realized when you had the opportunity to break out."

"We were captured for several days."

"I know. I've been looking for that entire time."

"What made you think we were outside the city?"

"It was the letter I got. It was the kind of thing Tristan would send. I was certain it was him. There was his sigil on the letter, after all, and the man he'd sent to give me the paper was this little rat-faced guy. He told me he'd been hired, but I knew better."

"What was that?" Wrenlow asked.

"The rat-faced guy or the paper?"

"Rat-faced. What makes you call him that?"

"Because that's what he looked like," Gavin said.

He still wanted to find him and wished he'd sent Imogen to capture him—then they could figure out who he'd been working with. As far as Gavin had learned, the rat-faced man had escaped, which should have told him all he needed about how skilled this person was.

"There was somebody like that among those who took

us," Wrenlow said. "I only caught sight of one face. It was strange looking and lean, with distinctive features, and there was something about it that seemed familiar."

"I would've remembered that face," Gavin said.

"I'm sure you would have."

Gavin sighed. "So, you were out here, and you managed to escape."

"We did. And I still don't know what allowed us to get free. All I know is that if we didn't escape, they... they'd made it clear we weren't going to live through this, Gavin."

Gavin moved the wooden boards around. They were solid—solid enough that Wrenlow wouldn't have been able to break out of them easily. He must have had some residual enchantment, unless his fear for Olivia had taken hold and made him stronger.

"That's funny to you?" Wrenlow said.

"Not at all." He turned to Wrenlow, trying to fix him with a serious expression, but failing.

"What are you grinning at?" Wrenlow asked.

"Just thinking," Gavin said.

"That gets you in trouble."

"You're starting to sound too much like Gaspar."

"I don't think that's all bad," Wrenlow said. "Someone has to keep you honest."

Gavin grunted, and he continued poking through the lumber. He started to feel a cold tingling along his skin. He straightened, peering around him in the darkness, and reached for the El'aras dagger.

It wasn't glowing.

"What's wrong?" Wrenlow asked.

"There's magic here. I can feel it."

Gavin didn't voice his worry to Wrenlow, but would he be strong enough to fight, given everything they had dealt with so far? He looked around once more, then handed the El'aras dagger to Wrenlow.

"Be ready," he said.

Gavin unsheathed the sword.

CHAPTER TWENTY

The sword didn't glow either. Gavin turned in place, looking for any signs of shadowy movement, but he didn't see anything.

Wrenlow clutched the dagger awkwardly, despite Gavin's previous lessons readying Wrenlow for the possibility that he might need to use it at some point.

"Just hold it out," Gavin instructed. "Don't be worried about the blade."

"That's easy for you to say," Wrenlow said.

Gavin looked all around him, worried about what was out there, but he couldn't see much in the darkness. He decided to move back toward the city.

What he needed was his enchantment.

He grabbed the ring from his pocket and slipped it on. For a moment, everything lightened around him, but then it faded.

"Shit," Gavin muttered.

"What is it?" Wrenlow asked.

"The enchantment failed."

He swept his gaze around him. Was something here that suppressed the enchantment, or had its magic simply faded? Gavin didn't know which one it was, and given how much he'd been drawing upon it to help with his eyesight, it was entirely possible that it had run out. Gavin knew better than to continue to draw upon that power, to risk depending on the enchantment, but he had needed it.

Now he would have to rely on his own ability to navigate in the darkness.

He crept forward carefully, searching, but he didn't see anything. Wrenlow watched him and mimicked Gavin's movements, staying close to him and holding out the dagger.

"You said you heard an attack out here," Gavin said.

"It was muted, but I was certain there was something."

Gavin glanced over to the debris. In the darkness, it looked like a looming shadow, but there seemed to be something moving near it.

"If this goes south, I want you to run back to the Dragon. Let Gaspar and Imogen know, then go to Davel Chan."

"I'm not going to the constable," Wrenlow said.

Gavin shook his head. "You need to let him know."

And Gavin needed to investigate. He didn't like the idea of moving toward whatever this was, especially if his enchantments had faded, but there might be one other way that he hadn't tried before.

What he needed was power.

Now was the time to use all the advantages he had—regardless of how much they might strain him.

He dipped into the sh'rasn powder and took a quick mouthful. As it flooded into him, a bit of power surged, enough that he could feel it washing over him. What he wouldn't give for the control Anna had claimed he needed in order to understand his power. Maybe then he wouldn't rely on the enchantments to help him see. It was possible that Gavin could simply use his own magic to enchant his eyesight.

But that wasn't the way his magic worked. He was the Chain Breaker, and that was it. That was all he'd ever needed to be.

Gavin had to come up with something else. He stepped forward and moved toward the darkness, toward the shadows that he saw. Wrenlow stayed close behind. Gavin shook his head at him, but Wrenlow ignored him. Together, they marched into the dark, into certain danger.

"You're going to regret that," Gavin said.

"I'm coming with you," Wrenlow said. "This is what you taught me to do."

Gavin wasn't sure if Wrenlow was ready or not, but he wasn't going to chase him away now. He also didn't want his friend to get into trouble by staying with him, but what could he do otherwise?

Gavin turned and searched along the street. Darkness. Magic.

This was the kind of thing Tristan would pull.

But why here? Why would he have released Wrenlow?

Only... he hadn't. Wrenlow had broken out. That

suggested to Gavin that this wasn't a test or that Tristan had *wanted* for him to think that Wrenlow had broken out on his own. Gavin didn't know what it was and was determined to figure it out, but he had to act quickly.

He darted forward, and a familiar tingling washed across his arms. He brought his sword up, sending his own magic into the blade, leaving it glowing.

"Oh," Wrenlow said next to him.

The power exploded out through the blade, causing everything around them to be cast in a bluish haze. Gavin searched around them to figure out what was there, but he didn't see anything. There had been something, though. He could feel it tingling along his skin.

"I know you're out there," he said.

If it was Tristan, then so be it. Maybe Tristan had called them here, using Wrenlow as bait. Obviously, the attack outside Nelar had not worked. So whatever else Tristan wanted, he still needed Gavin for it.

But what was it?

"Step out here and we can talk," he said. He didn't know if anybody would bother to emerge, but he wasn't about to wait around. "Show yourself."

"Gavin?" Wrenlow asked, nudging him from behind.

Gavin turned and held the sword out from him. The light that exploded around them was incredible. He was calling upon far more of his core reserve magic than he had before, which was coming from the sh'rasn that he had consumed. He should have known better than to do it, and he knew that there was a danger in holding on to that much power. But Gavin had needed it to see what was here.

A darkened figure came toward them, which must have been what Wrenlow had seen. Gavin held out the blade, ready to attack, when something caught his attention.

Smoke.

He had seen that kind of smoke before. It swirled around the figure, working from their feet up to their head.

Gavin groaned. "The Toral," he said.

So much for trying to send word to her.

The figure continued to approach.

"I have the feeling you don't want to fight," Gavin said. "But if you do, you'll find that I will be more of a challenge for you than the last time we faced each other."

The smoke continued to swirl around her as she kept walking toward them. Gavin struggled to see anything as the haze that generated around her obscured her features.

And then she stopped about five paces away from him.

"I don't know what you're looking for, but I can help you find it, if you'll stop this fighting." He was no longer sure if it *was* the dark egg. "You don't have to work for Tristan. Or the Fates. Or… whoever you're working for."

"You keep saying that name as if I should know it."

Gavin hesitated. He continued to push power through him into the blade, using that to eliminate the night. He would run out of his core reserves eventually, but for now, he would hold on to that power as much as he could.

"You don't know who you're working for?" he asked.

Gavin hid his surprise. That wasn't anything he would've expected from Tristan, who was proud and wanted people to know they were working on his behalf. He didn't try to manipulate them into working for him, at least that had not been Gavin's experience before. Tristan forced them to serve, and he coerced them, but he didn't manipulate. It was a fine distinction, but it was definitely one Gavin believed in.

The other woman let smoke swirl from her. It was faint, though when it touched upon her, it seemed to Gavin that she used it in ways to protect the Toral.

That was interesting.

"I know who I'm working for, but I'm not sharing his name with you," the Toral said.

"Careful," the other woman said. "You remember what happened the last time."

"I know what happened," the Toral said, though she kept her focus on Gavin.

She didn't try to wrap him in power the way she had the last few times.

And she didn't attack.

That had to matter.

"You don't deny that you're working for somebody, though."

"Not this Tristan."

"Not a half-El'aras man who sent you to kill me?"

She frowned. "I wasn't sent to kill anyone. We had word of an item of dark power in the city. A *t'ranth*. That's why we're here."

The smoke continued to swirl around her. She turned

and whispered something, and soon the smoke started to fade. As it drifted down, another woman's form was revealed. She was dressed in a black cloak, strands of her red hair hanging out from the hood, her pale skin practically gleaming in the light of his blade.

"You've said that before, but I don't know anything by that term. Is it the dark egg?"

"You know this device?"

"I might know something about it. It's safe. No one is using it." Again, he didn't want to add. And with Zella keeping it protected, it *was* safe.

It would stay that way, as well.

More than that, it would stay in the city.

That was how they would keep the Fates from attacking.

"Who *are* you?" she asked.

"I'm Gavin Lorren. You would have known that, though, if you were sent for me."

"I wasn't sent for you."

Gavin furrowed his brow, and everything he'd learned about her so far started to come together in his mind. "Your friend at the outpost didn't think you were sent to kill anybody either."

"That would be Char."

Gavin frowned. "His name is Char?"

She took a step toward him. Power surged, tight and painful along Gavin's skin.

He held his hands up. "Listen. I didn't do anything to him. Well, maybe I threatened him a little, but then I *did* pay him."

She cocked her head to the side, and she tapped something on her fingers. An enchantment. The smoke pressed upon her, and the dark-haired woman pressed the Toral back. They shared a look that almost made Gavin smile. It was one of warning to the Toral. And it seemed to work.

She let out a soft sigh and turned her attention back to Gavin. "Char sent word I was to find you. He told me what you did. And what you were after."

She'd come looking for him.

No, not him. For the ones Gavin had gone after. His friends.

Gavin looked over to Wrenlow. The fighting in the wagons. The sounds Wrenlow had heard. The fact that there been nobody there after he'd broken out. All of that seemed to fit together.

"You incapacitated his attackers," Gavin said.

"I wanted to find these people you spoke of," she said.

"Because you thought I'd be willing to trade for them?"

"I knew you'd come for them."

She'd been waiting for him.

She had helped Wrenlow. Gavin had seen that. And there was what her friend had said—and felt—about her.

This wasn't a violent sorceress.

She was powerful, but not evil.

And maybe she hadn't been used by Tristan the way he'd come to think.

She still wants the dark egg.

Or the *t'ranth*. Whatever that happened to be.

He touched his sword.

It couldn't be that. She would have tried to take it from

him during their first confrontation. Or their second. Even the third, when he'd been unable to do anything against her power.

"We've gotten off on the wrong foot here. I think maybe the two of us can help each other."

The other woman behind her continued to send the smoke swirling around her. It was an impressive use of power, and it was something so different than what Gavin had seen before. He'd never seen smoke magic like this.

"Your friend can come forward as well," Gavin said.

The sorceress glanced behind her, whispered something, and the raven-haired woman stepped toward them. She was dressed all in white. Gavin had a sense of heat coming off her, something he couldn't quite place, but it was an impressive energy. She kept her eyes on the ground, though the power around her suggested a significant energy.

"What kind of magic do you have?" he asked.

"She's not going to tell you," the Toral said.

"Then what about you? You're a sorcerer and a Toral, but I'm not quite sure who has gifted you their power."

That seemed to matter. It was something Anna had said, some aspect of serving as a Toral that seemed to make a difference. Gavin needed those answers.

"Where is the *t'ranth*? I know it's in the city. I feel it." She frowned. "Not as well as I did at first, though."

It had to be the dark egg. "Before we go into that, who told you I have it?"

"Ceran."

It sounded so much like Cyran that Gavin doubted it was a coincidence.

Could she be working for him?

"I think the two of us need to talk," he said.

Gavin looked along the street, and he continued to hold power through him, but he didn't want to keep doing that. If they were to attack, he didn't want to be trapped here, forced to keep summoning his magic. He had more of the sh'rasn powder and could use that to strengthen him, but that was a last resort.

She regarded him for a long moment before finally nodding. "Where do you suggest?"

She already knew how to find him. She'd already defeated him once. And he had a feeling she was withholding attacking him now.

It was a gamble. All of this was risky, and until he understood what she was doing, what she was after, and why she was working with Cyran, he needed to play this out.

"I know a place," he said.

As he started off, Wrenlow grabbed his arm and forced Gavin to look at him. "Are you sure that's a good decision?"

"No," Gavin said.

"Just so long as we're on the same page. I am not sure Jessica is going to care much for that."

"What's the alternative?"

"You could take her to the constables," Wrenlow suggested.

Gavin considered it. That was not a terrible idea.

Davel Chan, at least, had enough experience working with magic and enchantments that he and the constables might be able to help if she attacked again, but he'd be putting them in significant danger. But at the Dragon, there were only a few people there, and they had already faced these two before.

Gavin shook his head. "If it comes down to that, we will, but for now…"

Wrenlow nodded. They walked through the streets, and Gavin made a point of keeping his eye on both the Toral and the smoke woman until they reached the Dragon. At the door, the smoke woman ran her finger along the dragon etching on the door.

"What is this place?" she asked.

"It's a tavern. Called the Roasted Dragon," Wrenlow offered.

She looked back, and a bit of smoke swirled from her hand, tracing into the door. Gavin felt uneasy. The kind of power she had, the magic he detected from her, was unlike anything he'd ever seen before. At least with the Toral, Gavin had faced her before and had come away alive. In the case of this woman, he had no idea whether he would be able to face her and survive it. She was obviously powerful.

"What do you think, Eva?" the Toral asked.

So I have one name at least.

"This is not protected," Eva said.

The Toral relaxed, some of the tension leaving her shoulders.

Eva ran her hand through her dark hair. Something

metallic pierced her palm. It looked like an enchantment, but blood surrounded it. Smoke trailed from the blood, then swept outward, circling around her—and the Toral.

She protected the Toral.

That was interesting.

With as powerful as he'd seen the Toral, this Eva still protected her?

Gavin moved past and pushed open the door. As soon as he did, Imogen brought her sword toward him. He reacted by sending a burst of his core reserves out and caught the blade with his bare hands, the power somehow pushed *out* from his hands and protected him.

Imogen looked at him, and he looked at his hands. There was just a hair's width between his hand and her blade. And that was with him pushing as much power out of him as he could.

He offered a hint of a smile at Imogen. "I brought some visitors."

He stepped inside. Wrenlow hurried over to the table with Olivia and sat down next to her. He leaned forward and whispered to her, nodding to the Toral and Eva.

"What are you doing, boy?" Gaspar said, getting to his feet and flourishing his knives.

"They could have attacked at any point, but they didn't," Gavin said.

"You just *led* them here?"

"To talk. It sounds like she was hired by Cyran."

The Toral stopped, frowning deeply at Gavin. "No. Not Cyran," the Toral said. "Ceran."

"Well, Cyran is a powerful sorcerer. Is that what your Ceran is?"

She frowned, wrinkling her brow. "I don't know. Perhaps a sorcerer, but a Sul'toral regardless."

Gavin's eyes widened. *Sul'toral.* That was a word he'd only heard in passing from Zella. A powerful sorcerer.

"That's who you serve," Gavin said.

She nodded.

He looked over to Gaspar and shook his head. "That's not Cyran."

"No," Gaspar agreed. "Regardless of what power your friend has, I don't think he's anything like that."

Otherwise, Gavin wouldn't have been able to stop him. Cyran had been challenging, but he had not been so challenging that Gavin hadn't been able to defeat him. And if he was a Sul'toral, Gavin would've expected that he wouldn't have been able to.

The Toral looked around the tavern, her gaze lingering on each person, and Gavin had the distinct sense that she was using some form of magic he couldn't see. He couldn't feel anything either, which comforted him, though only marginally so. He had no idea how much power she had and whether she could use it against them without him detecting anything. At this point, the only thing he knew was that he was no longer convinced she was the one responsible for everything that had happened to him.

"Take a seat," Gavin said, motioning to the table.

She looked over to Eva before sitting.

Eva had scooped a mug of ale off one table and took a sip.

There was no smoke swirling around her, though he wondered when that would change. She drank the ale quickly, something in her seeming to relax.

It made Gavin relax with her.

That was one to watch.

She was powerful, though he didn't know how.

"You obviously have the wrong impression of me, and I obviously have the wrong impression of you," she said. "And I think we need to rectify that."

Through the enchantment, he could hear Gaspar's voice whispering, "What makes you think you have the wrong impression of her?"

Gavin twisted and made a point of putting part of his back up against the Toral, a marker of faith she wasn't going to hurt him.

Despite that, he still held on to his core reserves, which were diminishing gradually after as much power as he had already summoned. "Because of Char, the sorcerer who helped you," Gavin called over the distance.

She frowned as he turned back to her.

Gavin shrugged. "Your friend was reluctant to tell me anything about you."

"Char would not share anything about me. Not with you."

"Other than to say he didn't think you would harm my friends."

"I would not," she said.

"He thought enough of you that it made me start questioning everything," Gavin said.

And that was the part that he had to come to terms

with. He had to figure out what was going on here and what his role was in all this.

"You said that you're here for an item of dark power. Your Ceran must have told you about the dark egg, didn't he?"

"Egg?" She frowned and shared a look with Eva. "You've said that before. That's where I'm confused, and I'm rarely confused." Eva snorted and the Toral looked over to her. "But I don't know anything about an egg. What I'm after is something different—and dangerous for most who come upon them."

"And that is?"

She shared a look with Eva, then turned her attention back to Gavin. She rested her hands on the table. Her fists were balled up, and she held his gaze with a dark intensity. "I thought you knew and were hiding it from me."

"I've been trying to figure out what you've been after since I first met you. If it's not the dark egg"—and Gavin suspected he'd have to explain what *that* was now that she knew about it—"what *are* you after?"

"The *t'ranth*. It's the Toral ring you have."

CHAPTER TWENTY-ONE

It *was all about a ring?*
That was what she'd been after?
Not the dark egg as he'd feared.
At least it's protected. The enchanters need it to keep the city safe from the Fates.
If something were to happen to him, he'd want them to have it, if only as a deterrent.

Gavin looked across the table at her, and he tried to figure out what he was going to say. He'd been hired to retrieve a Toral ring years ago and had failed, but he wasn't sure she would even believe him. It would take far more explanation than what he thought he could share with her.

Gavin forced a calm smile, holding her gaze. "I don't have a Toral ring. I have dealt with several different sorcerers around here, but none are Toral."

"That is not what we understand," she said. "And it's

not what I have detected."

"I don't care what you understand. I am telling you what is true."

She cocked her head to the side, and Eva leaned close. A trail of smoke came from her mouth and drifted to the Toral before fading once again.

The Toral nodded. "I detect one in the city."

"What do you mean you *detect* one?" Gavin asked.

She held her hand out and slapped it on the table. The Toral ring on her hand looked like a band of pale white stone. As he watched, it started to glow softly.

But that was it. It did nothing else, and he saw no sign of magic. He still held on to his core reserves of magic, though, because he had no idea what she might pull.

"I have a Toral ring," she said. "And when I first came… there was a trail. We followed it. And we kept running into you."

"Sorry about that. It seems we've had a misunderstanding all this time. Probably about the ring you're looking for. I was once hired to steal one, but I failed. There's not one in the city, though, so unfortunately, your information is incorrect."

"Not information. It is what I detect."

"Then what you detect is wrong," Gavin said. "I'm not exactly sure what you think you're going to do, but I don't have this Toral ring. If I did…"

Gavin had no idea what he would do if he had one. Certainly not try to use it. That would be dangerous. Probably suicide, especially as he had no clue as to the kind of power within it, or how to use it.

Instead, he watched her, trying to figure out what to do or what to say to her, but he didn't come up with anything. She simply stared at him, an unreadable expression in her eyes, something that suggested a dark intention. Smoke swirled from Eva, and it headed toward the Toral again.

"It is here," she said. "Within the city. And everything has led me to you."

"Why don't we talk through this step by step? You weren't sent by Tristan," he said, and she shook her head. "And you aren't working with Cyran. But you are working with somebody named Ceran?"

She nodded.

"And this Ceran is your Sul'toral."

She nodded again.

"Let me guess. Your Sul'toral instructed you to claim this Toral ring from me."

She didn't make any expression.

"Or you received word that I had it," Gavin said.

She pressed her lips together in a tight frown before finally nodding.

Gavin leaned back, and he chuckled.

"I fail to see what is so amusing to you," the Toral said.

"Jayna," Eva said.

Gavin smiled to himself. At least he had a name now. He was tired of calling her the Toral. "Obviously, Jayna, you have a misconception. And, unfortunately, I think you've been used."

"I have not been used," she said.

"I'm sure you didn't want to be, but the type of power

that has guided you here is obviously using you against me."

He thought that he could piece things together, though it wasn't clear.

If it *was* about a ring, maybe it was still about Tristan's pursuit of a ring.

If there was one in the city, it would explain why everything kept coming back to Yoran. Magic was here. Powerful magic.

The kind that would make Tristan nearly impossible for Gavin to stop.

Anna had said he wouldn't be able to use it, though. Why chase it if he couldn't?

"Why would that be the case?" Jayna asked.

"Because I've upset powerful people," Gavin said.

What was worse was that the people he had upset were clearly powerful enough that they could send even more magic at him. He would've expected Tristan to have pulled that. *Why wouldn't he? Why wouldn't Tristan use somebody like her, somebody who had even more power than Gavin could summon?* To force it upon him, making him struggle with figuring out a way to stop it. He knew what Tristan was capable of doing, and Tristan knew that Gavin had come to understand his innate magic. That was exactly the kind of thing Tristan would do.

"Why don't we work together?" he said to Jayna. "We can figure out where this Toral ring is, and then maybe the two of us can figure out how to call my old mentor here. And perhaps—"

"You can't be serious," Gaspar whispered through the

enchantment.

"Why not?" Gavin asked, looking over to him. "It's a perfectly sensible thing for us to do."

"You and sensible don't go together very well," Gaspar said.

"Fine. Maybe it's not perfectly sensible, but it makes sense."

Having somebody like the Toral, with the power he'd felt from her, would be a boon when it came to dealing with Tristan. Not only her, but this Eva as well. He had no idea what she had other than the smoke magic, but he'd seen it in action and knew that it was different than sorcery, which made it powerful.

"I'm afraid I cannot be of use to you and your vengeance," Jayna said.

Gavin grunted, shaking his head. "It is not my vengeance. I'm simply trying to help protect the city." He frowned as something that he'd seen in Nelar came back to him. He was increasingly certain he was right about it. "You *protected* Nelar."

She was more like him. Powerful, but she wanted to protect her city.

"What do you know about that?"

Gavin realized he had the right of it. "Just what I saw when I was there," he said, shrugging. "There was an attack."

He watched her as he said it, and her eyes twitched. Maybe it was more than just an attack. Whatever it was, she'd been involved, and it must have been significant enough—and violent enough—that it had upset her. Gavin could tell that from her demeanor as she looked at him and from how she touched her Toral ring.

"If you don't want the same thing to happen here, you will help me," he said.

She grinned. "I doubt the same attack will happen in the city."

"Really? We've dealt with a sorcerer by the name of the Mistress of Vines, also known as the Tanran. She was a powerful creature and had nearly overwhelmed us; nearly destroyed others in the city who she saw as an obstacle to her rule. Then there were the Fates."

Her eyes narrowed.

When he'd mentioned it before, she'd kept her face neutral. Not this time.

Now he could tell that she recognized that term. Of course she would. He believed that she was a sorceress, so they were likely aware of each other. Most sorcerers came through the society, but not all.

Gavin would never have believed it before, but learning that Cyran had developed magic outside of the society suggested that perhaps there were others. Still, the Fates would be known by anyone trying to use sorcery.

"That is not of my concern," she said.

"No? You *are* a sorceress, are you not?" Gavin was taking a gamble now. "Don't you have any affiliation with the Sorcerers' Society? Don't you feel as if you need to ensure you're keeping the society from doing what they should not?"

She laughed lightly, and she slid back in the chair. Jayna glanced over to Eva, who continued to swirl smoke around her. It was a strange use of power, but Gavin started to think that it was some sort of defensive mechanism, as though she was using that smoke to protect both of them if they were concerned about what Gavin might do.

He wouldn't be surprised if they were. They had fought each other, and they knew each other's strengths and weaknesses—at least, as much as anybody could know his strengths and weaknesses. Gavin had faced her three times now, which was more than he had ever faced anybody else before without ending a fight.

"I have little use for the Society," she said.

"You have separated from them. Interesting. I didn't realize any sorcerers left it. I thought doing so meant you were banished from them."

"Only if I chose to embrace the Society in the first place."

Gavin glanced over, and he saw Gaspar watching her. Maybe there was something in all of this that Gaspar might be able to understand, but right now Gavin didn't know anything.

"Something happened," Gavin said. "And whatever you were dealing with is similar to what we're dealing with here. There's danger from magic in the city, the kind I'm trying to protect the city against. Maybe it wasn't coming from the Society, but it was definitely dangerous. This city has known what it's like to be under the rule of sorcery, and they do not want to go back to that time."

"It has nothing to do with what I'm here for," she said.

"Then what you're here for is the same thing that my

mentor was after. You're here for the ring, and I suspect he is as well. That has to be why he sent you after me."

"And I told you that he didn't send me after you."

"Maybe not directly, but he sent you in my direction."

Gavin shook his head. The distinction was minor, and even as he said it, he wasn't sure whether or not it was entirely accurate.

It still didn't strike him as completely right.

Knowing Tristan, that wasn't the kind of thing that he would typically do. Tristan tended to act directly, which was the reason all this bothered Gavin.

Ever since the first attack, ever since the testing had begun, Gavin had been troubled about it. None of this fit with what he knew of Tristan, other than the tests. Tristan would bring one of his own people to fight Gavin, and Tristan himself would too, as if he had been completely unconcerned about Gavin's abilities that had developed in the time since he had left him.

Of course Tristan wouldn't worry about Gavin. He had no reason to fear his abilities because Gavin had never been able to defeat him before. It was the kind of arrogance he expected out of Tristan.

Gavin sat back, crossing his arms, and he frowned to himself.

What if I'm wrong about this?

"What is it?" Gaspar asked him.

Gavin shut his eyes, his mind racing, trying to come up with what it was that bothered him. "Just a minute."

All along, he had believed that this was about Tristan, that the test had come from him. But there had been part of him that felt like this was not quite right. He needed to uncover what that was and why it would bother him so much.

He glanced over to Gaspar and shook his head. "I am not sure I had this right."

"What part of it aren't you sure about?" Gaspar asked.

"That we're dealing with Tristan."

A different thought came to him. What if it was *Cyran*?

He would never have thought that was the case, especially given that he'd believed Cyran was still being held by the El'aras. But he'd escaped. And the timing *could* work.

"Do you remember who sent you looking for me when you reached Yoran?" he asked Jayna.

"I followed the trail to the city, but once I was here, there was a strange-looking man who offered his help," she said.

"Strange looking how?" he asked.

"He had a thin face, narrow-set eyes, and—"

"A rat face," Gavin said with a sigh. "It's the same damn person." He looked over at Gaspar and Imogen. "Did you figure anything out about where he ended up, then?"

"No. I followed him, but I lost him," Imogen said.

Gavin glanced at Gaspar. "This is Hamish all over again."

"You think this guy that sat at the table with us was Cyran?"

Gavin couldn't put it past him, and he couldn't shake the idea that it was. And if it was, then he knew what he needed to do. Get to Cyran.

He leaned forward. "We're going to have to work together," he said to Jayna. "I know you have no interest in working with me, and to be honest, I really have no interest in working with you. But I think we need to."

"I am not after this Cyran," she said.

"No, but I suspect you are after the same thing that he is."

"Why would you suggest that?"

"Because he sent messages all tied to something that happened a long time ago."

Now that Gavin thought about it, he realized something and laughed to himself. "I think I was supposed to take *your* ring."

"You would not have been able to," she said.

Gavin shrugged. "You wouldn't be the first one I tried to target."

"You would not have been able to," she repeated.

Gavin looked over at Gaspar. "That's what this was about. I've been trying to figure out what reason he had for all of this. It's all about these Toral rings."

And if Gavin was right—and, increasingly, he thought he was—then it wasn't just about any Toral ring, but about the specific one she had. Cyran had tested Gavin to determine whether he would be able to take on a Toral and claim the ring from her. Cyran would've known Gavin had faced one of them before, and he would've known that Gavin had failed.

Which was why he'd tested him now, why he had brought all of the power to bear against him early on, wanting to know whether Gavin had discovered some secret part of himself that would allow him to fight back. Cyran had learned of Gavin's connection to magic.

Of course he had, though. Gavin hadn't hidden that from anyone. When Cyran had been in the city, Gavin had been learning about that connection, developing it. Cyran had even gone so far as to try to use his strange powder to mitigate it.

"Dammit," he whispered. "All of this because he wanted me to take a Toral ring."

"For Tristan?" Jessica asked, standing near the kitchen.

Gavin shook his head, looking over to her and smiling tightly. "I don't think this is about Tristan. At least, not directly." He rubbed his hands together, trying to think, but it had been a long day. His mind was tired, much like his body was. Cyran might want the ring, but Tristan had already gone after one before. "He might have wanted it for Tristan, though. Cyran had made it sound like he had gotten away from Tristan, but what if he hadn't?"

Tristan wanted a Toral ring. Gavin had been unable to get it for him, despite being Tristan's most skilled student at the time. In that failure, Tristan had been angry enough that he had almost killed Gavin because of it.

And Cyran had known. He and Gavin had spoken about it, which meant that Cyran knew that Gavin had gone to that house. He would know how to use him, how to guide and direct him, and…

It all made a sick sort of sense, but he didn't know what Cyran intended to do with the ring.

"You said something about not being able to use the ring," he said to Jayna.

"A Toral needs to serve a Sul'toral," she said carefully. She frowned as she did, and Gavin had the distinct sense that she didn't care for sharing even that much with him. "Without that, you would not be able to use the power of the ring. It would simply be a ring."

Gavin wondered if that was true or not. Maybe there would be some power that would be innate to the ring itself. "And without knowing the Sul'toral…"

"It's not a matter of just knowing the Sul'toral," she said. "You have to be granted the ability to use the power by the Sul'toral."

"And yours is this Ceran?"

"Yes."

"And would Ceran be able to help if we were to go against Cyran?"

She snorted, shaking her head. "Ceran only helps when he wants to."

"Why?"

"Do you even understand what a Toral does?"

"Other than serve a Sul'toral, I suppose not."

"We have a specific type of power. The ring allows me to access that power and add it to what I have of my own."

"Sorcery."

She nodded. "The Sul'toral is a person of incredible power—more than any sorcerer you've ever encountered, and the ring lets me sort of borrow his power."

Gavin found himself frowning. "I don't know. I've met some powerful sorcerers."

"The Fates."

He nodded. "And we chased them out of the city. If this

Ceran is anything like them—"

"He's not. He's far more powerful." The words hung in the air, leaving Gavin's mouth dry. He'd *felt* how powerful the fates were. "And there are those who would use that power in dark and dangerous ways. Most would, in fact. I am tasked to ensure that doesn't happen."

"You wouldn't misuse this power," Gavin said, hoping that was the case. He didn't know anything about this woman, other than the fact that she had stopped attacking him because she was curious and wanted a chance to learn more.

"If I wanted to embrace the darkness, I would have done so by now," she said.

"Then what?"

She shook her head, and she glanced over to Eva. There was something more going on here, something Gavin didn't know, but perhaps it didn't matter.

"So, if your Sul'toral won't help, then we're on our own," he guessed.

"Yes," she said.

"I suppose that's fine. I've been on my own for a while."

He frowned as he focused on what he might need to do, the power he might need to summon. But if it came down to figuring out a way to get Cyran to come, that was what Gavin had to do.

There was only one way to lure Cyran here.

Cyran had to believe that Gavin had the ring.

"He's pitted us against each other at every point," Gavin said, looking from Eva to Jayna. "And he believes I have enough skill to overpower you."

"You do not," Jayna said.

Gavin smiled. "Maybe."

He liked her confidence. It was possible he didn't have enough skill to win against her. She was more powerful than he had expected. She had managed to stop him more than once and had nearly overpowered him the second time he'd faced her. The first time, Gavin had gotten lucky by surprising her. The second time, without the enchanters, he didn't know if he would have stopped her. The third time...

The third time, she had broken up the fight.

Here he liked to think of himself as one of the most skilled assassins and fighters in all the world, but when it came to magic, he was not as skilled. When he fought those with magic, Gavin had limitations, even though he had his own connection to it.

"We have to convince him that I defeated you," Gavin said.

She frowned. "Why?"

"Because he's after the ring, and he has to believe I have it. If he does, then he'll reveal himself and come for it."

"There would be no way for him to know."

"Maybe not, but I think I could do something."

"What?" Jayna asked.

"He's phrased it so he knows I believe that Tristan has come for the ring. And if that's the case, all I need to do is figure out a way to convince him that I sent word to Tristan."

Send a message, get to Tristan. But where would he

call him to?

"We have to trap him. Somewhere," he said, looking at the others with them. "And it has to be believable."

"What do you propose?" Jayna asked.

Gavin smiled. At least she was willing to work with him. With enough time to prepare, he believed they would have enough of a chance to stop him.

"We can work through the details, but he wanted me in Nelar for a reason. Maybe we need to return."

If he could draw Cyran there, they could deal with him easily.

The Toral would be able to deal with him easily.

Gavin might not even need to do anything.

But this was Cyran. He *wanted* to be a part of taking him down.

"Why there?" she asked.

"Because that's where he thinks I needed to go. And if he's to believe I have your ring, he needs to believe you've been immobilized."

It was more than that, though. Nelar was where Gavin had been assigned to bring the ring when he'd taken it in the past.

"We should make preparations," he said, glancing to Gaspar and Imogen before turning his attention back to Jayna and Eva. "We're going to need to collect supplies."

"What kinds of supplies?" Jayna asked.

"Enchantments, primarily, but maybe other things."

She frowned. "I might be able to help with enchantments."

CHAPTER TWENTY-TWO

It was early morning, and none of them had slept yet. All of them sat around inside the Dragon, trying to figure out the next steps of their plan. Gavin could feel his eyes getting heavy. He looked over to Jayna and Eva, shaking his head.

"I think it's time for us to get some sleep," he said.

"It's time to finish this if you intend to use me in your plan," Jayna said.

"It's not a matter of using you."

He looked up as the door opened and Imogen slipped in. She set two pouches on the table.

"What are these?" Gavin asked.

"Enchantments. The enchanters were with the constables. It seems that there were more attacks while we were gone, and your constable friend requested their assistance."

Gavin had seen evidence of the attacks, though he'd

returned to the Dragon before he'd had the chance to learn more about them. Enchantments destroyed. Buildings targeted. Exiled magic again targeting the city.

"How many were lost?" he asked softly.

"They didn't say," Imogen said.

He breathed out a sigh. Davel knew the dangers, but the enchanters deserved better. They'd lived in fear long enough.

That was why he thought it good that the constables and enchanters work together. When they did, the city could be protected in a way that would not require Gavin's presence here any longer. The threat of the dark egg would remain, which would keep out the Fates, and maybe it would prevent other attacks as well.

"Where were the other attacks?" he asked.

"Scattered. So far, they have repelled them."

That had to be Cyran as well. Gavin gritted his teeth, and irritation filled him. All of this because he'd ousted Cyran from the city.

"What did they give us?"

"More enchantments," Imogen said. "Isn't that what you wanted?"

"I suppose it is," Gavin said. "And I should thank you."

"Don't bother."

She took a seat, and Gavin looked inside one of the pouches. Gaspar took another, slipping the satchel over his shoulder.

"I need rest," Gavin said. "If I don't get it—"

The door to the Dragon exploded open.

Shadows streamed toward them, stinking of a terrible

magic. Gavin clenched his fists and pulled on the power of his core reserves. All they needed was time to prepare, and they wouldn't even have that. And now the attack had come back to Yoran, to the Dragon.

All he wanted was to ensure the city's safety, but he continually failed. Anger filled him as he jumped to his feet, rage at what Cyran had done boiling up within him.

This was his doing; Gavin was certain of it.

"What is this?" Jayna asked, spinning and holding her hands out in front of her. She crossed her wrists and then began to form a tight spiral that blasted outward.

"This would be Cyran deciding he was impatient in waiting for us to come after him. Apparently, he must have known you were here."

Which meant that Cyran had some way of detecting the Toral ring, just like Jayna did. Gavin should've figured that.

He started forward, but Jayna grabbed him and threw him back. "Not yet," she said.

"I know how to fight in the shadows," he said to her.

"And I'm telling you no. You don't need to do this yet."

"Just wait?"

She nodded, and Eva strode forward, her hands clenched at her side. It looked as if blood dripped from her palms. As soon as the blood struck the floorboards, it started to smoke and swirl outward. The smoke drifted toward the shadows and looped within them, and then the shadows shattered.

A dozen figures emerged out of the darkness.

"Now you can do what you do," Jayna said.

Gavin growled as he lunged forward. Imogen was there as quickly as he was, her sword unsheathed, whipping it in such fast patterns that he could scarcely keep up.

Damn, he would love to spar with her again.

Gavin jumped in among the others. In close quarters, it was easy for him to choose which fighting style he would use. He darted with sharp wrist movements, chopping one man in the throat, bringing his knee up into the midsection of two, then twisting someone's arm behind him until it shattered. Gavin swept through the attackers, striking one after another, getting through them quickly until all of them were down.

It was easy.

Too easy—which meant it wasn't the primary attack.

He spun around, looking for Jayna.

She was gone.

"Eva?" he called.

She stood near the door, staring out into the street. "She's missing." Her voice was low and angry.

The Dragon was littered with a dozen bodies, and Imogen made her way among them, stabbing her sword into them, making sure that none of them got up again. Gaspar flicked his knives and grabbed another from one of the bodies, wiping it on the man's back before shoving it into his pocket.

"Where did she go?" Gavin asked.

"Somebody came for her," Eva replied. "I can follow her, but…" She looked over to Gavin. "If they were powerful enough to take her, I won't be able to stop them."

"Let me help," Gavin said.

She frowned, her brow furrowed, then she nodded. "She's saved me more times than I can count, and I'm not leaving her to them." Eva looked over to Gavin, and a pained expression filled her eyes.

"I'll help you," he said.

They stepped outside into the darkness of the early morning.

Gavin glanced over to the stone wolf still sitting there. "I thought you were supposed to protect me," he said. The wolf stood and looked up at him. "Great. And now you react?" He turned to Eva. "You'll need to ride with me."

"Ride?"

He climbed onto the back of the stone wolf, and the others emerged from the tavern. Gavin shot Gaspar a hard look. "Are you sure you're well enough?"

"I'm not staying out of this," Gaspar said. "If I ended up injured because of this bastard and now he's going after others, I'm not staying behind. You go ahead and try to stop me if you think you can."

"I'm not going to stop you."

Gaspar looked over to Eva. "Good. Then are we going to get going?"

Gaspar was angry in a way that Gavin hadn't seen before. Maybe it was because Olivia had been abducted, or maybe it was simply the continued attacks on the city, but whatever it was, Gavin worried about what Gaspar might do.

How aggressive would he be when it came down to it? And would this be more than Gaspar could handle?

Imogen climbed onto her strange stone creature.

"I'm coming too," Wrenlow said.

"You shouldn't," Gavin said.

"He captured me once. And I can be of help. You know I can."

Gavin clenched his jaw. Even though he didn't want Wrenlow to come along, he also wondered if maybe he needed the help. Cyran was going to be too much for him. In order for him to stop Cyran, it would take all the help he had. His team.

Not only the people that were there with him now, but the enchanters and the constables too. That was what Tristan would not expect.

Jessica stepped out of the tavern and handed the satchel of enchantments to him. "I was just bringing you this."

Gavin slipped it over his shoulder. "I need you to get word to the constables." He swept his gaze around the street. They were out there somewhere; he was sure of it. Jessica had been meeting with the constables to keep the Dragon protected for a reason. "I'm sure you have a way?"

"I might," she said.

"Tell them to hurry. I suspect the constables have enchantments for speed and strength that will work for that as well." He had hoped they would, at least. Otherwise, the fight would be just those with him, and it might be short-lived. "I'm sorry about the Dragon. I'll help restore it when I get back."

"I will hold you to that, Gavin."

He turned and looked over his shoulder at Eva. "Do you have some way of following her?"

"The trail is moving quickly. I don't know if we'll be able to move fast enough to keep up with it."

"Give these stone enchantments a chance."

The wolves raced forward, following something Gavin couldn't tell, but Eva obviously detected it and communicated with the stone creatures in some way. They darted through the streets and reached the forest beyond the edge of the city. They didn't go far before they stopped in a darkened clearing.

Gavin sorted through the enchantments Zella had given him. He found the small pebbles for speed, a couple of markers for strength, and then a ring. Enhanced eyesight.

He slipped it on. The dark forest brightened.

Gavin climbed off the stone wolf and patted him on the side, smiling at him. It felt foolish to do so since the wolf was not anything real or alive, but he had been helpful.

"Well?" Gaspar asked, getting down from his stone creature.

"Now we just have to—"

Gavin didn't have a chance to finish.

Shadows appeared out of the forest, flowing as if they were alive.

They had a foulness to them, an odor that filled his nostrils.

He much preferred the cold washing of a different kind of magic, though this was easier to destroy.

"This again?" Gavin muttered.

He rushed forward, readying for the attack, but Gaspar held on to him.

"Maybe try a different approach," Gaspar said. "When we charged in before, we were surprised by what he did."

"What would you have me do?"

"Be smart for once. You love to fight and prove how powerful you are, but maybe you don't have to."

"If not me, then who?"

Gaspar nodded to the stone creatures.

"I don't like that," Gavin mumbled.

"No, but we don't have much choice, do we?"

Gavin patted his stone wolf and frowned. "I'm sorry, buddy. I need you to protect me. Go in there, tear shit up, and then come back."

Gaspar shook his head, muttering under his breath, and he leaned down and said something to his own stone wolf. Imogen did the same, but then she slipped into the trees and disappeared.

The stone creatures sped forward. Gaspar pulled something out of his pouch and set it on the ground, then tapped it. A massive giant-shaped creature, looking something like a man, came to life and lumbered forward quickly.

"I feel more confident with you sending that one out there," Gavin said. "I don't want to lose my wolf friend."

"You do realize your wolf friend is not alive," Gaspar said.

"I know. That doesn't change the fact that I don't want something to happen to him."

"*It*," Gaspar said. "It is an *it*."

"I'm going to pretend you didn't say that."

Gaspar shook his head in annoyance before heading toward the tree line.

The creatures rumbled as they headed through the shadows, and there was something angry about the sound that echoed through the forest around them.

"She will be nearby," Eva said.

Gavin started forward, and as he did, the ground started to tremble. It was different from what they'd felt before, this one shaking everything around him. A stone creature hurtled toward him—a wolf racing at him.

Gavin watched it with a frown, and Eva shoved him to the side, the suddenness of it knocking him to the ground. He scrambled to his feet, and the smoke streamed off of her and swirled away. The smoke headed toward the stone wolf and stopped it from lunging at Gavin. The wolf continued to try to get to him and claw at him.

"What happened?" he asked.

"They have turned it," Eva said.

The ground thundered, and he looked up in time to see the giant stomping across the clearing toward them. Gavin had no idea what to do—other than destroy the very creatures they had sent in to protect them.

"Gavin?" Gaspar asked through the enchantment.

"I don't know how to stop them," Gavin said.

He had his core reserves, and he could go at them with the El'aras sword, but he wasn't sure if it was going to be enough.

He started sorting through the various enchantments he had, and as he fumbled through them, he couldn't find anything there that would be useful. Maybe he could turn another one of these creatures back against the shadows, but he ran the risk of Cyran just turning them again.

Gavin flipped through his pockets and found something he'd forgotten about.

The paper dragon.

He had no idea whether it would do anything, but he pushed out a trickle of energy from his core reserves and poured it into the paper dragon. It began to stretch longer and spread enormous wings, looking like a massive folded paper dragon, all angular but distinctly a dragon. Then it roared.

The sounds echoed through the forest, painful and overwhelming. The paper dragon swooped forward, grabbed the stone wolf, and flew outward.

Gavin blinked. "Well, I guess that answers what Alana's magic can do." He looked over to Eva. "Come on."

They started forward, and through the enchantment, he heard Gaspar. "There are others out here. Imogen and I will—"

Gavin didn't get a chance to hear what he and Imogen were going to do.

"Wrenlow," Gavin said, "help Gaspar."

"I'm on it," Wrenlow replied.

Darkened figures slipped all around them, filling the clearing. They were going to be too much for Gaspar and Wrenlow. Too much for Imogen. Too much for even Gavin.

How had Cyran managed to bring so many people to the city without anyone knowing?

Gavin turned, preparing to join the fight, when a flurry of movement caught his attention. He turned and smiled. Enchanters. Constables. Dozens of them. They must have followed the enchantment Zella had given him. They sped forward, attacking.

All around him came the clang of metal as constables battled with the Vuthyl. Gavin could scarcely see them, but that didn't matter. The constables and the enchanters could. With their enchantments for speed, strength, impervious skin, and enhanced eyesight, they would be uniquely capable of stopping them.

Gavin and Eva continued on, and they made their way into the center of the clearing. It occurred to Gavin that this was the same place he'd come before, where Cyran had brought them when he tried to force them into giving up Anna—the Risen Shard.

Why here?

Maybe it was a place of power.

The clearing around him was no longer quite as dark. Somebody lunged at him, and he drove his fist forward. He turned, and an attacker came at Eva, and Gavin started toward her to help. She somehow forced smoke into the man's mouth, and he coughed and gagged, then crumpled to the ground, trembling.

Gavin blinked. "Remind me not to go against you."

The darkness pressed upon them, a swirling sort of energy, and it tried to squeeze toward them. The power within Gavin was almost enough for him to see through it, but there was something different—some aspect of the shadows he couldn't quite penetrate. The smoke drifting away from Eva cleared that darkness and made it so that he could see.

A darkened figure lay in the center of the clearing. Power began to swirl around Gavin, and he tried to focus on that magic. He recognized it. He'd felt that before.

Jayna's Toral power.

But if he was right, then she was the one lying motionless ahead of them.

Eva moved forward.

Gavin grabbed her by the wrist, shaking his head. "No."

"You know who that is," she said.

"I do, but we need to wait."

This was all Cyran, all part of his plan. Gavin had no idea what it was, only that he needed more time to figure out just what Cyran was going to do.

"And here I thought you wouldn't make it," a voice said.

A strange-looking figure stood next to one of the trees. When he emerged from the shadows of the forest, Gavin recognized him. The rat-faced man. But the voice coming out of him was Cyran's.

"All of this for a Toral ring?" Gavin asked, shaking his head. "Is this because you want the power, or is to impress Tristan? Either way, I find it odd that you would go to all these lengths to find power you aren't even supposed to have."

The sounds of fighting rang out nearby. Someone shouted. Another cried out in pain. Each time he heard those sounds, a part of Gavin raged.

He would protect them.

That was why he had stayed in the city.

"No one is *supposed* to have this power," Cyran said. "Only those who claim it can use it. And I finally figured out how to claim one. Just draw off one of the more disappointing Toral, then dispatch her, and…"

Cyran stepped forward, spreading his hands on either side of him. With a flourish, his appearance transformed. Dark purple robes flowed down, his sharp nose stretched outward and became bulbous, and his brow widened.

Hamish.

Then he flickered again, and he was Cyran.

"Which of these do you prefer, Gavin? Or should I say, Chain Breaker?"

"I prefer none of them. Why are you so determined to come out here?"

"You decided to steal power from me once before, and it's taken me a while to come up with what I would do to get my revenge. Do you know what it's like staying inside an El'aras prison?"

"It's my understanding that it was a temple," Gavin said.

He tried to move his hand closer to the El'aras marker in his pocket, to summon Anna. She had come for him once before, but maybe she wouldn't come this time. Maybe the fact that Cyran had escaped made her unwilling to do anything more.

"A temple? Perhaps to them it was a temple, but to those of us who care about such things, it was torment. And you forced me there."

"After you used me, and then tried to kill me. I suppose we're even," Gavin said. "Maybe you leave Jayna alone, and we can call this a day."

"No. Now that I have her and the ring, we're going to summon her Sul'toral, and then—"

"And then what?" Gavin asked.

Something still didn't fit.

Jayna had come to the city for a *t'ranth*.

She'd followed a trail of it.

She'd felt that power.

It wasn't the one she had.

Cyran might have put her on Gavin's trail, but there was something else here.

Cyran smiled. "You can't even begin to understand what's going on. All of this is but a precursor to something greater."

"All of what?"

He chuckled, looking over to Gavin. "Haven't you started to question why you were trained the way you were? Why you had to be the Chain Breaker?"

"I have," Gavin said. They were the same fears he had, wondering what Tristan had in mind for him, knowing that Tristan would not have trained him to become the Chain Breaker had he not wanted to use him in some manner. "I also realize it didn't make much of a difference. I've done what I needed to do, and Tristan did with me what he thought he needed to do."

Another shout almost pulled his attention away, but refused to get distracted. The cold of magic washing over his skin ensured he kept his focus on Cyran.

"He trained you for a specific purpose. But you're still his failure. I'm going to be his success."

Gavin frowned. "What do you think you're going to do?"

"I am going to succeed where you failed. And then—"

Gavin laughed. "All of this is your way of trying to impress Tristan?" He shook his head, though the barriers around him made it difficult for him to even do that much. "I don't think Tristan cares whether or not you impress him. He doesn't care about any of us. You know he never did. We were tools."

"Tools. And yet, you never knew what you were built for. You never knew what he asked of us, how he intended to use us."

"And I never cared," Gavin said. "Not until I grew out of it, and not until he was gone did I start to care what purpose I had with any of it. And even now, he doesn't even matter."

As he said it, Gavin realized that what he was saying was true. He'd been wondering why he'd been trained to be the fighter, the Chain Breaker, but none of it really mattered. All that mattered was that he got to choose.

And he *had*.

By staying in Yoran, by helping his people, he had made his own choice. That was what was important.

"We were tools," Cyran said, "but he was building us, designing us, honing us, all while focusing on a specific purpose."

"And what purpose was that?"

Cyran looked down to where Jayna lay motionless, and

he smiled. Gavin tried to move and fight forward, but he could not.

Eva could, though. She strode toward Cyran, smoke swirling around her.

Cyran looked up, and he chuckled. "Don't think that I don't know about you, little one." He pressed his fingers together and twisted, then flicked.

It was a use of power Gavin had never seen before. Eva flew out of the clearing and slammed into one of the trees, where she crumpled. All of that power that he had seen of her, and there was nothing left.

Gavin struggled against the magic that was holding him, but he couldn't move.

"When she awakens, she is going to serve me," Cyran said, nodding to Jayna.

"She won't," Gavin said. "And if you think that you're going to strip the Toral ring off of her—"

"If I *think* I'm going to strip it off? What do you think I've already done?" Cyran held up his hand. The stone ring glittered on his middle finger, glowing softly with a pale light.

Cyran and a Toral ring were a terrible combination. Gavin had seen what a sorceress with a Toral ring could do. But Cyran…

Gavin couldn't stand and do nothing. But as he continued to try to move, he could not. Frozen in place, he was forced to face Cyran while hearing the sounds of his friends fighting around him. Without him.

He strained.

Gavin needed to get free from the power Cyran used on him.

Destroy him. Help my friends.

Those thoughts stayed with him.

"When I summon her Sul'toral, then I will take real power," Cyran said.

"Do you think Tristan is going to be impressed by any of this?" Gavin said, trying to delay him. It was the only thing he could think of doing.

Cyran shook his head and let out a bitter laugh. "You failed him. And then you failed him again. And now… even the great Chain Breaker is not going to be able to stop this now. Everything is too far gone, Gavin. You can do nothing."

Things didn't quite add up.

Tristan *had* been in the city.

Unless that had been Cyran as well.

The *t'ranth* had brought Jayna to the city.

A Toral ring.

Not hers, though Cyran was after it.

They were both still being manipulated.

Gavin focused on his core reserves, trying to summon the power inside himself. He could feel the energy there, just within reach. All he had to do was call upon it, then he could break free. He could be the Chain Breaker.

Only, this time, he felt as if it were even more significant than every other time before. He felt as if what he was doing now mattered much more than when he had stopped Cyran last time.

The power was there, and he just needed to reach for it. But he heard Cyran laughing.

"You think I'm not aware of what you're doing?"

"I was hoping you weren't," Gavin said.

"I'd heard the stories of the Chain Breaker when I returned to the city. I'd started to hear rumors about how you had defeated the Mistress of Vines, and I realized something. You had tapped into magic. I'd always known you had potential. The way you healed faster than anyone else and the way you were able to become the Chain Breaker suggested you were far more powerful than Tristan ever acknowledged, but I had never expected you to be quite as powerful as you proved to be."

"I'm not that powerful," Gavin said.

Cyran chuckled. "No, you are not."

Gavin tried to get his arms free. All he needed was one hand, and he could go for the powder. If he could get the sh'rasn, he could use it to break free, but even as he tried, Gavin couldn't do anything. His hand slipped and touched the sword, but there wasn't anything Gavin could do with it.

He tried to raise the blade.

Cyran twisted his hands in a pattern. A stream of pale yellow power struck Gavin in the chest, knocking him back. The sword scraped a rock, fraying the leather wrapped around the hilt of the blade.

Gavin strained against the bindings Cyran used against him.

He couldn't move.

If only he could get free.

The sword.

As his hand rested on the frayed leather along the hilt of the sword, Gavin felt something he'd never noticed before. There was a sphere on the end of the hilt. He traced his thumb around it, and the leather that wrapped around the hilt started to come loose. He pried it off, then flicked his gaze down.

A Toral ring.

The *t'ranth*.

Jayna *had* detected something.

She'd gone to the lair. She'd followed him.

And he'd had it on him the entire time.

The sounds of fighting around him grew distant.

How many of his friends had been lost already? How many more would suffer?

This was why the sword had been held inside the case before.

This would save his friends.

Gavin started laughing.

Cyran eyed him. "What do you think is so funny?"

"You. You were in Yoran for how many years? All that time, you were in search of the Toral ring you believed was in the city, and you never found it."

"There was no Toral ring here," Cyran snapped. "I used that rumor to draw *her* out."

"Are you so certain? She followed it. She *knew* there was something here."

That was the difference.

Cyran had started rumors, but the Toral had *real* power.

Only... he'd still defeated her.

Cyran grinned at him. "I'm completely sure. You forget, I was the one who called you to Yoran."

Gavin chuckled again. "That's right. And I found your little hiding place."

"Of course you did. I intended for you to find it."

"And I opened the chamber."

Cyran glared at him.

He needed to buy time. If he could distract Cyran, he might have the time he needed and might be able to overpower him.

The easiest way he knew to distract him was taunting him.

Cyran was proud. He thought himself smarter than Gavin.

Gavin would use that.

"I got the sword you couldn't get," Gavin said. He held his hand on the hilt, trying to remove the Toral ring. Would there be any power within it that he might be able to use?

All the time that he had been holding the sword, there had been something more to it. When he had first found it, Gavin had known there was something different about it, but he hadn't known just how special it was. Now that he had the blade, now that he had the ring, he could feel the unique energy within it.

"It doesn't matter. It was just a sword," Cyran said.

"An El'aras sword, held within a case you could not open."

El'aras.

Gavin frowned as his own words echoed. That had to matter. Somehow, the fact that this sword had been made by the El'aras, had been protected within a shield of El'aras magic...

And *he* was El'aras.

The *t'ranth*.

This wasn't just any Toral ring.

It was attached to an El'aras sword.

It was an El'aras Toral ring.

Gavin worked his thumb around the leather wrappings, and he finally managed to pry the ring free and shift it to his palm. It was slightly warm and smooth, much like how Jayna's looked like it would be.

"You can have your sword," Cyran said. "Unfortunately, the sword is no good to you against someone like me—somebody with real power."

"What makes you think I don't have real power?" Gavin asked.

"Because you are nothing but the Chain Breaker. And soon, I will be—"

Gavin didn't give him the chance to finish. He had slipped the ring on his finger and pushed his core reserves through it. Power exploded out of him very differently than it had before, unleashing a torrent of energy that was beyond what Gavin could fathom. When it poured out of him, it slammed into the barrier Cyran held and tossed him back.

Gavin started forward, but Cyran had already begun to move his hand in a tight pattern. Sorcery built from him, and Gavin had to push his core reserves outward through the ring. The combination granted him even more strength than he had managed before. It blasted and struck Cyran once again.

Gavin darted toward him and brought the sword back to strike but loops of power snaked around him. He focused, trying to summon all the strength within him, and struggled.

He couldn't let Cyran beat him. Gavin had already defeated him once, somebody who had been his friend. Facing him now, feeling the power that Cyran used on him, filled Gavin with anger.

Strangely, the ring on his finger began to vibrate, as if reacting to his rage. He had to push that down. He needed control.

If there was one lesson that Tristan had taught him, that Gavin had taken to heart, it was that he needed control. That was the key in all things. Even with a ring he did not fully understand and a strange power that filled it, Gavin knew he needed to manage his emotions.

He tamped them down, and then he looked over to Cyran. He had gone to his knees, and he moved both hands in a pattern that Gavin couldn't fully comprehend. His hands were moving steadily, slithering around him, as if the pattern was what caused the constriction around Gavin's legs and his torso.

Gavin focused on his core reserves, and he burst outward with them. But the power circled around him once again.

Cyran smiled, but for the first time, he had a look of hesitation in his eyes. Gavin understood the uncertainty.

He had no idea how he managed to use this power. All he knew was that it filled him.

He staggered forward, raising the sword.

"You might have gotten more training than I expected," Cyran said.

"Nothing other than what Tristan offered to me."

Gavin spun, barely avoiding Cyran's next use of power, darting around so that Cyran couldn't overwhelm him. In the distance, he could hear the fighting. At the edge of his vision, he saw the enchanters, the constables, and even Wrenlow and Gaspar taking down their opponents. Most from Vuthyl, which left questions in Gavin's mind about why they'd help Cyran. There were others among them, though Gavin couldn't tell where they were from without taking time away from Cyran. His friends fighting, all to protect Yoran.

This was up to Gavin now.

He stopped moving and faced Cyran.

"Are you done dancing?" Cyran asked.

Power circled around Gavin. He could feel the energy from within that ring. He had no idea what it was, only that it was there. He drew through the ring, and energy filled him.

Power exploded outward and struck the barrier that Cyran had formed. It threw Cyran back once again. He started to get to his feet, but Gavin raced forward, still holding on to the power within the ring. He raised the sword. Cyran tried to hold his hands up, and he twisted them in a pattern.

"What were you saying?" Gavin asked.

Cyran glared at him, and Gavin thrust the sword into his chest. Cyran wrapped his hands around the blade, eyes wide, and Gavin stretched one hand out toward Cyran.

"It seems you were wrong all this time," Gavin said.

Cyran coughed, blood gurgling from his lips. "How?"

"Because I'm the Chain Breaker."

CHAPTER TWENTY-THREE

Gavin stripped the Toral ring from Cyran's hand and held it in his palm. This one wasn't nearly as warm as the one he still had on his own finger, but it glowed. Was there some sort of power within it that he might be able to use again?

Gavin feared using something far more dangerous than he intended. There was no point in him trying to keep channeling that kind of power. He pulled on the Toral ring on his hand, but it would not budge. He tried prying the ring off his finger, but still it didn't come free.

The ring had come off Cyran's finger much easier.

He made his way toward Jayna, who remained motionless in the center of the clearing. In the distance, Gavin was aware of the constables and the enchanters securing the forest. They were working quickly and ensuring that others did not get too close. He breathed out a sigh of relief at that. This was over.

As he crouched down next to Jayna, he tapped on the enchantment. "Wrenlow? Gaspar?" He didn't have any way of calling out to the constables or enchanters, though he wanted to.

"We're here," Wrenlow said. "Guess what, Gavin? I killed a man."

"I wouldn't brag about that, kid," Gaspar muttered.

Gavin looked down at Jayna, and he ran his hands along her arms and legs, looking for any signs of injury. There was nothing there. He took the Toral ring that he had retrieved from Cyran and slipped it into her hand. She stared blankly, unmoving.

Smoke streamed toward him, and Gavin scrambled away from Jayna. Eva strode over to him. Blood trickled from her mouth, and where it dripped to the ground, it turned to smoke that circled all around her.

"I didn't do this to her," he said. "I brought the ring back to her."

"I saw what you did." The smoke swirled from her into Jayna, then began to flow all the way down her body.

Jayna coughed. She carefully sat up and looked over to Eva, taking a deep breath and letting it out slowly. "What happened? I was attacked. It happened so quickly and so suddenly, there wasn't anything I could do about it."

"That was Cyran," Gavin said.

She held out her palm, glancing down at the ring. "How?"

"How did I get it back from him, or how did he take it from you?"

"Both, I suppose," Jayna said.

Gavin shrugged. "Well, he's an incredibly powerful sorcerer, and he used that power to strip that off of you."

"He should not have been able to do that. I suppose that he was using dark magic." She got to her feet and looked over at Eva. "I had not detected it."

She'd mentioned dark magic before, though he had no idea what that meant. Gavin knew about several types of magic. There was sorcery, there was the power of the enchanters—which was like sorcery, though generally weaker—and there was El'aras magic. Maybe there was yet another kind.

Jayna closed her eyes. More of that smoke continued to swirl around her, starting at her feet, then working its way up. She breathed it in and opened her eyes, nodding to Eva. "Thank you."

"What is that about?" Gavin asked.

"That is nothing," Jayna said. "You have it. The *t'ranth*."

He looked down to his hand. "I suppose I do. I didn't realize that I did. I'm… well, I'm sorry."

She rubbed her neck, looking over to Eva. "All I can recommend is that you stay away from the darkness within it. Oh, and I should thank you as well. I don't know how you were able to do that…"

Gavin clenched his fist, keeping the El'aras Toral ring out of sight. He had no idea what to make of it—yet. It was another question he had. "I've been trained to handle people like that."

"That's a unique kind of power," she said. "And the fact

that you were able to overwhelm his magic is…" She shook her head. "Perhaps I underestimated you. And I misjudged you."

Gavin chuckled. "You don't have to sound so disappointed."

"It's not disappointed. It's a matter of me wanting to make sure I'm doing what's necessary. It's my responsibility to fight the darkness. Perhaps yours now, too. There is dark power in the world, and there are those of us who fight against it."

"The Toral?"

"Not the Toral," she said, glancing over to Eva before turning her attention back to Gavin. "At least, not many. You could help, it seems. I would welcome your assistance."

Gavin laughed and shook his head. "I'm not so sure that's my calling. I have other things I need to do."

And he still needed to know why Tristan had wanted the Toral ring. Why Cyran had gone after it for him. Why Cyran believed that calling the Sul'toral here would have made a difference.

Could Cyran have thought to claim *that* power?

"Be careful with it, then. There's a danger in what you now wear."

"You're not going to try to take it?"

She regarded him, then glanced to Eva, who shook her head.

Jayna sighed. "I guess not. Ceran will hate it, so maybe that's not all bad."

Gavin wanted to know more about that relationship, but she'd proven unwilling to share anything about him so far. "He intended to use your ring, to call your Sul'toral and..." Gavin shrugged. "I'm not exactly sure what else he was going to do, only that I suspect he intended to harm your Sul'toral. Maybe separate him from his power and replace him."

"That would not have been possible," she said.

"Just like separating you from your ring should not have been possible?"

Jayna's brow furrowed, and she shook her head. "We should return," she said to Eva. "Maybe I *do* have to call him. He's going to hate that, too."

"You don't like it much better."

"Only because of the things he shows me. And Char is going to be insufferable."

Gavin found himself smiling. It had taken him until now to find his team, but it seemed to him that Jayna had already found her own. Maybe there was still something he could do to help her, though.

"I could help with transportation," Gavin said.

"I think we'll manage," Eva said.

Smoke swirled around her, then Jayna. When it cleared, they were gone.

Gavin stared at the space where they'd been. He headed over to Gaspar and Wrenlow. A pile of stone littered the ground. There were bodies scattered all around them. Constables, enchanters. He didn't see anyone that he recognized, but the fact that some had laid down their lives to defeat Cyran's attack on Yoran—all for the ring—infuriated Gavin.

The ring vibrated again, and Gavin tamped down his emotions. All because of Tristan. All because of the magic that existed in Yoran. He let out a frustrated sigh, but it would do no good. They had to regroup. They had to be ready. This was not over.

Imogen rested nearby. She sat on the ground, her knees clutched to her chest, her face troubled.

"What happened to her?" he asked Gaspar.

"She had to kill her stone creature."

"I thought you said they weren't alive," Gavin said.

"And I didn't think they were. She obviously felt differently."

"I'm sure we could ask Mekel to make others."

Imogen looked over and frowned. "You would just replace them like that?"

"It's not a matter of replacing," Gavin said. "It's just—"

Gaspar rested his hand on his shoulder and shook his head. "Let her have her time."

"Thank you," Gavin said, looking back toward where Jayna and Eva had disappeared. "All of you. We made a good team."

Wrenlow smiled. "I know you've been trying to keep me away from this, but I think I did well." He looked over to Gaspar. "Of course, the old man doesn't think that."

"The old man thinks that fighting and killing are things that should be avoided. The old man recognizes that violence is not always the right answer. The old man—"

"Would you stop calling yourself the old man," Gavin said.

"Are you defending him now?" Wrenlow asked.

"Maybe I am," Gavin said.

He looked around and found Cyran's body lying motionless. There was a part of him that worried that somehow Cyran would have some way of using magic to recuperate, but he didn't think Cyran could truly do that this time.

"You three should get back to the city," Gavin said.

"Just us?" Wrenlow asked. "What are you going to do?"

"I'm not leaving, if that's your concern."

"I thought it a reasonable concern to have," Wrenlow said, "considering how you've—"

"I'm not leaving right now," Gavin said.

"Just right now?"

Gavin looked over at Gaspar, then Imogen, and back to Wrenlow. "Eventually, I might need to. I have questions, and…" He ran his finger along the Toral ring, feeling the warmth within it. There was something within him that hummed with power, a surge of energy he could feel without even having to tap into his core reserves. Once he did that, he would be able to call upon even more.

Gavin had felt that magic, and he had been filled with it. He worried that if he were to need to summon it again without having any way of understanding it, he might be too violent and dangerous with it.

He needed control.

Which meant that he would have to go to the El'aras.

Eventually.

He'd been avoiding it all this time, wanting to steer clear of the El'aras when he had committed to helping Yoran, but now…

Now Gavin didn't know anymore. He didn't know what he would have to do to fully gain control of that power. The more he thought about it, though, the more he began to feel as if he would have to.

He glanced over to Gaspar. The old thief watched him, as if he recognized the struggle Gavin was having.

Gavin forced a smile. "Get going. I need to bury Cyran."

"We can help," Wrenlow said.

"This is something I need to do myself."

Wrenlow opened his mouth to argue, but Gaspar grabbed him by the wrist and dragged him away. They left Gavin alone in the clearing, in the darkness, in the center of the forest. Everywhere around him was an energy, but one that Gavin didn't fear.

He wasn't sure if it came from within him or if it came from some external source like the Toral ring. Either way, Gavin recognized that there was something in that energy he might need to tap into, some aspect of power that he might need to call upon, to stop Tristan.

He reached Cyran's body and leaned down, running his fingers over the fabric of his jacket. He would bury him, giving him dignity he probably didn't deserve, but Gavin thought maybe it would be better for him to remember Cyran the way he once had been—not the way he was now.

And then he would go after Tristan.

Somehow, all of this was still tied to Tristan. All of this was still bound up in what Gavin had been when he was younger. He'd thought that by leaving Tristan, he would no longer be beholden to his old mentor. But with everything that had happened, it felt as if Gavin was being pulled deeper and deeper into a past he wanted to forget, something he'd believed he was beyond.

He found himself still indebted to Tristan after all this time. He wasn't all that different from Cyran, despite how he'd taunted him.

Gavin moved Cyran's body and prepared to lift it, wanting to carry it to the center of the clearing to bury it. "I'm sorry that it came to this."

"Why do you feel remorse at this?"

He spun. Anna stood in the clearing, watching him.

"How did you know I was here?" he asked.

"I felt the summons," she said.

"There was no summons." Gavin reached into his pocket and pulled out the marker.

"Not that one," she said, nodding to the marker, "but that one." She tilted her head toward his other hand.

He held out the ring. "Did you know that the ring was here?"

"The ring has been missing for many generations," she said softly. There was a note of concern in her voice.

He understood.

The *t'ranth*. A Toral ring.

And now *he* wore it.

"It is an El'aras Toral ring, isn't it? The *t'ranth*."

She nodded. "Something like that. The El'aras would

not refer to it as a Toral ring, but it does connect to a different sort of power. Similar to the kind of power the Toral ring taps into." She smiled at him. "You have been avoiding your calling, Gavin."

"I haven't been avoiding it. I've just known I have others that depend on me."

Despite the constables and enchanters now working together, Gavin still couldn't shake the feeling that he needed to be in Yoran, that he needed to offer a measure of protection. Without him, Gavin worried that something terrible would happen to the city.

"I've suggested to you the opportunity that you could go to the El'aras to learn."

Gavin nodded. "You have."

"But you have not wanted to."

"It hasn't been for me."

"No," Anna said. "You've been determined to take a different path, though perhaps that is just as well. Had you gone to the El'aras, then we may have had a different difficulty."

"What is that?"

"They would have demanded that you serve them."

"*They* would have demanded?"

"Not like your mentor had, though they would have required service. I understand why you would choose not to serve, but you would've found it difficult to refuse."

"I doubt that," Gavin said.

"More difficult than you can imagine." She looked around the clearing and shook her head. "Such darkness here."

"What do you mean?"

"This place. There is so much darkness here. Don't you recognize it?"

"Should I?"

She tilted her head. "Perhaps not. But that does not change that it exists. It is why he would've used this place to call to the Sul'toral."

"Would he have been able to steal that power?"

Anna frowned. "It is possible, though I wonder if there was a different motivation."

"What other motivation would there have been?"

She took a deep breath. "You've tapped into a dangerous power."

"The ring? Or my own?"

"Perhaps both," Anna said in a whisper. "It seems that fate conspires to bring us together, Gavin Lorren. I had hoped that…" She shook her head, and the sad smile that he had seen several times from her returned. "Perhaps it doesn't matter what I had hoped. All that matters is that we serve our purpose. But maybe there is something else." She regarded him for a moment. Gavin had no idea what she was going on about, but it seemed that she had come to some considerable decision. "And since you cannot travel to study, I think a different plan must be hatched."

"What plan is that?"

She arched a brow at him. "I think that I must stay and teach you. Since you now have the ring, you are a part of something much greater than you have learned, but I fear you will learn what that means soon enough." She took a long breath. "And it is time that you know your magic. It is time that you learn to be more than the Chain Breaker."

Read more about Jayna and Eva! Their story continues in Festival of Mourn, The Dark Sorcerer book 1.

Gavin's story continues in the next Chain Breaker book: The Paper Dragon.

SERIES BY D.K. HOLMBERG

The Dragonwalkers Series
The Dragonwalker
The Dragon Misfits

Elemental Warrior Series:
Elemental Academy
The Elemental Warrior
The Cloud Warrior Saga
The Endless War

The Dark Ability Series
The Shadow Accords
The Collector Chronicles
The Dark Ability
The Sighted Assassin
The Elder Stones Saga

The Lost Prophecy Series
The Teralin Sword
The Lost Prophecy

The Volatar Saga Series
The Volatar Saga

The Book of Maladies Series

The Book of Maladies

The Lost Garden Series

The Lost Garden

Printed in Great Britain
by Amazon